ELISE
or the Real Life

((Elise))

or the Real Life

by *Claire Etcherelli*

Translated from the French by
JUNE P. WILSON AND
WALTER BENN MICHAELS

William Morrow and Company, Inc., 1969

NEW  YORK

ELISE
or the Real Life

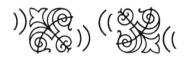

Whatever you do, don't think. Just as you say "Whatever you do, don't move" to someone with a broken leg. Don't think. Reject all thoughts, always the same, those of yesterday, of the time that will never return. Don't think. Don't repeat the last sentence of that last conversation, the words that our separation made final. Better say that it's mild for this time of year, that the people across the street are certainly late getting home. Lose yourself in details, lean out the window and watch the street below. Outside, people are walking, going home, going out. Workers carry empty lunch bags rolled up in their hands. The bars must be full; at this hour everybody is elbowing his way in. Tonight, there will be women, happy, adrift on a floating island in one room for two. Should I leave the window and go down? I am certain to find adventure in the street. The sidewalks are full of men with searching eyes. I don't like adventures. I want to leave on a boat that will never enter a port. Embark, disembark, that's not for me. I took this image of a boat from my brother Lucien. "I promise you a boat that will chart a course through the middle of the sea where no other boat will dare to follow." He wrote that for Anna. It must be seven o'clock. It's lovely out. A true month of June, with warm nights that make you think, "Summer, at last." The assembly line stops at seven, then the men move down to the locker rooms. I am beginning my last night. Tomorrow I leave this room. Anna will come for the key. I will have to thank her. She won't be surprised; she never asks questions. When she speaks, it's always in the present tense. She's not discreet or shy—only indifferent. Lucien wanted us to be friends, but she doesn't need a confidante, a counsellor or a benefactor. As for me, I've forgotten how. When I was thirteen, I had a friend "for life." At fifteen, I had only increasingly critical acquaintances. Besides, I was already committed to Lucien. The year I became fifteen, I gave him my room. Until then, my brother had slept in the kitchen on a bed that we put away every morning. To win him over, I surrendered what he wanted most—that little square room, filled with sun until noon, opening onto the court. Our grandmother was angry when she saw us moving our things. To make peace, I promised that I would share her big bed from then on. That made her happy, for she liked to talk all night. A year before the start of the war, we had come to live with her because she was to bring us up. In 1940, we were crossing the Pont de Pierre when the first German trucks arrived. "The Boches," I said to Lucien. He took up the word; he repeated it everywhere. We had to make him unlearn it. We were in high school then.

We used to argue in the evenings; I'd slap him and he'd tear up my papers. We wrote V's on our shoes with chalk. We were underfed; our grandmother had refused to let us be placed in the country. She didn't want us separated from her.

We didn't hide from a single bombardment nor miss a single line at the grocery stores. Every morning, Lucien and I set off together and, out of prudence, I left him only when we had reached the door of his school. After the war, I wanted to go on taking him. He could hardly stand me and I hung onto him. Since he walked fast, I had to quicken my pace. We were crossing the Place de la Victoire with its florists' bouquets. In every display, the conquering generals were enshrined. Lucien stopped to look at them. I stopped too. He had planned this moment. He dashed away, running, to shake me off. He seemed to me cynical and sly. I decided that my example would be the best lesson for him.

I had quietly succumbed to a religious faith that was both scrupulous and severe, and from which I drew all my happiness. My grandmother didn't care one way or the other. She had taught us our prayers, the words sin and sacrifice, but her faith—like her philosophy—was wrapped up in the one phrase she loved to repeat: "the good Lord has a big ladle and serves everybody." Emotion and pleasure came to me in the parish house garden —green as oases—where on Thursdays and Sundays under the wings of the calm nuns, I formed my taste for flowers, embroidered cloths, pale faces and an upright soul.

Our grandmother was still working as a cleaning

woman in harbor offices. Her main problem—always a difficult one—was providing for us. Once Lucien had his room, he locked himself in every evening. I was sorry I had given it to him. Sleeping with my grandmother became a chore. At sixteen, I quit school and went to work. Some shopkeepers in our neighborhood had advised me to rent a typewriter and teach myself to type, since typing school was beyond our means. Later on, with only a small outlay, I could do better. I had neither aptitude nor ambition. I dreamt of sacrificing myself for Lucien. I was guided by no one and thought myself better off than the girls in the neighborhood who at fifteen took the path to the factory.

I spent the mornings doing the housework and marketing. When Lucien came home at noon, I was proud that he found the table set, the house in order, and calm faces reflecting what I used to call upright living. This would instill in him the habit and therefore the need for this kind of equilibrium.

.   .   .

Tomorrow she will knock gently. "It's Anna."

I'll open the door and we will say hello.

"You're leaving? You don't need the room anymore?"

"No. I've packed all my things."

Then will come the hardest part. The thank-yous. Eager to be quit of each other, we will avoid lengthy good-bys. Will she mention Lucien?

.   .   .

At fourteen, my brother had two passions: his friendship with Henri—that was his noble passion—and roller skates which he put on the minute he was home from school. Every evening for months, we heard the sound of his skates rolling down the sidewalk. Sundays he got up early, gulped his breakfast, and returned at noon only to leave again until evening when he came home and got into bed, trembling with fatigue. One morning, out of curiosity, I stationed myself behind the Quinconces. A cold mist hid the rooftops, frost covered the branches of the black trees and the street lamps were still burning. I was worried about Lucien and decided to bring him home with me. I caught sight of him alone in the freezing fog wearing his tan coat that came down only to his thighs, with his socks pulled up over his knees and his skates on his feet. He had taken off his red scarf; I saw it on the ground near a tree. I watched him, his knees bent, the skin of his bare thighs red, arms out, ready to plunge forward. I guessed his happiness, the wandering through the mist, the sweetness of solitude, of life still asleep, the sensation of freedom rediscovered, the intoxication of running ahead, without obstacles, eyes wet with cold, hands frozen, feet burning. I thought of his return to the kitchen, Grandmother knitting, me reading, and him floating between us.

On several afternoons, I tried to go with him. Seated among the mothers, I waited for six o'clock, patiently, his snack on my lap, always finding someone to listen to. But I had to give up this pleasure, for, on the way home, he accused me of spying on him, annoying him; he threatened to go someplace else, or stop going out if I was going to follow him everywhere.

Grandmother and he argued often. She heaped futile

reproaches on him and he answered with insolence. He still talked sometimes of Henri, but with reticence, his voice changed, shy. This restraint made me feel how much he loved him. I got to know Henri one day at the close of school. Older than Lucien, his coldness gave him an air of authority. He spoke slowly, his voice solemn. He intimidated me a lot even though he was only seventeen. It seems he found me young. At twenty, it's true, I looked very young. I was proud of my pallor, I didn't wear bright colors and drew satisfaction from not being like the "others."

"You," Lucien told me later, "you are exceptional only to yourself."

.   .   .

The school games were coming soon. They were scheduled for the last Sunday in May. Henri, who was very athletic, was in charge of the gymnastic contest, and my brother hoped to be its star. He exercised his muscles in the evening when he thought we were downstairs. He was sure he'd be chosen; he mentioned it to me, but with indifference, as he did everything he cared about. He didn't get the honor. Henri chose a certain Cazale, who was no doubt better than Lucien.

"I'm to hoist myself up to the bar and sit there," Lucien admitted. "Cazale climbs up and starts his acrobatics. I stay near him and do nothing except give him a hand twice. I'm the fall guy."

He agreed to do it anyway. He came home from each practice, insolent and unhappy. He didn't want Cazale to be a success, he didn't want to see him bowing to the applause, or watch Henri tap him on the shoulder and take him for a drink after the triumph.

In his blue gym suit, he balanced nervously on the bar and held still. At the moment Cazale began his exercises, we saw Lucien lean back over the edge of the bar and, as if he had no idea of the danger, fall. Everybody screamed and jumped up. Cazale climbed down trembling. Lucien had won. Cazale could not perform. My brother was laid up for three months, his left leg broken, one wrist cracked, bruises on his head and face. He didn't take his exams, he never went back to school. Henri didn't come to see him; once, he sent him a card with excuses and best wishes.

No letters, no visits, only we three. Nothing to look at but the stones of the houses across the way. He read. He demanded many books. He played checkers. He smoked. During the morning, I stayed with him. He admitted the truth: his wild desire that Cazale not be the star. Touched by this confession, I dared not blame him. These were unforgettable weeks. He talked to me, called me when something he read excited him, laughingly tried to make me share his tastes and ideas, many of which shocked me. His bed was heaped with newspapers bearing in bold letters the name MAO-KHE. We fought, but it didn't upset me. He never opened a notebook and never spoke of going back to school. From time to time, he would say, "Let me get well, walk, and I'll enlist." Grandmother was beside herself, she saw him already in the rice paddies of Indochina. Slow to heal, he dragged through the entire winter.

(13)

Our deep understanding came to an end. It hadn't lasted long. Once again, he spent his days locked up in his room, and threatened us at the slightest reproach.

"If this keeps up, I'll enlist . . ."

He had tacked on his wall a map with tiny flags, some tri-color and some black. Impressed, Grandmother was afraid to say anything. When he went out in the evening, I knew he was going to look at the boats, and the water where the lamps on the bridge drowned their light. He had no money and rarely asked us for any.

Two years after the accident, his health was still poor. He did not enlist, he did not go away, he married Marie-Louise.

. . .

When Lucien appeared in the mornings, I turned my head away. He grumbled good morning. He resented our being there, our existence, our seeing him. He would have preferred us indifferent and blind, so that his appearance in the kitchen wouldn't even make us turn our heads. Like a small boy, awakened between our two smiles, he struggled: "No, no."

There was this difficult moment to get through; his coming in, his coldness, the heavy mood that was slow to break up. We had to make no mistakes, just find the right gesture, the word to soothe him. Getting up, sharing with us the intimacy of the morning ritual, cost him dear. I imagined him coming out of the bathroom, smiling and freshly groomed. I exhausted every means— sweetness, gaiety, jokes—for I wanted above all to make our first hour together pleasant. Because I needed a certain atmosphere of serenity, of kindness, I wanted him to share it.

One day, I suggested that he get a job in one of the companies that gave me work. "Come *on* . . ." he snapped, with the scorn of those who, never having worked, spend their lives waiting for an occupation worthy of them. A single passion had seized him: his new love. Without friends to tease or make fun of him, or vulgarize the first transports of desire and everything that eighteen-year-olds mean by the word love, he had blown it up all out of proportion, transfigured it. His fertile imagination and the indifference that cut him off from what he called "the others" kept him locked up within thick walls that protected him from us. When the windows were opened after the March rains, there was Marie-Louise, her arms raised in the early morning, combing her black bangs. At first a shadow, her contours imprecise, then with the coming of summer, golden against the light.

Grandmother came upon them one evening embracing behind the street door. She got angry and advised him to run after girls some place other than in our house.

I often rummaged through his room and his clothes. But his disorder was so well organized that he could hide things without risk. On the wall, the map was collecting dust. He could no longer bear us, he wounded us with his vulgar criticisms, and when he spoke—which was seldom—he launched into impassioned outbursts on his pride in being, in times like these, one of the oppressed.

"That's all very well. But Lucien, you do what you

want. Although up to now, it's true, you've elected to do nothing."

I had reached him. I could see it in his eyes. He would have hit me with pleasure. Then he went back into his room. In front of his eyes, Marie-Louise's window. He pressed his forehead against the glass, waited for her to appear, made her a sign and went out.

. . .

On Christmas Eve, he got dressed early.

"You're not eating with us?"

"Yes, but I have to go see a friend before dinner."

"You have a friend?"

"Yes, I have a friend."

We waited until late. Without him it was spoiled: the joy of Christmas Eve, the enchantment of the kitchen and its smells, the dishes covered until the last moment, the surprise hidden in the oven.

"He must be with her across the way," Grandmother said.

Then she began to evoke the dead as she ate the surprise.

When the holidays were over, I made up my mind. I went to Saint-Nicolas and saw the principal. Lucien had gone there in the early grades; it was customary for the parish to place its orphans in one of its schools. I explained my brother's case. The principal wrote me two days later to tell me he would hire Lucien to supervise the evening classes when school started again in January. He would be in touch with him before long. Lucien, when he received his letter, read it, reread it and disappeared into his room. He said nothing at the table, and went out as he did every day. That evening, I questioned him.

"You didn't receive anything important this morning?"

He gave me a hard look.

"So it was you? That's just like you. Can't you leave me alone? Can you see me a supervisor? If it was a question of money, you had only to say it, I could have gone down to the docks, the factory . . ."

He did go, however.

At the end of the month, he brought us his envelope and put it on the table.

"What is it?" Grandmother asked.

She opened it and smiled. "Your first pay check!"

He was afraid of the emotion that would follow and left.

After dinner one evening, when Grandmother lingered sleepily at the table, he said to her: "Listen. I know a girl. You know who. I want to get married. I'm working now. I know what I'm doing."

At first she laughed, then threatened, then beseeched, and finally one Sunday she received Marie-Louise and her father. The latter listed all his obligations and warned us he would be able to do nothing for them. Cheered by this discussion, which was more chicanery than agreement, Grandmother concluded with, "We'll see each other again. We don't live far."

.   .   .

It was a cold spring. The early morning dew froze on

the square. I wore my coat until May. It smelled of wet dog, heavy with rains dried before the stove. It was a time of wrangling in our house. The morning cold, the lifeless colors beneath a sun without warmth, the penetrating drizzle at the day's end, this heavy coat pulled on every morning, Lucien's surly obstinacy, his violence and his silence, the grating of the poker in the stove when Grandmother couldn't think of anything to say, our impotence, our defeat, the scaling plaster in the hall which followed us to our very threshold, the front door which banged shut with the wind—you had to knock three times, waiting in the downpour, answer the "who do you want?" then all those feelings of discouragement rose in my throat, the sensation of being mired, and I stood there for several seconds, head bowed, eyes full of tears and rain and waited, my neck frozen, for some imaginary relief—that was it, our spring.

.   .   .

"Make myself a little life all my own and not bother about him." I tried it for a day or two. It started with tidying up. I moved my things. Touching them, assigning them a new place gave the illusion of change. But I still had to live. And everything fell back into place, my place. I watched Lucien and suffered with him. One evening, he came home early, at eight o'clock. The days were getting longer, it was still light. He did not go out again, and sat with his back to the window, looking tired.

"Is it the work that wears you out?" Grandmother said. "Go to bed earlier. Look at your sister. She's in

(18)

bed every night at ten. All the same, Elise, I would have thought you'd marry before your brother."

I sighed. He looked at me and unexpectedly made a sign toward his door, got up, moved off and went in without taking his eyes off me. When I'd joined him, he started to laugh, rubbing his hands together.

"You can talk!" he said to the invisible Grandmother. But right away, we felt awkward being together, not knowing what to say. Stealthily, he threw a glance toward the window. Perhaps he had already had enough of my presence.

"It's true that you seem tired. Is it your work?"

He told me about the classes he ran. The children had liked him the first day. Now they were tired of him.

"It's dark, it's sad. Since I started to work, I see only a little sky. When I was laid up after the accident, in this bed, it was all I saw then. I spent days staring at it. I could almost see the texture of the sky, my eyes burned with it."

"That's over now," I said to encourage him.

"I know. And it won't come back. I was like something trapped in a glass bubble, and everyone could see me but no one could hear me. And what I wanted was to break the bubble so that someone would listen."

I thought: Is it Marie-Louise who is going to listen? But I didn't say it, I didn't dare yet. From his jacket pocket he pulled a rolled up newspaper which he unfolded.

"Do you want it? I'll leave it for you, you'll find it interesting."

"These days," I said, "I hardly have time to read."

Right away, I regretted my answer. I was disappointing him.

"Give me the newspaper. Is it a new one? I've never seen it."

"New and very important."

"Oh, really," I said as if astonished.

"They are completely against the war."

"Which war? The whole world is against war."

"You think so? You don't know that we've been fighting for five years?"

"Ah, but in Indochina!"

I remember the light tone with which I said that. A distant war, discreet, of imprecise origin, almost reassuring, proof of good health, of vitality.

"O.K.," he said, as if he knew he was wasting his time. "Now let's go to bed."

"When you go, I'll take back this room."

"When I go where?"

"You said you wanted to get married, or at least go away. I won't mention enlisting anymore, but after all, you'll get out of here someday."

"What about you? Grandmother is old; you'll be alone . . . don't you ever wish you could leave?"

His voice grew muffled as he pulled off his sweater by the neck—a bad habit of his. His arms still in the sleeves, he sat down next to me. I picked my words carefully. I wanted to be adroit, to avoid pronouncing the name Marie-Louise. Who knows? Perhaps one day his memory would happen upon these words, like dried flowers between the pages of a book.

"The real life," he said softly, "is like you. Serene, at peace with yourself. I'd like to be serene too. Believe me, Elise, the reason I want to get married is to get at that life. I'm sure to be happy—happier. And you will be happier too, and Grandmother."

He got to me. He knew I was vulnerable to these pictures of a quiet life, clean and simple.

After swearing "I will never say yes," after the tears, the scenes, the threats, Grandmother gave in. Tired of violent arguments, of Lucien's baleful expression, realizing she would never convince him and afraid he might do something foolish, she wearily chose to tell him one evening while ladling out the soup:

"Do what you like, get married, stay, go, I give you my permission."

She sat down, relieved, and talked of other things.

When Lucien, sad and tired, discussed his plans with us, she listened calmly. But alone with me, she often cried. Still, full of good grace, she went down our two flights of stairs and climbed the two floors at the rear of the court. There it was decided that Marie-Louise should continue working and that they should live with us. And thus the deed was done. The date was chosen, and Grandmother had only just enough time to have her black dress cleaned. The day before, she had her hair curled. She was certainly the most remarkable person in our meager cortège, eyes shining, no make-up other than her pent-up excitement, all in black: dress, shoes, hat, a cameo pinned low on her breast. Something fleeting and impalpable like a perfume, a certain air about her, made her stand out among us. She spoke little and

(21)

ate and drank with restraint, she who was so gluttonous at home. We were seven at the short benediction that followed the civil ceremony. The sacristan lit only one lamp. The priest called him in the middle of the prayers to ask for more light. Marie-Louise's parents left the same evening for the grape harvest. Lucien and his wife installed themselves in their empty rooms for a few days. That same evening, I slept in my brother's room with the feeling that I was trying to embrace something that was about to escape me forever. I had forgotten over the years that the sounds, even the smells, were not like those on the street-side. Through the middle of the night, boys called back and forth with loud whistles, their metal-tipped shoes clacketing on the cement steps. People talked from window to window and the sizzling frying pans of late-eating neighbors aroused the appetite.

They made a strange couple. She got up early, left before seven for the biscuit factory where she stood in front of her machine until evening. When she got home, Lucien was gone. She waited for him in their room, reading magazines. Sometimes, barely in the door, she would fix her hair, powder her nose and go off toward the Place de la Victoire to meet him.

Lucien ignored us completely. I was the first to guess there would be a child. I told Grandmother.

"I knew it would happen. From that boy, I expect anything. And I must say she was with him all the way in this. Now it's done; it's up to him to figure out how to earn their living."

"Do you like Marie-Louise?"

"She's not unpleasant, I expected worse."

Naturally, I didn't like her. I was even glad to see her deformed and heavy.

. . .

And the autumn passed by: gusts of rain, the first frosts, café-au-lait at four when the street lights went on, nothing that wasn't familiar, usual, expected. Life, my life, was broken down into four periods, the four seasons, which modified some of the motions in my well regulated schedule. But that particular fall with the hated stranger was the most unhappy of my life. It was also, although I didn't know it, the last before the crackup. With the smallest turns of the wheels, the carriage that was to take us on twisting trails to the slope where our existence would speed up for the final plunge, had begun to fall apart.

When we were all together, the elusive Lucien indulged in the most vulgar conversations. I had noticed that, alone with Marie-Louise, he changed tone and subject. The thin walls permitted many of their exchanges to filter through. After the meal, Lucien would get up, throw his napkin down, and from the door of his room, whistle to Marie-Louise, who would join him, laughing. The door closed, I could still hear them laugh. "They are laughing at me . . ." If I complained to Grandmother, she listened with boredom. Some time ago, her face had changed. Her eyelids were puffy, the irises of her eyes were yellow and, worst of all, her ears had grown immense.

Marie-Louise approved of everything Lucien did. I even came to pity her, so simple and undemanding, whose ideas were reduced to their palest expression, whose infatuation with Lucien had led her to us—the anxious, the hesitant, the dissatisfied arguers and questioners. Our problems, my brother's and mine, she doubtless considered a tiresome mania; but after all, to have Lucien, you had to put up with things like that. All the same, these ideas, these words ended by leaving their mark on her. She began by repeating them, without understanding—she was a born follower—then, as the habit took hold, she considered them her own.

Lucien read many newspapers. I picked up those he left around, sometimes also the books he forgot in the kitchen.

I read, and thick veils were lifted. It was like music. Unloose the shackles, understand, penetrate into the center of words, follow the sentence and its logic, know. I felt a physical satisfaction, I closed my eyes with pleasure. Improve one's self, I understood its meaning. I envied Lucien's running around libraries. I persevered, I multiplied the difficulties; it was like a complex canvas, each point making manifest the grand design. "I must talk to somebody." No one knew anything about all this pleasure I was accumulating. I had no opportunity to meet the spectator of my thoughts.

Lucien's books troubled me. With a terrible logic, these writings denounced everything that had seemed to me natural.

I quickly became involved. I saw my condition, I grew

proud of it. All around me, events traced their outlines, the port was immobilized by strikes, the longshoremen had been out twenty-three days, a young woman who had placed herself in front of a train loaded with arms was up for trial. It remained for me to understand the meaning of it all. Lucien rarely spoke to me, but that he did so occasionally was enough.

. . .

"I had not seen that I was sitting next to my sister. I had not seen the tree that bent toward the water, and I had not seen the water. I had not lifted my eyes when the barge advanced with the majesty of a fat woman. The water's eddies, little quivers that barely ruffled its surface, sent us its odor and I had not smelled it. I had not seen the colors, I did not even know that on that day the world was colored. I had thought it transparent, since my eyes had been arrested neither by the green bark of the yellow tree, nor by the grey water with its silver circles —its crazy eyes—nor by the barge, calm matron in black, nor by the opposite bank where the bargemen talked. My eyes moved across thick bodies, liquid bodies, my eyes looked only at me, and today, when I close them, the colors of that other time, of that day when I did not know there were any, dazzle me as if, having reached the top of a hill, I discovered a happy young boy sitting between his sister and his grandmother, facing the river, one evening in June."

This was written in Lucien's notebook—which I discovered in his absence—and dated March 1. Marie had been born the day before; Lucien had chosen her name. Every night we hung a line diagonally across the kitchen to dry her diapers. After a period of rest, Marie-Louise put her red sweater back on and once again went off to the biscuit factory. I didn't let her see it, but her predicament touched me. Lucien's demands confused her. He didn't hesitate to trip her up. He wanted, he said, to mold her, educate her. She followed without understanding, imagining sometimes that she might catch up, but when she said or did something that showed improvement over her past attitudes, he was already further ahead, or he had made a step backward and they never managed to meet. Among these contradictions of Lucien's, who could have found his bearings?

Except for his three hours of daily supervision, he had no occupation whatsoever. Marie-Louise encouraged him in his inaction. Was she jealous, was she afraid he would run after other girls? To her friends, she said: "He is a student." In our house, no one believed that anymore. I cannot figure out why all three of us trembled when he threatened to take the first job that came along. Did we think in the back of our minds that we could hold on to him better this way, use him to our advantage? Away from us, he would escape, he would have pals, a friend, other loves. He was so young, not yet twenty. He could still prepare himself, perfect himself, as he put it.

It was still light at eight o'clock, and in the evening, Marie-Louise went down to meet Lucien. He arrived, grabbed her by the nape of the neck; she caught the lapel of his jacket and up they climbed. One evening, I happened to go down to meet him too. Lucien was late. Finally, he came around the corner. The night was a little cold, moonless, and its only star the green neon light of a club newly-opened at the corner of the street. Three boys were heading for its door. The hard light shone on them, and the one on the left, who crossed in front of Lucien as he was about to join us, looked at him and stopped. Without enthusiasm, Lucien took his hand out of his pocket.

"Well!" the other one said, "I never thought I'd find you here after all this time! I recognized you right away. Are you going to the club too?"

Marie-Louise had come up to Lucien. I recognized the boy from his long curly hair. The green of the sign gave him a second face that lay in relief on the real one. I watched Lucien, I could feel what he felt. The accumulation of bitterness, the years of solitude, the broken friendship, the wound never healed, the quick vision of what he had not become, the humiliation of having nothing to say—I felt them all too.

"Good evening," he said finally.

There was a brief emptiness. I didn't dare move.

"I'm not going to the club. I live over there."

I breathed again. Over there; over there was the dank street, the broken-down house, the humid hall, the window where the clothes were dried, over there, among the grubby men, the old dotards chewing tobacco by the door, the old women with their soiled slips hanging below their smocks, the factory girls who lacquered their dirty fingernails, the poor people and the people who were poor.

"I didn't know that. What have you been doing?"

"I? I haven't been doing anything."

My brother's answer seemed to please the other. He looked at him, his nose wrinkled in a smile; a dog sniffing the scent, a conspirator's joy on his face.

"Come have a drink with us. There's nobody there at this hour; we can talk a little."

Marie-Louise came forward.

"Lucien, I'm going up."

"O.K. You go on up. Wait . . ."

He took her by the elbow. "I want to present my wife."

Before coming down, she had washed her face so that she would only have to wet it in the morning. Her night face, tired, chapped, was less impressive.

"You're married? Delighted, madame. I am a school friend of Lucien's."

Marie-Louise gave him a big smile.

"You go up," Lucien said. "I'll join you in five minutes."

"O.K. Let's go . . ."

Lucien shook his head.

"No thanks, I don't drink. What are you doing? Law?"

"That's right. Law. And I'm dragging it out at the moment to avoid the army. What about you?"

"I'm classified as physically disabled."

"Have you been married long?"

"A year soon."

They exchanged a few more words, then Lucien excused himself and offered his hand.

"Good night," the other said. "Perhaps another time."

"You, were you there?" Lucien asked when he saw me at the door.

"It was Henri?"

"Yes, it was Henri. You recognized him?"

"He hasn't changed."

Lucien nodded and we went up. The following evenings, he came home quickly as if he were afraid to meet Henri. They did meet, however. Later, my brother told me how Henri had been watching him and came up to him in front of our house. Lucien refused to go into the bar, so they agreed to meet one afternoon in a café by the harbor. Lucien promised himself he wouldn't go, then hesitation following on hesitation, he went. Henri questioned, Lucien talked. Henri listened. The unusual, the marginal attracted him. The rebellion of others, misery, the smell of poverty, were powerful stimulants. Belonging to a family comfortably off, without a history, he took delight in those he rooted out elsewhere. But for him, exoticism wasn't everything. He had arrived, through reasoning and analysis, at the same ideas as my brother. Henri lived with his parents and took advantage of his position, but only, he told Lucien, because "you have to cheat this society we want to destroy, and it is more effective to skirt around it and take advantage of it, the better to strike it down."

Lucien felt once again his old admiration. They quickly picked up the habit of meeting every day. One evening, Lucien brought him home. They shut themselves up in his room. From then on, Marie-Louise had to spend the evenings in the kitchen, with us. The first time, Henri's coming stirred us up. Grandmother thought vast cleanings were in order, linen on the kitchen table—which he would never notice—and Marie-Louise redid her make-up because he said good evening to her in passing. We didn't dare speak out loud, in the secret hope that we might pick up a few phrases. Henri seemed happy to come to our house. Climbing up, he must have taken in the smell of the stairs, choked on the décor.

Marie-Louise was sacrificed. Accustomed to Lucien's taking care of her, talking, questioning, explaining, she found herself whole evenings, whole Sundays, alone with Marie, whom she pushed the length of the quays when the sun was out. He left her at the moment when his mind, stiff, like an unused muscle, began to loosen. He had sown his seed in wild desperation, he had stuck with her stubbornly—he had nothing else—and he stopped suddenly. I can see her now, sitting on the bed on summer nights, useless, thinking but not understanding. Lucien and his friend had gone off to talk, smoking, at the edge of the river. He was happy. Henri encouraged him not to change his way of life. And we had hoped that he would bring his relatives into the picture! We already saw Lucien stashed away in a well-paid and important job.

One evening when he was late going home, Henri asked my brother if I would call his house to explain.

"My sister wouldn't dare go into a café to telephone. In fact, I suspect she's never used a telephone."

Henri looked at me. It was true. Who would I have phoned? We had no friends. When we needed information, we went out to get it. If we needed the doctor, we stopped by his place—he lived near by. A great sadness ran through me. I remembered the year when I had shown Grandmother two New Year's cards we'd just received, and she was ecstatic: "Oh, look at the cards!" It was such an event. Pitiable provincials. Isolated, awkward, poor with a hidden kind of poverty. I loved my brother at such moments for the way he would one day suffer, had already suffered. I loved him too because I was scared of life without him, my only bridge between the world of others and ours. After that incident, Henri showed me a certain deference. One couldn't say his attitude was dictated by charity. No, I was one of those unusual ill-adapted beings from whom his curious mind drew satisfaction. He granted me a few handshakes, little phrases in passing that I answered in a manner he liked, and Lucien, reticent at first, occasionally permitted my presence between them.

This was the period of my revenge, of the predicted and hoped-for moment: the abandonment of Marie-Louise. When I was around, she tried to stay in the picture, hanging on to Lucien with the kind of questions which, in the old days, would have delighted him.

"Tell me, Lucien, explain to me . . . tell me why . . ."

He came home around eleven, or later, and looked for her.

"Where is Marie-Louise?"

"I'm here."

"What's the matter?"

"Nothing."

"Well, if nothing's the matter, everything's O.K."

They went to their room, I could hear Marie-Louise's voice whispering, Lucien's louder. They talked a long time.

Every afternoon, Henri arrived around one o'clock, quietly sat by the door, waiting for my brother to come down; sometimes, he wandered back and forth in the court where the tree, greener than ever, spread its branches over the cobbles like an umbrella. Our windows stayed open day and night, and the walls dried. Sometimes Lucien sighed when he was with his friend:

"Someday, it'll be the real life, we'll do everything we want to do. We'll do everything we want to do."

Lucien was firm. Yes, we would realize our dreams, we would join those who felt like us. Our spirits had begun to stir, our bodies would soon follow.

.   .   .

The newspapers that Marie-Louise bought accumulated on the chair in their room. The lovelorn column, advice to the married, how to keep your husband, beauty recipes . . . She was trying to find in them the remedy for Lucien's metamorphosis. She was very gentle; at that time, I would have said very weak.

(32)

As for me, I devoured everything that denounced this dying, but not yet dead, war. I wanted Barsac's last article, which my brother had put away before I had time to read it. I couldn't find it. Once again, I seized upon the green notebook, hidden in a shirt stuffed with papers.

I looked it over quickly, skipping the sentences without interest, descriptions or philosophical observations. I was looking for some kind of clue, for the evening before, this is what had happened: After a long discussion—it was almost eleven—Henri had said good night. In the kitchen, Marie-Louise was glancing through a newspaper. Lucien called to her:

"Marie-Lou, ready for bed?"

"I'd like to go for a walk with you."

"At this hour?"

"Why not?"

She had risen slowly, she had folded the paper, then, suddenly, she had run toward him.

"Lucien, darling, take me for a walk."

"Not now."

He tried to shake her off, for she held him by his shirt collar.

"All right," he sighed, "get your jacket. Elise! Come, we're going for a walk."

I didn't move, I was too stunned.

"Come on," he repeated, "get going."

Marie-Louise hadn't dared say anything, but her face showed her disappointment. Lucien had gone to Grandmother's room; that's where we put Marie's bed until Henri was gone. She wasn't asleep; he picked her up.

(33)

"And you, my daughter, you're coming too. Everybody ready? March."

It was a mournful walk. Only he talked. He headed for the square, and I asked him why we couldn't walk along the banks of the river.

"No," he cut me short.

When we had done a tour of the square, he pointed to a bench. It was deep night, the grass glistened, mosquitoes buzzed around the lamps. Marie had fallen asleep in my brother's arms. He had said whatever came into his mind, banal observations about spring, winter, addressing himself to us both, and I had answered distractedly. I was being used; he took me along when he didn't want to be alone with Marie-Louise.

"Women, we're going home now," he commanded as he got up.

There had been no argument in their room, unless they spoke in very low voices, for I heard nothing; and I knew how to listen.

.   .   .

I found the letter in the green notebook. Folded four ways, it marked the last written page. I was almost caught, for the letter was long. Today, I have it again, for I have recovered all Lucien's belongings. It marked the end of an era. From then on everything changed.

"You told me tonight: 'You're like all the girls.' I am like all the girls not when they're good but when they're bad. Listen, I've never met a boy like you. Yes, that's something you've been told every time. This time, it's true.

(34)

"You showed me your door and you said, 'See, that's where I live. It's a little dark. It's old.' You asked me if I lived far. 'Beyond the swing bridge.' After the swing bridge, you walk a good fifteen minutes in open country. What country: a few stalls, some small houses, some gardens. You know them, Lucien, and the pure air of the gas factory, and the black earth and the muddy paths, for it is always raining in that kind of place. You have to put basins inside.

"That's where my room is. Finally, my room. Five of us share it: my father, his wife, his first wife, my brother and me. My father is sixty. We arrived here the second year of the Spanish Civil War. My mother died quietly, on the third floor of one of those harbor houses, in her bed, which had been placed in the window. Leaning forward a little, she could communicate with the neighbors across the way. A little while later, we got a new mother. She took better care of us than our real mother who was always sick, and we loved her the way she loved us. The one who brought us up is too gentle to get angry or to walk out. Where would she go? And besides, she attached herself to me with the anxiety of a fat woman for someone fragile. I went to school for awhile. But a cold was enough to make me stay out. When I was fifteen, I spent my days in the sun, when there was any, listening to the women talk. I didn't go out; my father was strict, he disapproved of dances and walks. My brother's friends came and peered at me. One of them went to night school. I wanted to go and my father gave in. We would come home together. We would stop in the darkest corners and smother each other with passion. I dreamed of

a life with him, of preparing his meals in a kitchen full of flowers . . . all the thoughts that girls have on that subject. Then he began to avoid me, ignore me and I suffered. I looked at men with rage, the rage to be noticed, chosen, loved. Just as boys do, I set off on the chase. I wanted a man. I soon learned that the only way to have one is to 'give one's self,' as they say.

"A long time later, one Sunday, I was accosted by some women. They were taking up a collection for the longshoremen on strike. I understood the reason for our scanty meals. I hadn't paid attention. My father didn't talk about those things.

"The women led me into a small building. I listened, I stayed, I returned. Finally, one evening, we joined up with the men. They were simple, poor, young, old, dirty, well-dressed, courageous, noisy, proud, a real May Day parade.

"I became the section's secretary. I learned a lot because I was in love with the treasurer, a hard man and pure. But the times were against sentiment, the men were struggling, most of them had no work. Why does no man want to keep me? Why, after a few dates, does he look bored and announce that he won't have enough time to see me? To begin again each time, each time settle into a love affair as if it were for always and each time pack the bag of memories. The waiting, the meeting, the first day, the second, the afternoons in the dimly-lit hotel rooms, quiet, those beds that are covered with smooth sheets, soft blankets. The others, outside, and I, protected from life, in the arms of the man who is to be my birth

and my death. To make them happy, I have done every-thing they wanted, everything that might please them.

"And yet they leave me. Maybe my silence displeases them? At the start they are happy that you listen. Then after that, they ask questions. What can you say? So, I shut up. I think they become suspicious of me. I cry when I leave them, I cry when I meet them again. Everything falls apart. I spent four years this way. The day before yesterday, I was going down the street parallel to yours when you suddenly appeared and offered me a cigarette. I had just left a man, I had to take the streetcar before ten. It was dark, the street was noisy. I stopped. You spoke first, I answered as I walked and we parted with the promise of a date.

"What's happening to me, how can I explain it? You would be quite right to say it's not love. Or to say it is love for the sake of simplicity. I have trouble with lan-guage; I'm not used to 'communicating.' I had forgotten that word. I read it one day in a magazine at the Maison Populaire. I learned it.

"I have the failing of taking everything I find. I love to have things. Books, especially. And I read them. That is how I picked up this word 'communication' from the magazine. It's that and it isn't that. It's to exist, for a few moments, and to know it through someone else. Without that, the only way I can discover anything is by suffering, by doing without. When I'm sad, when I can't find work, when I sleep badly because there's no room in the bed, when I see myself in the shop windows, that's when I feel me. But with you, I have felt me. Saying

(37)

all this to you would not have been easy, I would have had to hunt for words, like a liar in trouble. Lucien, will we see each other and be friends?

Anna"

. . .

"Don't wait for me tonight, I definitely won't be coming home. I'll sleep at Henri's, like the last time."

I didn't believe him. Marie-Louise looked at him, uneasiness in her eyes.

"Come home, Lucien. Even if it's late; come home."

"How can I, if the streetcars have stopped running?"

She shrugged her shoulders and went back to her room. But when the front door banged shut, she rushed out and ran after him down the stairs. Grandmother, who had been watching, went to the window and looked through a crack in the half-opened shutters.

"Ah, no, she didn't succeed. There she comes around the corner."

She started to laugh. We shut up. Marie-Louise was coming back. She closed the door, then broke into a dance step. She was smiling and we were confused, no longer positive that she hadn't caught up with him. But he didn't come home that night either.

. . .

Henri is sitting on the edge of the bed. He is rummaging through the pocket of his jacket which he has hung on the door latch. His face, as always, is calm. Does he owe this apparent serenity to his somewhat thick features and his colorless eyes? I think it is just that he is happy. He is conscious of his motions. He savors them:

to hang a jacket on the window, place a foot on the bed, bend an ear to catch the obscenities of two angry men down in the courtyard. He demolishes one world and, in fifteen minutes of exposition, builds another where a warm place awaits him. He finds a place for himself everywhere. He savors the newspaper that provides him tonight with three or four hours of conversation. He has put it down next to him on the bed; I decipher, upside down, the headlines in enormous type: "DIEN-BIEN-PHU FALLS." He has one hand on the table. He is at ease, he sniffs the sauce we are reheating and which we would never dare offer him.

"This is big enough to regroup the entire left," he said. "But who, in France, is ready to profit by these events? We have to find enough young people to create a permanent agitation. It wouldn't be revolution, of course; Paris is the capital of America's fiftieth state; nothing doing there, unless it's guerrilla warfare like the Viets."

Lucien drank to this possibility. He agreed fervently.

Henri was in permanent readiness for the revolution. It was the logical conclusion to his daily and nightly discussions. These were planned in his comfortable room and his horror of the society in which he was forced to live fortified his dreams of an overthrow. In Lucien he found the very embodiment of the system's victim: an orphan, unlucky, poor, thin, married too young, without roots. My brother's physique fascinated him: that beautiful gaunt face, straight out of the archives of the October revolution or an album of heroic anarchists. He envied him this and resented all the more the fact that Lucien wasn't completely committed to the goal, the struggle. Lucien was, but intermittently. We were born to trouble, our difficulties multiplied, choking us like ivy, from which we were unable to extricate ourselves without help. Lucien bore them with rage, but in order to survive, he had made for himself an impregnable refuge: a kind of laziness, the search for a special kind of love.

I became the unfeeling spectator of Marie-Louise's suffering. She wasn't as stupid as she pretended; from then on, around me, she affected an air of satisfaction and tranquility. The only honest thing my brother did was to warn us when he wasn't coming home. This happened two and even three times a week. The other evenings he came in late and found Marie-Louise up. They talked in low voices, but I was always careful not quite to close the door of our room. I could hear well enough. Marie-Louise covered him with sad caresses. He no doubt put on his solemn and distant look so she made an effort to talk about something that might arouse his interest.

"What about the war? Is it over?"

"What about the war ... read the papers, you'll know as much as I do."

All the same, he launched into a long dissertation from which I also profited, for his voice rose and I could even guess his gestures. Heroic Marie-Louise listened without blinking, Marie-Louise who had to get up at six and stay riveted to her machine until evening. She had married a "student," she was paying for it. The hardest part was that she couldn't even complain to her group of women who told each other everything. At one time, she had been envied. Now she was less popular with her friends. She used Lucien's language, his expressions. "She's always finding fault, she's stuck up," they were saying at the factory.

. . .

We were following, as you might a rescue operation, one man's bid for peace in Indochina. Marie-Louise too was caught up in the feverish atmosphere Henri and my brother had created; generously, she forgot her woes and shared our impatience.

On the fourteenth of July, Lucien asked me for some money. This had never happened before. I gave him a little, without asking questions. I learned that Marie-Louise had made the same request of Grandmother.

"I told her, ask Elise; she's the one who keeps the accounts."

She hadn't dared ask me. I wouldn't have been able to give her any.

One night, in the darkness of our room, Grandmother confided in me:

"Do you know where Lucien spends his nights, where he spends his days? Not with Henri. You're such a stupid thing, you believe everything that comes out of his mouth. You've spoiled him, you always backed him up. And that Henri is on it, too. And Marie-Louise, if she knew, my God . . ."

She sniffed a little and went on: "He's going to make trouble for us. Marie-Louise, her father, that nasty mother of hers . . ."

Lucien met a girl every day at noon at the streetcar

stop. Together, they went into one of the hotels on the docks. They had also been seen coming out in the early morning.

"Several people have met them, longshoremen who live on that street, who know the girl's father."

The Hotel des Docks. The girl was the one who had written the letter, Anna. The money was to pay for the hotel. Henri knew all about it. Had he read the letter?

I couldn't sleep. I kept seeing the quays at midday, the background of boats and the display of oysters and gray shrimp . . . two shadows holding hands, breathing the smell of parting that rose from the gutters. I was seized with such anxiety that I decided, come what may, to stick by Lucien. I wanted him to come home immediately so that I could tell him. I told him nothing, for he didn't come home and it was a good thing; he would have seen it as an obvious trap.

. . .

Money. Now we are three sweating for money. Lucien needs it for his afternoons. This is summer vacation; he isn't making a cent. He doesn't talk about going to work anymore, he hasn't the time to work. He goes to bed from noon 'till night in some harbor hotel where, in his downy nest, he can hear the clanking of the cranes. Then, at night, he goes to bed again, here or elsewhere. But he needs money. It's Marie-Louise who brings home the most. What she keeps, she shares with Lucien. That means neither has much. She too is seized with a lust for money; since Lucien's desertion, she spends a lot on newspapers, cosmetics, ribbons, jewelry.

She's read in some stupid advice-to-the-lovelorn column that you must be several women in one. But recipes for pleasing a man come high. I've caught her complacently sticking flowers in her hair, in love with her own image. Marie-Louise needs money. I miss terribly what I loaned to Lucien. Ten thousand francs. Enough to live on a whole week. We are the respectable poor. Those who hide their poverty like a shameful disgrace. We must keep it to ourselves.

.   .   .

Our faces in the shadow—it was now black night—I felt as if we could say everything, to the bitter end. It was hot but we had to keep the window closed—the other people in the house might hear.

"As for the three of us, first we must spend as little as possible, temporarily give up buying anything except food, and somehow increase our income by every means we can think of."

"You mean work."

"Yes, work," I said.

"O.K.," he said. "We didn't need a family council for that. But since we're here . . . At this time of year, I won't be able to find any job that will pay. Besides, I've tried . . . well, I don't have to give the details now. Right now, I need all my spare time. By October, it'll be better. Until then, I have to ask you to help out and have a little patience."

"All right," Marie-Louise said, thinking the discussion over. She must have resented my cutting short one of the rare evenings when Lucien was with her.

"No, it's not all right!"

Anger overwhelmed me; suddenly, I was so hot I had to explode.

"You don't understand. I have no money."

"But . . . I haven't either."

"I ask you, Lucien, to give me back what you have, the little you have. You too, Marie-Louise."

"But we haven't any," Lucien howled. "What are you trying to get at?"

I kept quiet. Outside, we could hear the screams of children who didn't want to go home. Marie-Louise turned on the light. Now that we could see each other, I wasn't sure I dared go on. He took a few ten franc pieces out of his pocket and, smiling, placed them on the table.

I no longer hesitated.

"Marie-Louise, your father knows everybody who does any hiring on the docks. Lucien, can't you ask him to help you find work for a few weeks? It's a temporary solution, I know you can do it and we'd be saved."

"Not that," said Marie-Louise, pouting.

"No, not that," Lucien repeated in a low voice.

Across the table, he grabbed the collar of my blouse.

"I see that madame, rather mademoiselle, has discovered a new world, she has learned about strikes, the unemployed workers. She has a new religion. Therefore, for her moral well-being, she fancies having a proletarian in the bosom of the family. It's easier than being one herself. Why haven't you ever worked like the others? What's your excuse? That you had to bring me up? You're lying to yourself. And if it was to bring me up, why send me to the docks today? It's a little late. Why didn't you do it when I was sixteen?"

And with a single blow, he let out all his bitterness. He had been sent to school. At the beginning, yes, at the beginning, he'd been happy. But after? He had paid a high price for our vanity.

"You should have raised me according to our means!" he cried.

"All the same," I said sadly, "think of the sacrifices we made for your sake. So that you could have more, I practically lived in penury. Think back, Lucien. So that you could have a new shirt for the holiday or the contest, I wore a faded blouse, a made-over skirt."

"And that's exactly what I hold against you!"

"Keep quiet. Keep quiet."

Grandmother opened the door.

"Come now," she said sharply, "they can hear you downstairs. What is it?"

No one answered.

"It's none of your business."

Lucien pushed her toward her room.

"What are you doing?" she said.

And she held the door wide open.

"I want to know."

This made him furious. He lunged forward and closed the door.

She opened it again.

"The door is to stay open."

He hooked the latch violently.

Grandmother cried out: "This isn't a prison! You can't lock people in."

They had now both lost control and the door was opened and shut several times. He grasped the knob tight while she banged on the door, screaming. I fell on him and tried to pull his hand off the latch. He pushed me with his left elbow but this motion loosened his grip and Grandmother succeeded in opening the door.

"Shame, shame!" she cried. "For years you've been hanging around here; nourished by others, you drink our sweat. You're lazy, vicious. I know everything," she spat out, "yes, everything."

"Be quiet." I pointed at Marie-Louise.

"I don't care, I'll tell everything. You can leave. You can go to work. We don't ever want to see you again."

Lucien grabbed her, shook her and threw her on the bed. Would he have strangled her? I held him from behind so that he'd turn against me, for he had her by the throat. Then he let go of her, pushed me aside and lunged toward the kitchen. I was scared. He was going and what would he do outside? I ran toward him and stopped him. He misunderstood, he pushed me away. I fell against the table. He came toward me and slapped me twice, with hatred, then he grabbed the oilcloth where the plates were stacked, and pulled. Without looking at me, her daughter in her arms, Marie-Louise went out with him. As I pulled myself up, I stepped on a peach that had rolled out of a broken bowl. Our neighbors, what would they think of us? We had been so proud of being the only ones who never made a spectacle of themselves.

"Did you see him? He might have killed me . . . He's no good, Elise."

"Just so long as no one heard."

. . .

It was a week before we saw him again. One evening, he arrived with Henri, which spared us explanations. Marie-Louise paid me back some of the money. "This is an installment." There was nothing else to say. Once again, the kitchen was scattered with newspapers.

Henri announced his departure. He was to spend three years in Paris. This news made me think. What a revolution he had brought into our midst in these few months! Our windows had been opened. With him had come names, countries, men, and Indochina was suddenly as near as the hills of Verdelais. All those newspapers he left us, whose names now filled my mouth and which I recited like a magic formula! A few days before his departure, in November, Henri came in out of breath, a paper in his hand. He threw out a name to which I paid little attention; the name was Algeria.

For the first few days we were distressed, but we ended by adapting ourselves to Henri's absence. He wrote to Lucien at length, who would say as he shut himself up, "I'm answering Henri." My brother and I became closer. I soon learned the reason. He had always been aware of my hostility toward Marie-Louise. She was beginning to be a nuisance, she was taking the place I had filled during his youth. And she, who somehow felt it without knowing the cause, was growing closer to Grandmother; the bond was Marie. But Lucien expected me to pay for this return of affection with my complicity.

During this school year, he started his duties at four

and had managed to obtain two sessions every Thursday. Sometimes I felt ashamed of my triumph when he called me into his sanctuary, which I entered only with permission.

Marie-Louise followed me in. He didn't see her. He talked to me, read me some article or other, made comments: ". . . what racism is in North Africa, to what extremes it is carried . . . but we are ashamed, some kinds of brutality leave no trace."

"What do you mean, brutality?"

"Oh, come on, Marie-Louise, don't interrupt."

And he explained it to me, without so much as a glance at her, and took out a letter from Henri from which he read me certain passages. I looked at his table. On it, a row of books lent by Henri before he left hinted at a life that I found fascinating.

"This war . . . we must do something."

"This isn't Paris. I do know a few isolated types like us . . ."

Lucien said "us." He and I.

"I want you to meet a friend of mine. Her name is Anna. She is involved in several movements. She is not very active now, she is too busy. What's the matter with you? Why are you looking at me that way? You're all red in the face."

"Nothing," was all I said.

I didn't dare say more. I would have started to tremble.

. . .

I am sitting across from my brother. The bar is called "0 20 100 0." When the door opens, a cold fog freezes

(48)

our legs. I'm about to see Anna. I'm scared. She has become, without my knowing her, something huge, fantastic.

Someone has arrived who is suddenly at our table. Lucien doesn't get up; it's I who get up without looking at the person in front of me. I see two feet wearing broken-down pumps. I fold the paper eight ways; that takes a few more seconds. All the same, I must raise my head. She looks at me. There is no shock. The face before me is ordinary. She unwinds an immense scarf that envelops her head, Sahara-fashion. She has long brown hair that hangs inside the collar of her coat, or is it a jacket? I can't tell which. She shakes it loose with her fingers. It hangs low over her forehead in uneven bangs. The rest of her face is narrow and pale. Lucien has ordered three coffees. He introduces me with some nice phrases, that much I hear. From then on, the conversation remains total confusion. I am thinking and cannot follow what they say. She has a whispering voice, which irritates me. She plays with her hair and I ask myself if long hair would become me. I say yes to everything. Lucien offers her a cigarette, he shows her a cartoon from the *Canard Enchaine* he has pulled from his pocket. She laughs and looks at me. I am now used to her thin face. I begin to discover a certain charm, her light hazel eyes are large and beautiful. Where does she get such long, black lashes? Looking at her profile, I see from their stiffness that they are laced with thick mascara.

Marie-Louise is prettier: regular features, texture of skin, shape of mouth. Anna has to work on her face

(49)

constantly to arrive at beauty. She lights up like a lamp and her seductiveness turns on. Her thinness is no handicap. The hair of a drowned person, Grandmother would say. But on her thread-like body, it has the charm of wet grass. There is something magical, something mysterious in this seductiveness that goes against all the usual forms: frail body, child's wrists, flat breasts, face pale and serious. One of those people you don't distrust. Anna wears a black sweater, gray skirt, a black smock with big pockets. We get up. She adjusts her long scarf. Lucien makes his excuses. He must go back to Saint-Nicolas; Anna is going in the same direction, isn't she? I leave alone.

. . .

"You'll see, some day the real life will begin," he often used to say. "The main thing is to get there intact."

What was it, that real life? More agitation? A better furnished gallery of human portraits to surround us? What would change? How would we know that the real life had begun?

"Why aren't you like the others?" Marie-Louise complained.

One Friday, she was brought home by two women. She had become dizzy in front of her machine. When Lucien came home, he found his wife in bed. I was at her side; we were waiting for the doctor. He patted her hand and she started to cry. He asked her questions without being able to hide from me a certain gleam in his eyes that I knew well and that took my breath away. He had just begun to hope that she might die.

The doctor arrived very late, ordered examinations

and analyses. He diagnosed Marie-Louise as very weakened and advised us to act quickly. While he was packing his kit, I called Lucien aside.

"Have you any money?"

"No. Have you?"

"Very little. We must keep it for the prescriptions. You haven't even five hundred francs?"

"Not a penny."

Shamefaced, I had to make excuses which were all too familiar to the doctor. We would pay him the next time.

Lucien had a thousand francs. I knew it; he had unintentionally pulled them from his pocket with his handkerchief that very morning. I renewed my demand; he continued to pretend he had no money.

This illness irritated him. It got to the point where, for Marie-Louise, it was a period in hell. But hardly had she returned to the biscuit factory when she collapsed again.

"What can be wrong with her? Elise, do you think she'll get well?"

Grandmother, torn between her natural goodness and her calculations, went in over her head, panicked, fashioned nourishing desserts for Marie-Louise, lit candles in church, pulled me behind the door to take stock of her efforts and, since they were proving useless, leveled an unjustified rancor against Lucien's wife.

Marie-Louise finally gave in to our pressures, my brother's, mine and Grandmother's. She agreed to go. She was admitted to the Cestas rest home with her daughter for three months. I think she became afraid when she saw the purple and yellow skin around her eyes. Rested—therefore pretty, the magazines said—Lucien might desire her again.

"And it won't cost you a penny," Grandmother threw in.

This, she found admirable.

. . .

Strange sensation to find ourselves three again, like the old days.

Lucien became almost tender with me, or at least as tender as he could be with someone he didn't love. I served as interpreter between Grandmother and him, for they no longer spoke. She was profoundly unhappy. She had to bear the hostility of those across the way who were informing anyone who would listen that Lucien was killing their daughter. She had to suffer through our conversations when Lucien ate with us—politics and war didn't interest her. She missed Marie. I, she said, had "moved over to Lucien's camp." She imagined that when she went downstairs, people turned and talked about us.

Winter started off cold. The windowsills were covered with ice. When night came, Grandmother went all the way to the greengrocer's who threw empty crates outside his door. She would bring home several and we'd make a big fire every night after dinner. She fell one icy night and had to be hospitalized with three fractures. People looked at us strangely. "Everything happens to them," they said behind our backs. "They attract bad luck."

We had never been alone, Lucien and I, and we

weren't for long: two days after Grandmother's accident, Anna made her entrance. She checked our three rooms, liked Lucien's very much and he—never doubting my neutrality—closed the door in my face. I found myself alone in the kitchen every afternoon, while they whispered together in the next room.

Visiting hours at the hospital started at one o'clock. I arrived punctually and stayed until three, giving encouragement to Grandmother, who cried because she wanted to get out. I went home. Anna arrived, left at seven, some time after Lucien so that curious neighbors would think she had come to see me.

But she sometimes spent the night with us. For fifteen days, I had been going to the hospital every day. This particular day, I stopped by Puesh's who gave me copy to type, and went home. Was Anna already there? What did she do with her time when she wasn't with Lucien? So there were people with no fixed occupation, who could make dates, loaf, make love in the middle of the great ant heap where all the others exhausted themselves.

From the first floor, I recognized their voices. They must be having an argument. I ran up the last steps. Anna had her back to Lucien and was leaning against the door with one hand and putting on her shoes with the other. Her skirt hung down.

Lucien was talking. They didn't hear me.

"I've taken risks; I've had you come here; I've managed to get rid of my wife by making her life impossible. Now, what do you want us to do? There is nothing

(53)

left here. Let's go to Paris. I'll leave first, you wait here, at my house, if you like . . ."

"Listen to me, Lucien. You've always said we'd leave together. Now, you're ashamed to admit it, but you want to join your friend, alone. You'll leave and I won't hear a word from you. So let's get this straight, I'm going. And the hurt you're doing me you'll feel some day. So I'm going, good, but before I go, let me give you some news, nothing important, only that I'm expecting a child. I've known it three weeks."

"What? It isn't true . . ."

She let go of the door and turned to him. She was crying.

"It isn't true? You know me well, you see me naked every day . . . look." Lucien had moved up to the door. Leaning now against the table, she dropped her skirt, pulled up her sweater. She had no slip on and her belly showed. From a distance, it looked slightly stuck out.

"Look closely," she repeated several times, her voice choked with tears. "See it, this little swelling, it's a child, your child. Look closely, it's the first time you'll see it but also the last. And it's all you'll see of it."

She adjusted her skirt, sniffling. Trembling, she couldn't quite button the belt. She threw a scarf over her head, put on her jacket, gathered up her shoes. I heard her moan and breathe hard. She ran to the door and fled down the stairs. Lucien went into his room and I left the corner where I had hidden. A sudden disgust took hold of me. They made themselves at home everywhere. Once they had made love in a place, they made it theirs.

I had need, just like Grandmother, for respectability, for consideration. "He is going," I said to myself. "Anna joins him or she doesn't; she has a child or she doesn't. They get angry or they don't. In three months, when Marie-Louise comes back, we'll take stock. He is going. No more scratching this wound that won't heal. With courage, I'll get out. Haven't I always been alone? It will be less terrible than a scandal, which couldn't fail to explode. What happens far away won't reach me."

.   .   .

There was still a little gray snow around the door of Les Glycines, the rest home in Cestas. Marie-Louise greeted us with exclamations of pleasure. She had not been quick to regain her strength and her face was still yellow and mauve. She reproached Lucien for not writing her. He closed his eyes for a few seconds without answering. They brought in Marie. She, at least, seemed very well. Lucien didn't know what to say. He kept repeating the same questions about the food, the care the schedule. Then he talked a great deal about the political developments that preoccupied him, about the racist mentality that was furiously developing. But Marie-Louise couldn't make the effort to listen for long.

"I'm here for another forty-one days. When I'm ready to leave, will you come for me?"

Lucien didn't answer. I felt like an accomplice to the silent crime he was preparing to commit. I was uneasy and redoubled my thoughtful questions so that she might retain from our visit the feeling of being loved. The room we were in resembled the parlor of a boarding school. Marie was sitting on the floor playing with a doll her father had brought her.

"I'm sorry about your granny," Marie-Louise said. "Why didn't you tell me about the accident? I would have written; it would have given her pleasure."

Lucien made a skeptical pout and said in a low voice, "No time."

He was playing with Marie's wrist and turning the little chain she wore. That suddenly gave me an idea. In a drawer of our closet, Grandmother had stowed away her treasures: her husband's wedding ring and watch, a ring, two gold pins, our mother's earrings. Would she let us pawn them so Lucien could go to Paris? I doubted it.

"You're keeping me away," Marie-Louise complained.

I moved toward the window, afraid that one or the other might appeal to me for support.

"Take this to Elise," Lucien said, giving his daughter the newspaper he held in his hand.

He wanted me to come back. Marie-Louise realized this and for several seconds said nothing. The pleasant features of her face had contracted, she was trying to keep from sobbing. Then she put out her arm to Lucien, to lean against him. He jumped back brusquely. As she straightened up, she moaned.

"No tears," he said stonily, "or I go."

She looked at him, but he averted his eyes.

"Lucien," she said in a soft voice, "I'm your Algeria, too."

He shrugged his shoulders but said nothing.

This comparison had spontaneously come to her lips; it disturbed Lucien. It disturbed me too. For a long time, we each held on to this little phrase—the last Marie-Louise was to say to my brother.

. . .

I took the jewelry, pawned it and got twenty-five thousand francs which I gave to Lucien the day before his departure.

He said thank you, assured me that he would pay it back some day. I asked him to write to me often and began to cry in spite of my resolutions. He seemed moved. Several times, he made the rounds of the apartment with small steps. Despite the cold, he opened the window and looked for a long time at the black tree hung with icicles. I insisted he eat something but without success. He went to bed early, for he was to take the seven o'clock train the next morning. I wanted to go with him but he wouldn't let me; so I didn't know whether he left alone.

When he got up, he found me in the kitchen. His suitcase was packed. I couldn't believe it. Naturally, I said none of the things I had prepared in the warmth of my bed. Was this departure real? He was playing at going, he would unpack his bag, I couldn't stay alone. To hell with the real life. And who could say that it wasn't here, in the long daydreams, in the waiting and the wanting to go away? He put on his jacket, lit a cigarette and then my heart really beat hard. The moment had come. He kissed me absentmindedly; he had already left. He said nothing to staunch my bleeding wounds, not even a pat phrase to give me hope. But on opening the door, and as I touched the cloth of his jacket, he winked at me and looked back. The last seconds lengthened, grew, shrank and the door was closed. On the stairway, his steps slowed as he turned the corners. There was still the window. I ran to it; he had just stepped out, there was a thirty-meter respite before he reached the corner. Would he look back? Like so many ants, men were leaving their black houses. One of them obscured Lucien. He was gone. I turned back toward the kitchen, went back to bed, got up again, sat on the side of the bed, opened his empty drawers. It was later that I began to suffer, as daylight lengthened the angles, gave back to the walls their real dimensions, illumined the emptiness around me. I did not go to the hospital. I spent the entire day in retreat among the memories of my brother.

. . .

I suffered much and for a long time, until the first letter. He wrote on the twentieth day after his departure, six dry lines, without details, to reassure me about his health, his morale, his occupations.

I was left with two disagreeable jobs to do: first, to tell Marie-Louise, prevent her from joining him, calm her, urge her to be patient. Second, to get back Grandmother's jewelry, for which I saw only one solution: economize and do without. And if I didn't succeed before her return, what then? I had an uneasy conscience and preferred that she know nothing about this affair. This fear led me to a decision that was to change my whole future. I thought in three months I could find the necessary money. Therefore I had to keep her hospitalized as had been ordered. That turned out to be difficult. She cried, she implored; I swore that it was only a question of a short stay and that I was already getting things ready for her return. She called me names, threatened to die, then sank into a hostile silence.

I went to see Marie-Louise and announced Lucien's departure as if it were good news. He would find work, he would be able to support his wife and Marie. She was indifferent to this argument. I sketched a brilliant future for my brother. I lied, talked of a few weeks' absence. She seemed resigned and I left her, relieved.

I worked hard, sometimes in the exaltation fed by self-contemplation, sometimes in the search for the drunkenness of fatigue. In the evening, I ate early and went to bed early. It was a moment I enjoyed to the hilt. Finally the day was dying. Tomorrow there might be mail. Sleep would deliver me for a few hours. The solitude of evening was not painful. I felt myself secure. Security. I liked that word and what it evoked. It took the place of happiness. The sense of well-being throughout my stretched-out body, the lights I dimmed, the book I opened . . . what did my brother matter at such a moment?

For a whole month, I had no news. I thought several times my life might dissolve in the vertigo I felt before the letter box. Then Lucien wrote several pages. He was working.

"I have found myself driven by necessity to take on a difficult job, but very exalting. I am going to join the real fighters, share the inhuman life of factory workers.

Among Bretons, Algerians, exiled Poles, and Spaniards I'm going to make contact with the true reality of the movement. And when I've finished the day at the factory, I'll go back to my papers and my notebooks, for—my old Elise—I will bear witness for those who cannot."

Then came several polite and forced references to Grandmother's health and a curious postscript:

"In the hotel where I live, there is a room that should be free for quite a while. If you would like to use it, let me know as soon as possible and I'll pass the word to the manager. You could live in Paris for a few weeks during Grandmother's absence.

"I hope you will say yes, for I miss my sister."

. . .

An end to sleeping, eating, working. Temptation seethed through me; the pictures that came to my mind followed me everywhere, too many thoughts boiled: to leave, to live near Lucien. Paris, the real life, Lucien in the factory. This last vision saddened me, but it was really as a martyr he had made this choice.

Leave? How? And Grandmother, who will visit her? Lucien specified, "a few weeks." And after that? And how would I live there? And the jewelry I had almost bought back? I opened the window and leaned out. Some women were laughing at a baby's first awkward steps. Across from our house, the voice of drunken singing issued from a bistro. Girls not unlike Marie-Louise were teasing a boy. "Everybody lives like an animal, wakes up only to defend the interests of his corporation,

(60)

his clan—longshoreman, workman or mason. There is nothing here. One must look elsewhere." That's what I was thinking when a soft wind began to blow from the river. I felt it on my face and could not fathom the reason for my sudden joy. I will go. That same morning, I wrote to Lucien. It took me a whole week to get organized for my departure, so fantastic was the event. With a new tone of assurance I informed Puesh that I would be away for two months. I tidied up our three rooms, sprinkled insecticide on the baseboards to discourage the cockroaches who were sure to come, washed and ironed all the clothes I possessed, but could not find the courage to tell Grandmother of my imminent departure. I would write her from Paris, I would lie, there was nothing else to do, I would invent a sudden illness of Lucien's.

"And anyway," I said, coward that I was, "I will be back in two months."

· · ·

I was laughing as I got on the train. People were hectically pushing their way and I was taking the train for the first time. But it was the train of revenge. Now the real life could not fail to begin.

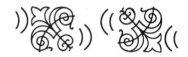

The man who feels his socks, stiff with the sweat of the
day before, and puts them on again,
And his shirt, stiff from the day before,
And puts it on again
And who says in the morning that he'll wash in the evening
And in the evening that he'll wash in the morning
Because he is too tired . . .

R. Desnos

I listened to the rain. It fell on the metal elbow of the gutter just under the window. It had been raining for a week. I had arrived twenty days earlier and the hotel manager, on reading my registration slip, had said scornfully, "Ah, you've come to the country of rain." I had only seen Paris drowned, glistening with water, under lowering skies. Around the small perimeter of the window, the room was light. The bed, covered with a maroon velvet spread that hid its iron feet, darkened the corner to the left of the door. Two floors below Lucien and some friends were discussing my fate. I waited. The raindrops flattened on the window sill. I went to the night table and turned on the record player. I fixed the sound so that the music came out softly. It was a Portuguese song whose title Lucien had translated for me —*When the wind rises*. I loved the trembling and syncopated beginning. What would they decide? I sat down on the bed. The period of grace was coming to an end. They wanted the room back and I didn't want to give it up. They were discussing it without me.

The rain had just stopped. I opened the window and leaned out. Here there were no trees, no vegetation, only straight lines, crossing, and black or white smoke rising between them. This landscape had a desolation that moved me. The hotel was many stories higher than the neighboring houses. In the evening, at the hour of mist and street lights, the room seemed suspended, floating in an unreal universe that frightened me.

Lucien came in, after shaking the latch.

"Come, Elise. We're going to show you how things can be arranged."

"Do I have to give up the room?" I asked as we went down.

"That, yes. But we've found a solution."

He went before me. His room was on the second floor at the end of a dark hall. He opened the door and signaled me to follow. There were two boys who appeared to be my brother's age seated or, more exactly, sprawled on the bed and a woman who at first showed only her back.

"All right," Lucien said. "Vera, you take Robert's room."

Vera agreed. She was handsome but unsmiling. Her clothes seemed elegant. It was hard to imagine her without a room.

"I'll go sleep with Michel for a while and you, Elise, can take my room."

Timidly, I said all right. I was disappointed. The room was larger than the one I had but it was dark and its window opened on the street. Through the curtains, I could read the sign across the way: "Bakery of the Basilica."

"One more thing," Lucien said. "Our funds are getting low. I have to pay you back for what you gave me. I'll do it before you leave. But while you wait . . . do you want to work?"

Why did he ask this question in front of strangers? And how could I say no? He had done it on purpose and calculated the results. I pointed out that I would be going in a few weeks. Could he keep me until then?

"Of course I can. But I thought that work might be an interesting experience for you. And besides, money disappears fast around here. But . . ."

I felt caught in such a vice that there was nothing to do but give in.

I suddenly hungered for my familiar town, Grandmother and our cloistered life. People scared me, life scared me.

In my room, Vera, paying no attention to me, was opening every drawer. I quickly packed my bag. I wanted to cry. I stole a glance at the window. The rain was falling on the gutter again and the sound of it touched me. Vera took an ash tray. I put out my hand. Hers was white, with little oblong red flowers at the end of each finger. They were spread apart as we shook hands and I found the gesture graceful.

. . .

I hadn't seen Lucien for three days when I found him one evening at the door to my room.

"I was waiting for you," he said. "So, is everything O.K.?"

He was dirty. He was wearing his gray pants, still the same ones, wrinkled and stained. His jacket was greasy and his socks were covered with mud. But even more than his clothes, the neglect of his person struck me as he sat down. He had several days' beard and layers of dirt behind the ears. His hands especially and his long fingernails were filthy. He guessed my thoughts.

"You think I'm dirty? I'm so tired I think of nothing but sleep. I'll wash tomorrow; it's Sunday. So, tell me what you're doing."

I gave him a resumé. I knew he hadn't come to hear my news. Was he bringing me some money? His sunken eyes looked swollen. He seemed to be getting almost no sleep. They were lifeless and sad like the rest of him. Even his voice was changed. It was less dry and high pitched. He expressed himself with great economy and spoke in murmurs of which I caught the essentials: "I've been around, come on, let's get started, go on, O.K., I've had it, so long, you've gone too far" and a few newly-learned obscenities.

Tonight, he was forced to really talk to me and it boded ill for me that he wouldn't come right to the point.

"You remember Anna?"

"Obviously."

I was about to add something caustic, but stopped myself just in time. His cold eyes held mine. I had said "obviously" in a tone that put him on guard. I went on:

"Yes, of course."

And this time my voice was very natural.

"Anna is coming."

I hadn't expected this and I realized that I was blushing. "It would take too long to explain . . ." This, for years, was his favorite alibi, his cut-off, the height of his absurd pretense. I expected it every time he launched into the semblance of a conversation.

"Yes, she will be here tomorrow or the day after. It's not worth my trying to explain, it would take too long . . . Only, you see, there's the room. I'm terribly sorry," he said hypocritically.

"Why did I have her come?" he must have wondered. What an idea! He had sat down, his legs spread apart, arms dangling between his thighs. The beard, the empty eyes, the deep hollows under his cheeks, the two sullen furrows between his eyebrows, the dirty shirt—a wreck, Henri had said amicably. I pictured him, alone in the morning, looking around for the boiling coffee he was incapable of fixing for himself. I was losing, but I resolved to put up a fight.

"Do I have to move again?" I asked, to put him on the spot.

It was hard for him to say yes.

"What can we do?" he said craftily.

We sparred for several seconds and I felt he was getting impatient.

"Where are you sending me this time?" I asked.

He didn't answer. He seemed spineless. Where were the fireworks of old?

"I'll pay for a room by the day in a hotel near here so that you don't feel too isolated. Then, during my free time, I'll look for something better. I'll see Henri and another friend . . . Michel knows a place not far from here."

"And meanwhile?"

"Meanwhile, you stay here. I'll take a room by the day."

"No," I said, softening. "I'll have to pay less than . . . you two. Do you know an address?"

"Anywhere will do, in Paris, here."

"I don't know anywhere. Do you still have any of the money . . ."

"Yes, here is five thousand. After that, I'm broke."

"What will you do then?"

He made a gesture of indifference.

"Don't you think that money is important?" he asked.

"Not really. What I really think is that we end by losing sight of the important things because of money."

"It comes to the same thing," he sighed.

For a few minutes he tried to interest himself in our conversation but I soon realized that he was talking aimlessly. His staring eyes gleamed. Anna's arrival occupied his imagination.

I was wild with curiosity but didn't ask him any questions.

"Do I have to leave tonight?"

"Of course not," he protested. "Leave the key downstairs, in the office. That's all. By tomorrow night, I'll have found you something else."

The next morning, I packed my bag. "It would have been fairer to leave me here. She is used to hotels. I get the impression he likes to shake me up, to make me live outside my aquarium. I'm going home."

.   .   .

Anna is nothing but scenery, a cleverly devised construction, a lie, an illusion. Anna stripped bare is a body, thin as a pole, budding breasts, the pasty color of ardent girls, large eyes too far apart, large marks on her neck, left-over adolescent ailments, enormous laziness, a pride that thrives on spectacular humiliations, a permanent need for the bed, warmth, sleep, an unfeigned indifference to food and a few long locks crowning the whole. Anna is an uncontrolled imagination who sees herself as she isn't and builds on what she sees. Anna, for Lucien, is fragile. Everything is manufactured. The hair she curls, the eyelashes she colors, the face she fashions by pasting the hair to her cheeks to achieve a well-calculated shadow, the painted eyes, the fake complexion, the pointed breasts under the sweater. Is Lucien such a sucker? Is it the image he loves or the real Anna, botched by her creator, touching in her efforts? And the prisoner of her efforts, she displays herself to him only when she is ready to play her role. She gets up in the night to take off her face; she gets up at dawn to put it back on.

They have left their bags, each containing the

other's letters. She writes "Your timid antelope" or "Your child-wife." He answers ". . . like a liana in my arms . . ."

But this morning, when I went to pick up my things, I found her still in bed. Since Lucien left at five o'clock, she had no need to budge. She bounded toward the chair to wrap herself in her coat. I saw her shoulder blades as sharp as wings, the skinny thighs and the face, sad like a beach at low tide.

We never know what to say to each other. She offered me some coffee. I accepted, watched her, scrutinized her belly; it looked normal and flat. All the same, I guessed her embarrassment and that gave me pleasure. I asked:

"Is the weather better at home than here?"

"I have no idea."

"Forgive me. I thought you'd come from there."

"Oh, no."

"Did it take you long to get used to Paris?"

She will tell Lucien if I question her anymore. We talked about Paris; we made excuses for the room. Lucien, she said, had insisted that I come and eat dinner with them whenever I wanted. Was I staying in Paris long?

She puts me off the track and intimidates me. With Marie-Louise it had been simple. Imagine missing her . . .

.   .   .

Michel took me to the Women's Residence Hall. A room with two beds, separated by a heavy curtain. A shelf, a hook, a wash stand, a window on the street.

Three thousand francs a month. This seemed great to me, almost luxurious. On the ground floor there was a big kitchen open every morning at six where everybody would have a café-au-lait prepared the night before.

"Ab-so-lu-te-ly great," Lucien said. "You have enough to live on for about a month and enough time to get to know Paris."

"And what are you going to do?"

"Oh, me," he said, "I've lost quite a lot of time these past few weeks. I'm going to look up Henri. Perhaps he can help me out. Is there anything left of that five thousand? I'll pay you back Friday . . . You know what we should do? Send Grandmother a little souvenir. What do you say? An Eiffel Tower, a handkerchief . . ."

I looked at my brother, his eyes were shining.

"Oh, Lucien . . ."

"Buy it for me and I'll pay you back next pay day."

I was so touched that I offered to help out.

"That would be great," he said without enthusiasm. "I still owe you money, right? A month from now I'll be in the clear. I may even be able to send a little something . . . back home."

"How much do you need in the meantime?"

"Well, two or three thousand."

I gave it back to him.

. . .

I had received two letters from Grandmother in answer to mine. She felt sorry for herself and begged me to come for her. One evening when I had been in their room and was on the point of leaving, Lucien suddenly asked me:

"Elise, do you want to work with me?"

"But Lucien, I'm about to go back home!"

"Really? You want to go back there?"

"What kind of work is it?"

"They're hiring girls to figure out the coupons, the bonuses; it's what they call auditing. They pay one eighty-five an hour."

"No, Lucien, I ought to go back. Did you read Grandmother's letter? Let's say I stay until November and try to earn the money for my trip back. You just can't go away like that, leaving others behind."

He moped for the rest of the evening. I left them at nine and walked to the Residence Hall. In the gentle rain, Lucien's proposal was intoxicating. Not to go away, to see him every day, to be involved, a part of his life . . .

"It's beginning," I said to myself, without being able to define what it was.

I had finally realized that he wasn't going to pay me back. Anna wasn't working. She had bought herself some books; together, they studied I'm not quite sure what: English, journalism, photography, oriental civilizations, a whole hodge-podge that made them think they were superior.

"Do what you like. If you want to go . . ."

"You know I don't have enough money. All right, I'll do it. I'll work here two months."

"That's four pay checks. I can pay you back . . ."

"I don't want anything. Just think of yourself. Do you think you've made progress?"

"I'm enriched, but not financially, no."

"You've been saying that for five years. And what about your health? You're thin. If Grandmother could see you . . ."

"She can't see me and that's what's good about it. I'm never going back there. Besides, things are happening here."

"Pasting up posters, does that satisfy you?"

"That's none of your business," he broke out impatiently. "I'm no business of yours."

He passed me the fruit bowl.

"Go on, eat, and be quiet," he said gently.

"This auditing, are you sure I can do it?"

"Try it. If you can't do it, you quit."

"Will you take me tomorrow?"

I was scared.

. . .

The trip was endless. We took the bus at the Porte de la Chapelle and got off at the Porte de Choisy. The day began clear and pure. Gaiety spread from tree to tree along the Boulevard Masséna where the birds were waking up. I had taken great pains with my looks and was satisfied with the results.

"Hi, hi," my brother said to everyone who stretched out his hand.

We were in front of an enormous wall and enormous iron gates.

"You wait there."

"Lucien, don't leave me alone."

"I'll be back in five minutes."

I huddled in a corner by the door and the men and women who passed by didn't notice me. The sun was climbing; not much bigger than an orange, it was above the roofs across from the factory.

Lucien returned with a large man, square, straight, and smiling.

"This is Gilles, the foreman."

He shook my hand firmly.

"You wait around until eight o'clock and then present yourself here."

He indicated a glass door marked "Employment."

"Tell them that Monsieur Gilles knows about it. I'll confirm it. They'll check your papers, interview you and you'll be taken to Shop Seventy-six. It's the assembly line," he said. "Lucien has told you about it?"

"Yes, sir."

"O.K. then, see you later."

"And what if they don't take me?"

He burst out laughing.

"You'd better say '. . . and what if I don't take them.' They'll take you. See you later."

Lucien came back to me.

"Don't worry so much."

"I'm all right."

And I really felt all right. Gilles, Lucien . . . they were taking care of me. I had forty-five minutes to wait. I set off on a side street without thinking. It led to a large vacant lot beyond which were several new buildings.

At quarter to eight, I returned to the employment office. A few men, foreigners for the most part, were already there, waiting. They looked at me with curiosity. At eight, a guard opened the door and slammed it behind him.

"What do you want?" he asked one of the men leaning against the wall.

"I'm here for a job."

"There are no jobs," he said, shaking his head. "There's nothing."

"Really?"

Skeptical, the man didn't move.

"We're not hiring," the guard repeated.

The men shifted their legs a little but stayed in front of the door.

"It's in the papers," one of them said.

The guard went up to him and yelled in his face: "You know how to read, write, count?"

They began to move away from the door, slowly, as if with regret. One of them spoke, in Arabic no doubt, and the name Citroën was often mentioned. Then they scattered and made for the gates.

"What do you want?" the guard asked as he turned to me.

"I'm supposed to register. Monsieur Gilles . . ."

"For a job?"

"Yes," I said, intimidated.

"Go on in then."

And he opened the glass door.

In the office, there were four women writing. I was questioned; I answered. One of the women made a phone call, had me sit down and start to fill out the papers she gave me.

"You know it's not for the offices," she said when she read my form.

"Yes, yes."

"O.K. Go out that way, cross the street, through the door marked "Social Services," it's on the second floor, the office for medical examinations."

In the waiting room, we were five—four men and me. There was a sign saying "No Smoking," and under it the same message in Arabic. There was a two hour wait. Eventually, one of the men sitting near me lit a cigarette. The doctor came in, followed by a nurse with our forms. The examination was quick. The doctor asked questions, the secretary took down the answers. He asked me embarrassing questions, didn't insist when he saw me blush and asked to see my legs, for I was to work standing. "X-rays," the secretary announced. I mussed my hair taking off my sweater but there was no mirror to see myself with. The Algerian who had preceded me was called back by the doctor. He had moved in front of the machine.

"What's your name? Say it again? It's hard to say. Your name is Mohammed?" and he began to laugh. "All you Arabs are called Mohammed. O.K., you pass. Next. Ah, a lady . . ."

When he'd finished, he took me aside.

"Why didn't you ask for a job in the offices? Do you know where you're going? You're going into the assembly line, with a whole bunch of foreigners, a lot of Algerians. You won't be able to take it. You're too good for it. Go see the assistant and find out what she can do for you."

The guard was waiting for us. He read our forms.

(75)

Mine read: Shop 76. We went up to the second floor in an enormous elevator. There, a woman sorting out small pieces of metal called to the guard:

"Are there a lot today?"

"Five," he said.

I looked at her and would have liked to see her smile but she looked right through me.

"You go here," the guard said to me.

Gilles was coming toward us. He was wearing a white smock and signaled me to follow. A rumbling sound reached me and I started to tremble. Gilles raised the latch of a heavy door and let me through. I stopped and looked at him. He said something but I could no longer hear; I was in Shop 76.

Machines, hammers, tools, the motors of the assembly line, saws, all mingled their infernal noise, and this unbearable racket made of rumblings, whistles, and shrill sounds that pierced the ear seemed to me so inhuman that I thought there must have been an accident, that since these sounds didn't harmonize with each other, some would have to stop. Gilles saw my astonishment.

"It's noisy!" he cried in my ear.

He didn't seem to mind. Shop 76 was immense. We moved forward, stepping over various carts and crates, and when we got to the row of machines where a number of men were working, there rose a howl which spread and seemed to be picked up by every man in the shop.

"Don't be afraid. It's for you. Every time a woman comes in here, it's like that."

I bent my head and walked on, followed by that roaring "ah" which now came from everywhere.

At my right, a snake-like file of cars was slowly moving forward, but I didn't dare look.

"Wait," cried Gilles.

He went into a glass cage in the middle of the shop and quickly came out with an impeccably clean young man.

"Mr. Bernier, the head of your section."

"It's Letellier's sister!" he yelled.

The man made a sign with his head.

"Do you have a smock?"

I indicated no.

"Go down to the coatroom. Bernier will take you, leave your coat there. But I'm afraid you're going to get dirty. You don't have sneakers either?"

He seemed irritated.

While we were talking, the howls had stopped. They started up again when I went by with Bernier. I concentrated on looking straight ahead.

"It'll take them three days," Bernier whispered.

The guard had the key to the coatroom. It was always kept locked because of thefts, Bernier explained. I hastily put down my coat and pocketbook. The coatroom was dark, lit only by two barred skylights. It was dank with the smell of urine and artichokes.

We went back up. Bernier led me to the very rear of the shop, in the section that looked out over the boulevard. It was lit by windows painted white and scratched in various places by the workers no doubt.

"This is the assembly line," Bernier said proudly.

He made me climb onto a sort of bench made of wooden slats. Cars were passing by slowly with men busy inside. I saw that Bernier was talking to me. I couldn't hear him and apologized.

"Don't worry," he said, "you'll get used to it. Only, you're going to get dirty."

He called a man who came over to us.

"This is Mademoiselle Letellier, the sister of the guy over there. You're to take her to the control for two or three days."

"Yes? So, it's the women who are going to do the control now?"

Annoyed, he made a sign to follow and we crossed the assembly line between two cars. There was little room. Thrown by the motion, I stumbled and grabbed him. He grumbled. He was no longer young and wore glasses.

"We'll go back up the line a bit," he said.

It dropped sinuously in gentle stages, carrying on its belly well-fastened cars in and out of which men were rushing. The noise, the motion, the tremor of the wooden slats, the comings and goings of the men, the smell of gasoline, dazed and suffocated me.

"My name is Daubat. And what's yours again? Oh yes, Letellier."

"You know my brother?"

"Naturally I know him. He's the guy over there. Look."

He pulled me to the left and pointed his finger in the direction of the machines.

The assembly line dominated the shop. We were at its starting point; it ended far away, after making a tour of the huge shop. On the other side of the aisle were machines where a large number of men worked. Daubat pointed to a silhouette, his head covered by a beret, a mask protecting his eyes, wearing canvas overalls and holding in a hand enveloped in rags, a kind of paint gun that sprayed small pieces of something. It was Lucien. From my position, partly hidden by passing cars, I watched the men working in that section. Some were painting, others banging on pieces they then hooked onto a cable. Then the piece moved on to the next man. It was the dirtiest part of the shop. The men were dressed in soiled blue overalls and their faces were smeared with grease. Lucien didn't see me. Daubat called me and I went to him. He held out a metal sheet on which rested a clip board.

"I'll give you a pencil. Are you coming?"

He went back to the head of the line. I followed him like a shadow, for I felt many eyes on me and forced myself to look only at things. I was also concentrating on how to place my feet sideways on the wooden slats. You had to climb up and down. Daubat took my arm and placed me in a car.

"You examine this."

He showed me the dashboard covered with a plastic material.

"If there is a defect, make a note of it. See? There, it's improperly stretched. So, mark it down. And there? Look."

He examined the windshield wipers.

"They're all right. O.K. And the sun visor? Torn! You write down: torn sun visor. Ah, but you must work fast. Look where we are."

He jumped from the car and made me jump with him. We were far away from where we had gotten in.

"We won't be able to do the next one," he said, discouraged. "I'll tell Gilles; it's too bad. Let's try that one."

We started again. He went fast. He kept saying "there, here," "there's a wrinkle," "no rearview mirror," or "badly placed rearview mirror." I understood nothing.

For a few minutes I took refuge in the idea that I wouldn't come back tomorrow. I couldn't see myself going up and down the assembly line, getting into the car, noting everything in a few minutes, writing, jumping, running to the next one; in, jump, look, write.

"Is it clear?" Daubat asked.

"A little."

"A little won't do," he said, shaking his head. "I can't understand why they have women do this. I'll have to see Gilles. If this goes on, my bonus is out the window. I've let three cars go by."

We went further up the line.

"There, that's good," Daubat said.

In the car we were facing, five men were at work. One screwed, another hammered the stripping around the doors, the others placed padding on the dashboard.

"Hey," Daubat said, "you're late!"

He shoved them out. Anyway, the men had stopped to look at me.

"So now it's women," one of them said.

"Yes, and what next? Get to work, you're already one car behind."

The one who had spoken—he was an Arab—laughed and spoke to the others in his language.

We were now seven in the shell, crouching on the metal floor; rugs and seats wouldn't be installed until much later.

"Think you're getting it?" Daubat asked.

"Yes, I think so."

"The next one you do alone. I'll be right behind you."

Stumbling—which made one of the boys laugh—I got out of the car and waited for the next one. Sheet in hand, leaning on the door to keep my balance, I tried to look around. My arm brushed the back of a man hammering. As I leaned toward the dashboard, I almost fell on the man who was getting ready to screw on the rearview mirror. He smiled and helped me straighten up. I got out quickly without seeing Daubat. I had to put something down. I couldn't rest the sheet on the trunk of the car—they called it trunk, I had just learned—I wrote down, guessing: rearview mirror missing, because I had seen Daubat put that down on each sheet. But after that what? Without Daubat, I was lost. He got out of the car that had moved in front of me.

"How's it going? You take the one behind," he said.

He went toward the car in front and read my sheet. I concentrated on the new car. I saw wrinkles on the ceiling and put down "wrinkles." A man near by touched me. I looked at him sternly until I realized that he was asking for room to get by. I hadn't heard him.

Someone got into the car. I turned around. It was Gilles. He made some rapid explanations that mostly escaped me.

"It's near the lunch break," he said.

Oh, deliverance . . . and not to come back this afternoon.

The men had already stopped and were wiping their hands. I wondered where I should go during this hour. When the bell rang, everybody dashed toward the exit. Daubat had joined me again when Lucien came up.

"How are you doing?"

I looked at Daubat for his assessment.

"It's a beginning. She'll have her troubles. It's the same with the kids; it isn't easy. If you point out their poor work, they give you excuses. But I'm here. If any of them bothers you, you tell me. All the same, it isn't woman's work. I've told Gilles already."

"Yes," Lucien said absentmindedly. "Where are you eating?"

"I don't know. What about you?"

"I'll go to the canteen. Do you want some tickets? I can lend you some."

"I'll get my coat."

"If you must, but hurry. I'll wait for you."

I went into the coatroom where a few women were sitting on benches, talking and eating their lunch. They stared at me. I said hello and left.

Lucien said nothing. I didn't either. *It's tough work.*

I'm tired . . . how absurd. What could that mean?

The outdoor air stirred desires sharper than hunger.

"Forgive me," I said to Lucien, "I'd rather take a walk. It's too beautiful out."

"What a sun!" he said. "I'll do the same. That's it. We'll walk."

We walked on the sunny side of the street. Workers were passing by with bottles and loaves of bread.

"Those men there eat in the factory. Mostly Algerians, on account of the pork they serve in the canteen."

Once on the boulevard, he turned in the direction of the Porte d'Italie. We found a bench and sat down, side by side. We had the sun on our backs. My legs trembled and I had worked only two hours. I would have to go back for another four and a half. Lucien stretched out, legs straight, arms crossed behind, head back.

"O.K. Tell me the truth," he said in a low voice. "You think you can hold up?"

"I'll hold up."

In the sun, relaxing, it was easy to say.

"You weren't scared when they let out that howl this morning?"

"No, not scared," I lied. "But why do they do it?"

He sat up and crossed his legs.

"When you work like that, you go back to an animal state. They're beasts sighting the female. They bellow. It's the animal expression of their delight. They're not bad. Just a little eager because they have no women here."

"All the same, I was frightened by what I saw."

"What did you see? You haven't seen anything at all.

(83)

If you hang on, if you stay, you'll discover other things."

"But what about you, Lucien, do you think you'll stay long?"

"Ah," he said, "that I don't know. I wanted to go through it, to see it. But sometimes I'm afraid I'll break down. I can't eat anything, I'm drunk on the paint. And the people around me, what a disappointment . . ."

"What about Henri?"

"What about Henri. You're always talking about him. What do you want him to do? When he's passed his exams, he'll start a brilliant career, and that will be that."

"He hasn't been able to do anything for you?"

"That's not the problem," he said, annoyed.

I didn't press him.

"Come on, we've got to eat something."

We went toward the Porte d'Italie. When some men went past us, they winked at Lucien.

"It's like summer!"

"I know. I'm thirsty," I said.

We sat on the terrace of a café. Lucien was wearing his filthy overalls and I hadn't taken the time to wash my hands. What of it . . . It was our break; we had to recuperate.

My brother ordered a sandwich which we shared. He drank two small coffees. The sun licked us. The fresh air cleansed our lungs. "Joy of living" seemed to hang suspended in that pure, clear autumn sky.

"You see, a worker's life begins the moment he finishes work. And since you have to sleep a little, there's not much time left for living."

He got up and stretched.

(84)

"Forget it," he said with disgust. "It isn't worth sticking out. What do you get out of it?"

I asked him once again why he himself didn't quit.

"And what would I live on? What else do you want me to do? If I weren't such a stinker, I'd send a little money back there. And live here."

This conversation had plunged me into a deep depression. I started back to the shop without courage.

In front of the factory entrance where a few men were waiting for the siren, some sitting on the ground, some leaning against the wall, it was all right that they should whistle and call to me. In the shop, I succeeded in going about unnoticed. The siren hadn't sounded yet, and men were scattered here and there, smoking. I moved forward between crates, columns and machines. I got lost and found myself before a group of men discussing something. Daubat recognized me and beckoned.

"This is my little student," he said to the others. "Come here."

He took me by the shoulder.

"This is the sister of the dark-haired guy, Lucien."

They were all three about the same age. Their overalls were neat, mended, almost clean.

Daubat introduced them: "This is our timekeeper."

The man removed his cigar butt and spat out a piece of tobacco.

"And this one here, he's the only professional in the shop."

He was fatter than the other two and above his round cheeks showed two sparkling blue eyes.

"We," he confided to me, "are the only three Frenchmen in this section. Think of it. Nothing but foreigners. Algerians, Moroccans, Spaniards, Yugoslavs."

"Your brother loves them," said the timekeeper bitterly.

"Lucien loves everybody."

"He's wrong. This will make trouble for him. You can't work with people like them. Anyway, if they bother you, we're here."

"What about Gilles?" said the fat one.

"Gilles, you can't be sure of him."

Daubat showed me a kindness that was in sharp contrast to his bad humor of the morning.

"We've got to stick together."

And he tapped the timekeeper's shoulder.

"The siren's going to go off," he said.

I took my place, passing some cars in which men were asleep. Some were even lying on the ground on spread-out newspapers.

"Look at that," said Daubat.

He pointed to a body rolled up like a cat on a heap of glass wool. Having brushed against it that morning, I knew that any contact with it caused unbearable itching.

"You think these are men? They have hides instead of skin."

The siren startled everybody. The sleepers stretched, slowly.

I picked up my board, pencil and paper and started once again. Gilles came and told me he would check three cars with me to show how it was done.

I listened carefully. He was fast, he discovered at first glance the defect or omission.

"Look."

I repeated, yes. I was beginning to understand, but I wished he would explain what was done to the cars before they got to me.

"Mademoiselle Letellier, I'll try to do that some day, I hope. But as you can see, it's hard to explain here. If I stop, the cars move on, the whole line is slowed down."

"So," Daubat asked when he had gone, "did the boss explain everything?"

"Yes, he's terrific. He sees the defect right off."

"That's not surprising, after all, the boss . . ." He had an ironic expression on his face.

"Quick," he said, "we haven't time."

I had annoyed him. But he cheered up when the time-keeper who was passing by called out something about his student. It gave him a sense of importance.

"What time is it?" I asked him.

"Three o'clock. Are you tired?"

"No, no, I'm all right."

"Will you look at that!"

Daubat pulled me to the car and showed me the sun visors. Above the hinge, the material, stretched too tight, had ripped.

"They go too fast. To get ahead of the game, they do ten cars in a row, any old way, so that they can sit down in the washroom and have a cigarette. That one, especially."

He pointed to the round back of a man crouched before the window.

"Hey, you, come here and see what you've done."

The back didn't move.

"Look at that, look at that," Daubat said to me. "So

much for his bonus. In any event, those people don't stay. It used to be professionals who did this kind of work; three cars an hour. Now, seven. Put down, 'color of the trunk does not conform.' "

I wanted to rest, and asked permission to catch my breath. My legs were as hard as wood, rusty in the joints; I was moving slower. And when I climbed into a car behind Daubat, I hurriedly squatted a few seconds. He noticed that I wasn't following very well.

"Why don't you rest a moment. Then you can take my place and I'll have a smoke."

There was no provision for sitting down. I wedged myself between two small drums of gasoline. There, I wouldn't be in anyone's way. Weariness cut me off from everybody and from what was going on around me. The motors of the assembly line rumbled in four-four time, like music. The sharpest sound came on the third beat. It penetrated the temples like a needle, then reached into the brain where it exploded. These explosions then fell like sparks above the eyebrows, then behind, in the nape of the neck.

"Mademoiselle, it's all yours."

Daubat handed me his board.

"Go to it, I'll be back. Watch out for the sun visors."

Climb in, crawl, crouch, look to the right, to the left, behind, above, see at first glance what isn't right, carefully examine the contours, the angles, the hollows, pass your hand over the stripping on the doors, write, attach the sheet, crawl out, get down, run, climb in, crawl, crouch in the next car, and do it all over again, seven times an hour.

I let many cars pass. Daubat said it didn't matter since he'd be with me for two or three days. Gilles had confirmed this.

"After that, they'll put me in manufacturing."

On his wrist I could see the hands of his big watch. Another hour and a half . . .

When there was less than an hour left, I began to get my strength back and I did a good job on two cars in a row. But I collapsed on the third. For the last fifteen minutes I couldn't even articulate the words to tell Daubat where the defects were. Some workers were cleaning their hands in the gas drums nearby.

"Those men there always stop before it's time," Daubat said.

I envied them.

We went on checking until the very end, and when the siren went off, Daubat carefully placed our boards in a cabinet near the window.

An intense joy seized me. It was over. I put questions to Daubat without even listening to the answers. Above all, I wanted to leave the shop in his company; I was afraid to go out alone through all those men.

In the coatroom, the women were ready to go. They were talking in loud voices, and in my joy at leaving, I gave them all a large smile.

At six o'clock, there is still a little daylight, but the lights on the boulevard are already turned on. I walk slowly, breathing deeply the street air as if it contains a hint of the sea. I am going home, to stretch out, place the bolster under my ankles. To bed . . . I'll buy something, anything, fruit, bread and the newspaper. There are already thirty people ahead of me in line for the same bus. Some buses don't stop, others take only two passengers and move on. When I reach the shelter, I'll be able to lean on something; it will be less tiring. On the bus platform, squeezed between the men, I see nothing but jackets, shoulders and I relax a little against their soft backs. The jolting of the bus reminds me of the assembly line. We move to its rhythm. I hurt in my legs, my back, my head. My body has become immense, my head enormous, my legs beyond measuring, and my brain tiny. Two more floors and there's my bed. My clothes fall off. That's good. Washing one's self, I always told Lucien, relaxes, revives, cleanses the soul. No matter, this particular evening, I give in to my first desire; I go to bed. I'll wash later. Stretched out, my legs hurt less. I look at them and I notice little nervous twitches under the skin. I let the newspaper drop and look at my stockings; the black heels remind me of the assembly line. Tomorrow, I'll wash them. Tonight, I hurt too much. Then, sleep.

And then I wake up. The light is on, I am on the bed; next to me are two banana skins. I mustn't sleep any more. If I doze, I'll dream that I am on the line; I'll hear the motors' noise, my legs will tremble with fatigue, I'll imagine that I'm staggering, that I'm slipping, and I'll wake up with a start.

. . .

The newspaper man was still setting up his stand when I bought my paper. He was hooking his gas lamp to the canvas that he used as a roof. The F.L.N. and its offshoots took up three columns. Every day there were arrests. But they came back. Extraordinary measures were demanded. Around me in the bus, there were lots of Algerians. Did they belong to the F.L.N.? Did they kill in the night?

I liked the long trip. Occasionally, there were agreeable views, glimpses of the Bois de Vincennes, lighted windows behind the trees where I imagined the smell of coffee and of perfumed soap. I finished waking up en route.

In the coatroom, I was one of the first arrivals. The other women weren't talking to me yet. But a young girl, hired after me, had already penetrated their group.

I had brought along an old smock, long and enveloping, to protect me from stains and dust.

It was the fourth day and I was beginning to see beyond myself and my weariness. I was discovering that the arms and feet that moved around me belonged to men and that these men also had faces.

I arrived in the aisle—early, to avoid the howls of the men—and I saw a young man lettering a sign. When he was finished, he placed it on the strippings hanging from a hook—snap-ons they called them here.

Passing by, I read:

DO NO TUCH

The siren went off. Many workmen were missing. The sickening smell of the motors warming up blended with the smell of gas. You had to conquer your nausea and limber up your legs. The boy draped a few snap-ons over his shoulder and climbed into a car. He attached them to the two front doors. He was slight, small, and in his oil-smeared face gleamed the round, black eyes of an inquisitive animal. He looked at me severely. Mechanically, I said good morning. He stopped his hammering.

"You're saying good morning today. Why not yesterday?"

Astonished, I didn't answer. I had never thought about saying good morning or good night. He shrugged. He wasn't handsome. I wanted to justify myself.

"Forgive me," I said.

But he was already finished and running to the next car. Other men got in, hammered, got out. No one greeted me.

Daubat came toward me.

"So, you're all alone today? It'll be all right. I'll come see you in a little while."

He was nice to me. I appealed to him. I was serious, I didn't joke with the men, I kept myself apart.

When the little snap-on boy got out of the car, he spat to one side with disgust. I suddenly realized that he might have taken my silence for a racist reflex and I went up to him.

"Excuse me," I said.

He turned around.

"What? What do you want, madame?" he asked with impatience.

I said louder: "Forgive me, but I was afraid to say good morning."

"You have no manners," he said, leaning toward me. "Then why do you say good morning to the bosses?"

"Forgive me," I said again.

He stopped hammering.

"Pardon me, madame," he said ceremoniously. "Will you please let me pass?"

I felt his hostility and was upset. He went to where the snap-ons were hanging—the sign was still there—and beckoned to a man who was approaching. I wanted to watch what was happening, but my car was taking me past; I had to get out and take the next.

I found him again a little later and smiled at him.

"Why do you make fun of me?" he asked me angrily.

I turned away and promised myself I would avoid him.

We observed each other all morning. I hid my fatigue and my panic when I missed a defect.

He stopped work at twelve-twenty, put away his tools, cleaned his hands in the gasoline and waited for the siren.

At half-past, he ran for the door and I lost sight of him.

I never ate in the canteen. Lucien had told me, "You won't like it, and besides, there are only men. And my table is full."

I brought a few things which I ate in the coatroom and then took a quick walk around the factory. My loneliness was great and I felt it intensely. At a quarter to two, I came back in, went up to the shop and resumed my place, being careful not to wake those who were asleep.

Near the gas drums there was a projecting stone, and

I had discovered it with delight. That is where I rested and escaped observation.

My enemy of the morning discovered me there. He came toward me.

"You are Lucien's sister?"

"Yes, I am."

"I thought you were his wife. Why," he went on with the eyes of an inquisitor, "do you wear such a long smock? The other women don't."

I looked at him, stupefied. He was already gone. Everybody was back at his post. The assembly line was about to start up. Each time we resumed work, I asked myself: "Will I make it?" There was no allowance for a break or the call of nature. The men succeeded in getting a breather by cheating, but I hadn't managed it yet. The car was there, and then the next and the next.

The snap-on boy accosted me once again. He was sitting on the frame of the door, and when the car reached my level, he slipped toward me, saying:

"Why don't you stop for a while?"

Always the same angry tone, and without waiting for my answer.

From time to time, Daubat would come leaping in my direction. I had become his protégé, his pupil.

"I would like to see how a car is made," I said to him. "Why don't they have the new people visit each shop so that they will understand?"

"Look out, you let a wrinkle get by. Why?"

"Yes, why? I don't understand one thing about the work I'm doing. If I could only see the stages the car goes through, where it comes from, where it goes, I could get interested, and understand the meaning of my efforts."

He stepped back, took out his glasses, wiped them and put them on.

"And what about production? Can you imagine what would happen if we conducted a tour of the factory for every new employee? Admit it, that's another one of your brother's ideas!" he said, laughing. "Watch out, there's a car."

He jumped into the aisle.

Watch out, watch out. That's what everybody said from morning to night.

"Where did you work before?"

It was my friend of the snap-ons. His head was bent toward the shoulder that held the strips.

"I lived in the provinces."

He turned away to start hammering.

"Why did you put that sign on your strips?"

"What?"

I repeated the question.

"So that nobody would touch them. I get them ready ahead of time. The ends turned in. See."

He showed me. Then I understood the meaning of the message:

DO NOT TOUCH

I felt a surge of sympathy for him.

"What's your name?"

"Why?" he said with surprise.

Then he jumped off.

(95)

I found him in the next car. He was banging hard and got out when I arrived. He was waiting for me in the third car and said:

"My name is Mustapha. And yours, what is it?"

"Elise."

"Elise? Is that French?"

At five o'clock, when the big lights came on, all my strength vanished. A dangerous numbness destroyed any possibility of thought. One idea possessed me obsessively: to sit down, stretch out. For four days, when I reached my room after nine hours in the line, one hour on the bus, ten hours of standing, I threw myself on the bed, and the thought of trying to wash was painful. I had begun with neglecting my shoes. I stopped shining them. The first day, I disgusted myself. But, imperceptibly, I slipped into the habit. I leafed through the papers without reading them. One evening though, I spent an hour shortening my smock and making a belt out of the hem I'd cut off. I was hoping that my body would get used to fatigue, and fatigue was accumulating in my body.

. . .

That evening, Lucien had come to tell me, before quitting time, "Stop by tonight. Come to dinner with us."

Anna opened the door. She was beautiful. She must have spent the afternoon getting ready. Lucien was lying on the bed. He sat up:

"And here is comrade Elise, head of the factory shock troops . . ."

"Be quiet, Lucien, or I'm going."

"Don't get angry," he said.

He stretched, got off the bed and came toward me.
"No kidding, how's it going?"

We discussed our work and for the first time, he was interested in what I had to say. Anna sat down on the bed and listened. I told Lucien about Mustapha. He knew him, had worked on the line with him. He was nineteen, he said. He was the youngest on the line. The worst, too.

"Someone's at the door," Anna said.

Lucien opened. Henri came in.

"You," he said to Lucien without saying hello, "I'm disappointed in you. Two months without a word. So, Elise, you're here. I had no idea. Good evening. Hello, Anna. You can't write or come see me?"

"No, my friend," Lucien said calmly. "I'm working. I have no time."

"But still . . ."

He took off his raincoat and placed it on the bed. We were all a little uncomfortable but not he. He began to talk to my brother about books, meetings, the theater.

"And what about you? What are you doing?"

Lucien proudly described his nocturnal activities, the number of posters pasted up, the slogans painted on walls. Henri kept silent.

"So," he said after a moment, "you're pleased with yourself. All your ardor, your great ideas, your potential, you've found nothing better to do with them than paste up posters. I've been listening to you. For you, it's a sport, a game of hide-and-seek with the cops. Is it effective, scrawling on walls?"

"Not as much as writing books or producing banned

plays or organizing meetings. But what do you want, those things aren't in my blood. This is what I'm good for, scrawling on walls. Later on, when the war is over, they'll remember you, while those who paste up posters . . ."

"Why don't you go to bed at night instead of running around with a pot of paste in your hand. You're nothing but skin and bones!"

Lucien turned pale. Henri had gotten to him.

"So it's the dictatorship of the proletariat? I knew it; there is nothing more to say." Henri turned to me; "And what do you think of Paris, Elise?"

We exchanged banalities. Where were our evenings back at home, with the smell of soup and the garlic sauce, the noise of the street and the courtyard? What had changed? Anna was in Marie-Louise's place, I was still here. But the time for wishing was over. We were at the center of life, "in the thick of it," Henri said. We were on stage. My brother cheered up. Henri and he went out together, like old times, but I guessed they'd continue the controversy outside.

"What do you think of Henri?" I asked Anna.

"Lots of things, all contradictory."

Her hair hid half her face. I envied her for knowing how to be beautiful.

"Ah," I sighed, "I'm going to bed. It's already ten o'clock. That doesn't leave much time for sleep. How does Lucien keep going?"

She smiled at me. I found it annoying, this obstinacy about avoiding conversation. "Shifty, lying, false, false."

I imagined her on the assembly line with her long hair. Would she appeal to Mustapha? I had long hair too. I would like Mustapha to know it, that puny, wicked little monkey, asking me: "Why do you wear your smock so long?"

.   .   .

To watch the horizon between the heads and turned-up collars through the windows of the bus, to follow the movement of the fog. What I had read in school on the subject of fog came back to me. Melancholy. I saw a bent head leaning on a hand.

I had fifty minutes of unreality. For fifty minutes, I shut myself in with phrases, words, pictures. A wisp of fog, a tear in the sky exhumed them from my memory. For fifty minutes, I let go. The real life, my brother, I'm holding on to it! Fifty minutes of calm, of dreams. Mortal awakening at the Porte de Choisy. The smell of the factory before you even get there. Three minutes of coatroom and hours of assembly line. Chained to our posts. Without understanding, without seeing. And each depending on the others. But fraternity is for later. Now I dream of autumn, of hunting, of mad dogs. Lucien calls this state: romanesquery. But he has Anna; between the grease and the sludge, the tar paint and the fetid sweat, slides hope made of love, made of flesh. In the old days, a few months ago, there had been God. Here, I am looking for Him; therefore, I must have lost Him. People have come between us. A great invisible fire. So many new beings have come into my camp, and so quickly; the fire has exploded into a thousand tongues and I have come to love these beings.

Mustapha was whistling. I was afraid he wouldn't notice my shortened smock and above all my hair. It was tied at the neck with the checked belt of the smock. Mustapha was distracted. He was working fast, too fast, I had already noted three badly attached strippings.

I was examining the trunk when someone got into the car. Mustapha let out a cry of joy and dropped his hammer. A man was crouching next to him, his back to me. They embraced each other. Mustapha laughed and clapped his hands. The car moved on while they were talking.

What should I do? Remind him of his work? Mark down "missing snap-on, missing . . . ?"

I went toward one of the men who, higher up, installed the dashboards. I tapped his arm. He turned and smiled.

"Warn your friend," I said. "He has let four cars go by. I don't want to get him in trouble."

He shrugged.

"Leave him alone. He's a loafer."

One of the men leaned over to listen.

"Who?" he shouted at the other who answered in Arabic while pointing at Mustapha.

He put down his tool and ran toward the car.

I returned to my place. Little by little, my muscles were getting used to it. But I still dreamed at night that I was endlessly walking up gigantic assembly lines.

Mustapha called me over.

"What's the matter?"

(100)

"I wanted to warn you," I said. "You let four cars go by."

"It's none of your business."

He was annoyed and made the gesture of writing.

"You just mark down, that's all."

The man had rejoined him. I looked away but I felt they were talking about me and I didn't dare budge.

They moved away from the door. I got out and stopped for a few seconds. I was seized with a sudden thirst. Successive emotions, timidity, Mustapha's scorn merged into this brutal need. It was about three hours until the break. I went and leaned on a wall. Mustapha came by at that moment. His strips around his neck, he looked like a snake charmer. The man was still with him. From his profile, he looked dry and when he spoke, hollows formed under the cheek bones. Under his thick eyebrows, his gaze was a black fire. He smiled and rested his hand on Mustapha's shoulder.

I had to get out. I couldn't stand it. The smell of the gas was like smoke swirling around me and into my mouth. I had let several cars go by. How could I get out? I thought of Daubat. He was somewhere near the top of the line. Threading my way along the aisle, I saw him stretching plastic with the help of two boys. He saw me and looked surprised.

"I'm sick," I said. "Can you take my place for a moment?"

He looked at me, round-eyed.

"You've left the cars?"

"I'm sick."

"Ah, la la la la!"

I felt I was the center of attention. I was frightened. To be sick wasn't all that simple. It wasn't planned for. I wanted to go back to my place. There is a certain security in being a wheel that never goes off the track, but to stop the works, to become an unhappy stomach, a heavy head . . .

"Little one," Daubat said—and he squeezed my arm —"go ahead. You're like a ghost. Ah, women on the assembly line! When you go out, tell the foreman. He'll put someone in. As you see, I can't move. It's going too fast. Saîd," he called out, "take her to Bernier."

Bernier was sitting on a high stool before a desk that almost reached his chin. Wearing a smock that was too long for him, its sleeves rolled up, he looked frail. His face, with its turned up nose, his little round and deep-set eyes, was naturally prone to laughter. He always looked happy. Occasionally, he would make a big noise to remind the men, who otherwise had little respect for him, of his function. But his noise sounded only like yapping and intimidated no one. On the other hand, he trembled when Gilles summoned him.

"O.K.," he said when I had explained my problem, "O.K., O.K."

He was trying to figure out the right thing to do.

"Well, yes. I'll give you a permission slip to go to the infirmary. There. A quarter of an hour, is that enough? It is now eight fifty, so, until nine fifteen. And," he added sadly, "I myself will take your place."

He put down his pen. He was lettering placards in

gothic script: BRAKES—GLASS WOOL—PULLS No. 2.

"Where is the infirmary, please?"

"Across the street. But . . ."

He got down from his stool and carefully selected a pencil.

"But don't go outdoors. Take the underpass."

I didn't know the underpass.

"You can figure it out downstairs," he said with annoyance.

Mustapha's friend approached the desk at that moment.

"Hello, Rezki," Bernier shouted. "So you've come back?"

"Yes, I'm going to take my papers over to the medical office."

"Perfect, you can take her to the infirmary," Bernier said brightly.

I took the slip he handed me and followed the man named Rezki. When we reached the door, a clamor greeted us.

"Hou, hou," the men howled. My companion stopped and went over to them. There were about a dozen men, black Africans and Algerians, loudly hooting at us. I moved forward a few steps and found myself at the same level as my guide. He yelled something in his language and pushed me toward the door. When it had separated us from the noise of the shop, he said to me gently, "Forgive them." Then he added, like Lucien: "The factory turns men into savages."

He didn't speak to me again, and seemed to have forgotten me. I followed him in the underpass that joined together the two parts of the factory.

"How long have you been here?" he asked when we were outside again.

"Nine days."

He pointed out the stairway that led to the infirmary and continued on his way to the offices.

It was a small room, bright and well heated. In front of a gas stove stood an old lady in a white smock.

"What's the matter?" she asked.

"I feel sick. I'm nauseated."

"Are you pregnant?"

I said no with indignation.

"Sit down."

Gently, she took my wrist and when she had finished, went back to the stove. She lifted the lid off the sterilizer, took a glass from a shelf and put it on the table in front of me. I noticed that she had on fur-trimmed slippers.

"There, little one, drink this slowly."

It was an infusion. I savored the moment. I was being cared for, given a tisane. The infirmary, warm and sunny, with its human objects, the sterilizer, the spirals of steam, the white enamel sink, the glasses, made me feel a horror for the ill-proportioned world of the shop, the assembly line, the metal pillars and the smell of the warm gas. "I won't stay. Five more days, my pay check, and I go."

The old woman looked at the time.

"I'll sign your slip, young lady. When you feel better, you can go."

I drank slowly, puffing on the infusion. My fingers warmed on contact with the glass. The telephone rang. The nurse went to the phone hanging on the wall. While she talked, her hand plucked a hairpin out of her hair and with it she scratched the inside of her ear. Grandmother had often done that.

The warmth, the light, the windows disappeared. My lying letters, and hers, written by some fellow patient to whom she dictated, her accusations, her maledictions and the final entreaty: "Come get me!" And I answered: "Patience, I'm earning money here. When I get home, I'll have everything painted and I'll buy you a radio."

Someone knocked at the door. The woman put down the receiver and called: "Come in."

"You again," she said to the man who appeared.

He was small, dark skinned, with curly hair.

"What have you dreamt up this time?"

"It's my throat," the man said.

"All right. Sit down. And watch out for my bottles."

I got up, thanked her and went out. The hecklers were otherwise occupied. They noticed me too late. When their muffled wolf-calls reached me, I was already far away.

"You're sick?" Mustapha asked when he saw me.

"I'm better."

"What?" he said capping his ear.

"I'm better!" I shouted.

The timekeeper who was passing by looked at me

disapprovingly. I climbed up on the assembly line. Bernier saw me and came to collect my pass.

"Are you better?"

I nodded. It was true. I felt better. My post, my little corner of the universe in which I already had my small landmarks, those things we call habits, gave me the reassuring feeling of a fox hole, a retreat, a refuge.

Around ten o'clock there was a shift. Mustapha's friend arrived and Bernier called for the worker who installed the rearview mirrors. He was a foreigner. Mustapha called him "the Magire." Daubat had told me "a Hungarian"; Gilles was more precise: a "Magyar." He spoke no French and worked without saying a word, jumping from one car to the next with a kind of desperation. Imagine the solitude of this man who had contact with nothing, not even the vulgarities, rough but real, that men hurl at each other. I considered myself lucky.

Bernier glanced into my car.

"Rezki!" he called.

He grabbed my arm and said in my ear:

"He's the one who's going to install the rearview mirrors now."

He started to laugh. He looked like a delighted little pig.

"Rezki," he yelled, "be careful, she sees everything."

"She sees everything in how many minutes?" the other one asked coldly.

Bernier let go my arm and got out. The Algerian worked rapidly and, without looking at me, left the car. I watched him the whole morning. He worked well and fast. We never found ourselves together. He was always ahead of me and I looked for him without finding him. Mustapha was slow, forgot a car and ran swearing to the top of the line. From time to time, he signaled to me and caught up with the car where he installed his stripping in a few seconds.

I closed my eyes to his haste and noted down nothing. In a car where I happened to meet him, I asked him the time. He put down his hammer and put up ten fingers, then two more. Noon, another half hour. Mustapha had placed his box under the dashboard and was smoking complacently. It was forbidden. His eyes were closed. I moved toward him.

"Your friend works fast."

"Arezki?" he said in a sleepy voice.

"Is his name Arezki? I thought it was Rezki."

"Same thing."

He dragged on his cigarette and started to get up.

"Get moving," he said. "You'll lose your bonus."

I ran to the next car. I was getting out when Arezki came along looking for the can of gasoline to clean his hands. He took a big ball of glass wool, wadded it and passed it along to his neighbor.

"Bon appetit," Mustapha came to tell me.

My appetite is good. I eat in the coatroom where a single faucet trickles, drop by drop. Sometimes, impatient, I eat without washing my hands. I fall on the bench. When I've eaten, I'll lie down, my coat rolled under my head. A carnal pleasure, rest.

In the afternoon, Gilles came to see me. It was a

pleasure to look at that handsome face of militant suburbia. Resolute, hard and clear, his even gaze penetrated to the marrow. He made a discreet little sign and we moved to the side.

"Mademoiselle Letellier, what's going on? There are eleven cars without snap-ons, and it was not reported. O.K., get going," he added, pushing me toward the car now coming up. "Check it quickly and then come explain."

I climbed in and looked around mechanically. He was watching me. The defects vaporized at my approach, and when I half turned away, they reappeared. In big, trembling letters, I put down anything, and went back to him.

"This morning, I had a pass for the infirmary."

"Yes, I know that, but Bernier took your place. No, it was later on, toward the end of the morning."

I was silent. There was no anger in his eyes. The next car approached.

"Go."

I checked it, and when I got back, he continued:

"Listen, Mademoiselle Letellier, you are here to check *their* work. . . . That's what they're here to do. I would have liked to talk with you about it the way I did with your brother. Unfortunately, that is not possible. Keep going."

I went, I checked, I got out.

"Here, conversation is impossible. In the evening, I'm busy, I have other occupations. Keep going."

While checking, I considered skipping the noon meal.

I spoke to him about it. He shook his head and said no, Lucien could explain why.

"It doesn't matter," he said.

And he told me to cheer up.

"But," he added, "do your work well. It's tough, I know, and I'm against the speed-up. There are ways to change some things. Do you understand me?"

He left me and called Mustapha. I got into the car he was leaving. Arezki was in it. He looked at me with complete indifference.

They were bitter, cold, discouraging, these contacts without results, these phrases spoken at random, these sympathies stillborn. Riveted to the assembly line like so many tools. We ourselves were tools.

I was about to get out; Mustapha stopped me. He seemed irritated.

"There's no point in you not marking it down when I don't do the work. Later on, the foreman will get after you and maybe he'll fire you. And it doesn't help me any."

His fingers made the motion of writing.

"Mark it down!"

Arezki had turned around. He questioned Mustapha, who made sweeping motions explaining himself. I left them together.

In spite of my weariness, I concentrated. But Gilles' remark burned a hole inside me. Like Mustapha, he thought it was some kind of charitable gesture and both of them were displeased. But what could I do? Be tough, like Daubat?

"I must see Lucien, talk to him. I'll tell him every-thing. The fatigue, the noise that isolates us one from the other, the filth between my fingers that I no longer bother to scrape off, the modesty that falls away in shreds."

"Look out!" someone near me shouted.

I turned around quickly. It was Daubat.

"I wanted to scare you," he said, bursting with laugh-ter. "How about it? Is it going better?"

He inspired in me a kind of respect and he knew it. Flattered, he felt a certain obligation to me, running over to encourage me, to ask me questions. Precious seconds he could have used to rest, to steal a smoke. His Parisian accent enchanted me.

"I must leave you," he said. "We mustn't fall behind. And don't be frightened. Mark down everything."

His eyes sought out Mustapha.

"Seventy-two. Three more."

Mustapha was already gone. He was getting ready to leave five minutes early. I let the last car slip by without checking. The line was about to stop, it wouldn't go any further. I had to see Lucien and rushed off at the first wail of the siren.

He was slowly going down the stairs. I grabbed his arm.

"I want to talk to you, Lucien. Can I see you tonight?"

"Tonight? It's not possible. There's a meeting. But you could come too. There are never too many. It's for peace in Algeria. Rue de la Grange-aux-Belles. You know it?"

"How should I know it?"

He suggested I go with him. Anna was waiting for him at the Porte de la Chapelle.

"Will it be over late? I have to get up tomorrow . . ."

"That way you'll never do anything!"

"You're right. Wait for me."

"O.K., but hurry. I'll be at the bus stop."

I moved fast. Hair, hands, they'd have to stay as they were. A meeting, that meant a crowd. A meeting, the word excited me.

Fatigue had rolled up into a ball somewhere inside my body. Slyly, it awaited its hour. My legs supple, I ran lightly toward the bus.

My brother was waiting for me.

"You haven't any friends you'd like to bring along?" he asked.

His question struck me as stupid.

"You understand, we need a crowd. But people don't show up. They haven't the time."

"They're tired," I said.

Lucien shrugged. In the bus, I filed after him, but we were separated and I found myself up near the driver.

The spectacle before us was like a fairyland. We were moving down the Boulevard Masséna on the hill this side of the Pont National; in front of us were dozens of cars, like comets with dazzling tails. A cluster of interweaving threads, red and green, illuminated the bridge, and the towers of the cubist city to the right were irregularly pierced with square lights.

But after the Porte Dorée, the land was flat and the fairyland ended. Lucien was now next to me. His hand held on to the metal bar and I saw traces of mercurochrome where his skin was broken; his swollen and wrinkled finger joints were those of an old man.

I looked from his hands to his face. I stole a look at his eyes. They had a familiar gleam and I suddenly wondered if he ever thought of Marie or his wife. And if he did think of them, how he could stand it.

"We're there."

We got off. Anna was standing in the shelter. She noticed my hair tied back with the checkered belt. Lucien suggested taking the métro. I walked a step behind. Under the many-colored neon lights, Anna was beautiful, but her appearance looked neglected. She must need money. Her battered pumps made her feet look ugly. Together, she and Lucien had the careless look of nature's children, citizens of the world, nonviolent, those who make people smile. They made you want to protect them. But I knew how ruthless they could be.

Going down the métro stairs, Lucien whispered under his breath: "Do you have a ticket?"

I didn't. Anna, smiling, held out hers. Her eyes were yellow and gentle.

At Stalingrad, we changed lines. On a bench, an old crone was holding on to four bursting bags, one of which was stuffed with newspapers. We watched her. Her head, wrapped in several shawls, leaned against the candy machine. Suddenly, she pulled away. Was it the contact with the cold metal or the sudden awareness of what she looked like? But did she know what she looked like, and did she see herself as we saw her?

Lucien started to laugh.

"See her?" he said to Anna. "That's you in another thirty years."

Anna didn't laugh. She looked at the woman and agreed.

"Yes, some day, I'll be like that."

Lucien had wanted to make a joke. But Anna's solemn tone removed our smiles. She examined the woman as if she were seeing her future.

The métro arrived, we got on silently and I forgot to read the names of the stations. I thought of Anna, after Lucien, after someone else, after still others, suddenly old, her hands as empty as they are today. Her somewhat foetal nature, and society, would push her oh so gently back to the byways whence she had come. No one spoke until we had left the métro.

"It's a memorial for a boy who died in Algeria. If there were only five hundred of us . . ."

There were thirty. Waiting for more to arrive, a few men argued near the platform. Anna had sat down at the end of a bench and I went over to join her.

"There aren't going to be many people," she said.

"You've already been to some of these meetings?"

"Yes, of course. Haven't you?"

"This is the first time my brother has asked me. Don't you think," I said, taking advantage of this tête-à-tête, "that Lucien looks badly?"

"I hadn't really noticed."

She got up. My question annoyed her. She saw in it an indirect reproach I had not intended. I couldn't seem to make myself understood by either of them. In her eyes, too, I was some sort of sister of charity. Her splendid disdain for health, rest, food—I wished I had it.

One of the men, holding some papers in his hand, mounted the platform. There was no loudspeaker or table and the lighting was dim.

"Comrades," he began.

Everyone gathered around the platform. I looked back. We made up a few thin rows.

"Comrades, last Saturday, the family of Jean Poinsot learned that he had been killed in Algeria. Jean was a young worker at Lavalette and lived in the neighborhood. In one of his last letters, he expressed the hope that he would soon return to France.

"On this painful occasion, the trade-unions of the C.G.T. and the local unions in the neighborhood share his family's grief over this young life snuffed out by the war."

We applauded.

The speaker coughed and went on in a stronger voice:

"The war in Algeria must end as soon as possible!"

Everybody shouted and clapped very hard.

"Workers of the tenth, we depend heavily on your union for the establishment of peace and the reconciliation of our two peoples."

What was Mustapha doing this evening? What would he think if he saw me here?

There were two more speeches. The last speaker, having looked over the audience, spoke without raising his voice. He told us that our small number shouldn't discourage us; that the death of this young worker would leave its impression on the working classes, that it would not be in vain if it unified us in the demand for peace.

As we left, we found about ten policemen posted along the street. Thinking we were more numerous, the cops waited to see if there wouldn't be more people coming behind us. Lucien shook a few hands and then we were four in the night on the Quai de Jemmapes. The boy who came with us proposed we have a drink. He led us into a quiet bar; he knew the neighborhood well.

"Sandwiches?"

"Yes."

"Yes."

At last we were going to eat. Up to then, no one had seemed to care. Lucien and his friend argued together with great animation. We were brought foaming beers and the bread came soon after.

The beer made me talkative.

"Her!" Lucien sighed. He turned to his neighbor. "It's taken her twenty-eight years to wake up; now she wants to go faster than anybody."

"I still think it's shocking that no one makes the slightest allusion to the principal victims, the Algerians, the people over there and the immigrants here."

"But what counts," the boy broke in, "is to shake people up. You want to shake them up with the suffering of the Algerians? You have to talk about what matters to them. A young kid who dies in Algeria, that matters to them; tomorrow, the same fate awaits them—them,

(115)

or their son, or their brother. Paris's compassion is a short-lived phenomenon. You can arouse the whole city to help the homeless, if the homeless are in style; you can also arouse it against a war, an injustice, but the wave soon passes. Between the waves, you have to give people time to live."

"There was a danger," Lucien remarked, "that this might excite their anger and provoke a desire for revenge."

"Look," the boy said.

He picked up a newspaper lying on the bench. On the front page there was a boldly drawn picture of some men sitting around a table, and one of them, bound and gagged, was guarded by two armed men. From each head floated a balloon explaining what each man was:

"The Judge."

"The Condemned Man."

"The Executioner."

"The Jury."

And the caption read in bold type:

"Condemned to death by the F.L.N., this man is about to be executed before his judges."

The drawing was moving. In an inside page, there was this:

"In the middle of Paris, people are being killed in the cellars."

"They're going a little far, don't you think?"

"That's their job," Lucien said. "Conducting a clandestine movement in the heart of the enemy territory, you have to use certain methods . . ."

"Yes," our companion agreed. "You can't make a

revolution in white gloves, but the people are completely hostile."

With the beer, weariness had pervaded my whole body to the ends of my fingers. Lucien mentioned paying, the other boy protested; we finally got up and he accompanied us to the métro. Lucien and I were sleepy. My brother asked how I was doing on the assembly line, if I would be able to hold up.

"Oh," I asked him, "can you explain to me what Gilles meant?"

And I told him what had happened.

"Why doesn't he want to discuss it at noon, neither in nor outside the factory? That's simple. If anyone saw you go off together, everyone would say that Gilles is running after you, or that you're running after him. That would make trouble for him, and for you, too."

"Here? In Paris? Working people would think that?"

"Of course, what would you think?"

We walked fast. The fog was getting thicker.

"Here you are."

I still had a hundred meters to go. I went to bed quickly. It was almost midnight. The alarm would go off at five; the night would be short.

.   .   .

I pushed open the door of the shop. Someone called me. I turned around. The timekeeper stamped out an unfinished cigarette. He was with a workman I had occasionally seen pass by.

"Hello," he said. "You're the new one?"

"Well, she's been here two weeks," the timekeeper said.

"It's eleven days," I said.

"I am the shop steward."

"That's interesting."

I gave him a big smile.

"Write down your name and tomorrow I'll get you your card and the stamp."

"Do I have to pay right away?"

He started to laugh.

"On payday, if it's better for you. Where do you come from?"

"I was in the provinces."

The men were arriving. We moved on. I talked to him about my brother. He told me he knew him, that he was a hard man.

Daubat, who had just arrived, gave me a friendly tap on the shoulder.

"Good morning, mademoiselle. A piece of advice. You are very nice and serious, just as you should be. Don't go putting yourself in the hands of a union. And don't talk too much with the Algerians. Have a good day!"

The motors started up and the great mechanized serpent got ready to devour once again. I got into a car. Arezki, Mustapha's friend, was already at work. He turned to me.

"I've just put the rearview mirror in the car in front. If you had checked it last night it wouldn't have been there."

"That's true. Thank you."

Arezki worked very fast and stopped from time to

time. That morning, his eyes kept searching for Mustapha. I was uneasy too, and the drawing in the paper came to mind. Had they forced him into a cellar? Had he forced them?

One by one, I looked at all the men working around me. Arezki seemed concerned; he spoke little.

Finally, Mustapha showed up. He wasn't in work clothes. He wore an overcoat of a bold black and white pattern.

"Good morning," he said very loud.

Arezki was annoyed.

The foreman approached.

"What's going on? What happened to you?"

"I overslept!" he said.

"Get down to the coatroom and get back fast. There'll be a penalty. Move . . ."

"Gently," Mustapha said.

And, full of dignity, he got down and went toward the machines.

Bernier grudgingly started to hammer some snap-ons. The white smocks were crossing the shop, one must take cover, they might come our way.

Mustapha returned and Bernier held out the hammer.

"Take it. Your tool box is in the car. But you've lost your bonus."

"Oh, well," Mustapha said haughtily, "I wasn't counting on it."

He was wearing a thick blue and white sweater; I had never seen him wear overalls. None of the Algerians on the line wore them. Mostly they worked in tweed jackets and greasy blue-jeans. Arezki wore a black polo shirt with rolled-up sleeves.

Mustapha began to hammer, then stopped to warn me.

"Look out, here comes the chrono."

"The chrono? What's that?"

He shrugged; I moved to the next car without waiting for his answer. He arrived with his shuffling gait, shoved the little Moroccan, struck a few blows with his hammer and stopped.

"Your hair . . . you've put it up again? You don't know what the chrono is? Well, it's the chrono. You must work quietly."

He gave me a demonstration, interrupted by Bernier who asked me to follow him.

"Come look at what you've let slip by."

The car he pointed to was moving way up ahead, in the locks section. Bernier climbed in, crouched down and showed me a large tear in the cloth next to the left door stripping.

I apologized.

"Pay attention the next time. If Gilles had seen that, or one of the foremen . . ."

His little yapping dog's face wasn't suited to serious statements.

"Get back there fast or they'll all go right past your nose. The defects, I mean."

Mustapha was watching me. He was curious.

"I've been stupid," I said.

"It was my work?"

"Yes."

He turned away and seemed to be thinking.

"Wait," he shouted.

He caught up with me, and with his finger pointing, his eyes earnest, his nose wrinkled with the effort of thought, he explained:

"This is the fourth car I've done this morning. He led you to the locks? Then," he shouted, overwhelmed, "it was him who did it!"

He clapped his hands with glee. I was annoyed. Disappointed, Mustapha shook his head.

"You're afraid of the boss?"

Yes, I was afraid.

Until noon, we worked without talking. From time to time, I leaned against the wall and closed my eyes for a few seconds. How could Lucien stand it?

I stayed in the coatroom to take a nap on the bench. A woman came in and told me it was twenty to two. I put on my coat and went down. Some coffee would pick me up. When the motors were still and the men were gone, I loved to walk through the enormous shops and look at the sleeping machines.

In front of the door, as I passed by, some men whistled. I was beginning to get used to it. Lucien was there too, talking to them. In the daylight, his face was gray. I made a sign and he joined me.

"Where are you going?"

"To get some coffee."

"It seems that you had a run-in with Bernier this morning."

"Who told you?"

"The little guy who works with you."

"Mustapha?"

"Yes.

"I've been here five months," Lucien went on. "I've been at your station, at others. And I've gotten to understand the system. Whether you go or stay, what I'm about to tell you will help you. Three days, a month, it makes no difference. Don't be humble. Here, humility is an admission. A little insolence puts the others at ease. The bosses are gripers. Don't take away their pleasure. Don't work too hard. Be a good tool, that's all you are. Never try to understand what you're doing. Don't ask what this is for or that is for. You're not here to understand but to go through a few motions. When you've gotten into the rhythm, you'll be a steady mechanic who sees no further than the end of the line. You'll be classified as a good worker and raised three francs an hour."

"I have no intention of staying," I said, raising my head.

We were on the Boulevard Masséna. I looked along the second floor for our shop windows.

"It's ten to. We must hurry."

We drank in silence and rapidly. Lucien paid. As we left, he asked:

"Have you any news?"

"I had some last week."

"Don't give them my address. It's time, we've got to hurry."

I heard the siren as I climbed the stairs.

The line is a giant boa constrictor that rolls along next

to the walls. An enormous mouth vomits the vehicles from the paint shop; a cauldron one floor above us pours out, via the elevator, seven cars an hour. As it moves down, the car is dressed in plastic and, in the course of its slow voyage, it is successively embellished with headlights, snap-ons, rearview mirrors, sun visors, dashboards, seats, doors, locks.

Gilles saw me as I passed in front of the boss's office. I saw him too, our eyes met. My lateness must have displeased him. I picked up my board, my pencil and my check list.

A chord in Mozart leapt from my memory. Lucien had played it so often when he was home from school that it had stuck in my head. My humming was lost in the noise of the line. I wished I knew the whole symphony so that I could sing it like a flute against the thunder of the machines.

Mustapha put his head in the rear window.

"The chrono, the chrono, look out!"

The chrono was there. He wore a gray smock and with him was the shop foreman, his hat on his head as always. The chrono had a big notebook, two pencils and, naturally, an enormous chronometer which he held in his open palm.

He planted himself next to me and watched. I tried to work slowly but, in spite of myself, certain motions were fast, my well-trained fingers went straight to their task. I took my time checking the dashboard. I tried to lose a few seconds. But it was pure ingenuousness. The chrono guessed it; the chrono was not interested in how many minutes it took to do a certain piece of work, but decided for himself the necessary time for each motion. His coming was the signal of an imminent change. He put away his clock when Mustapha approached.

"Sir," he asked, "do you have the time, please?" The other man bit his lip and moved on without answering.

The next day, Gilles came to tell us the new ruling. My job was now to include the checking of head and rear lights. The Magyar was to screw them on, Arezki was to install the heating controls on the dashboard.

"It's too much," Gilles said. "I tried to make them see it. But I'm the only one who says anything. You will soon have company. After the fifteenth, four women will start checking. One there, the others further down. Your brother is going up to the paint shop."

"Lucien? Why?"

"Boss," Mustapha asked as he came up. "What more do I have to do?"

"You, nothing," Gilles said, laughing. "Just do what you're doing but do it well."

Arezki was angry. He grabbed Gilles and they argued for a long time. Cars went by. I put down "rearview mirror missing."

"What the hell," Arezki said, taking his place again, "I've lost my bonus."

The fourteenth day was payday. Bernier brought the envelopes. Everybody stopped work for a few seconds to check his raise. A few went over to Bernier to protest. He sent them on to the shop foreman.

Why didn't I quit at that moment? Take my winnings, as they say? I didn't dare ask Lucien for the money he owed me. Now, if I took out the cost of the trip, I would have enough left to feed me a few days. I had written in my letters to Grandmother about economies, money earned, the radio I'd buy her . . . O.K., I'd do another two weeks. By that time, perhaps Lucien could give me something. I would economize . . .

I thought about it as I waited for the bus. The pay check I had stuffed into the bottom of my bag was a disappointment. So many motions, so little money. I walked away from the crowd and moved along the boulevard in the direction of the Place d'Italie. A taxi let a woman off. I came up and signaled it to wait.

Marvelous, marvelous. Collapsed in the seat, I took in the nocturnal fairyland. It filled my eyes; the luminous sparks of the Pont National, the factory chimneys transfigured by the horizon's glow, Paris at the edge of its suburbs, the blazing foundries and the giant tanks splitting the night sky, lowering, velvet, as if suspended at the level of the street lights. I savored all that, sitting, sprawled, hoping for ten thousand red lights to protract the festival.

That night, I took off my clothes, washed all over, my hair included, put on my nightgown, a wool sweater and lay down on the bed. I felt a sense of total well-being. I took a hard look at my expenses. So much for food, so much for the room, and I hid five thousand francs, which represented my first savings.

. . .

Often in the morning, assaulted by the noise and invaded by fatigue, I had violent headaches. I bought aspirin and got into the habit of swallowing a tablet around nine o'clock when my neck began to hurt. I also bought a little bottle of lavender which I sniffed from time to time. I had put these in a small box on which I had written: *E. Letellier,* and which I had tucked away in a corner.

One morning, Arezki put down his tools and ran over to Bernier's desk. He returned a moment later and went back to work but I noticed that his face looked pinched. We never spoke to each other. Mustapha came over to tell me:

"He's sick, he can't work."

"He should ask to leave or go to the infirmary."

"The boss says no."

"Where do you hurt?" I asked him directly.

"I have a headache. I can't see what I'm doing."

I got out of my car and went to look for Bernier. He was just approaching us.

"Sir," I said, "one of the men is sick. He can't work."

"Who?" he asked cheerfully.

"The one who installs the mirrors. Arezki."

"So what?" he asked.

"He should go to the infirmary."

"Sure, they all want to go to the infirmary. Before that, it was the men's room. Don't put yourself out for him, mademoiselle."

He patted my hand.

"I'm not giving out any more passes. It's orders. Only for accidents or if the guy collapses. All the others are fakes, put-ons. I know them."

"But that's inhuman."

"Relax, Mademoiselle Letellier," he said, dropping his nice smile. "Get back to your place and don't worry about such things."

I returned to the line, furious, rushed through two checks and looked for Arezki. He was slowly screwing on the knobs and Mustapha was installing the mirrors in his place.

"Do you still feel sick?"

Mustapha answered yes.

"Would you like some aspirin?" I shouted.

Arezki raised his head.

"You have some?"

I brought him two.

"The Tunisians have some milk," Mustapha said. "Go . . ."

Arezki took the tablets and got out of the car. Mustapha attached his strip with the fewest possible tacks, ran to the next, to the rear where he hammered his snapons.

I was checking a dashboard when Arezki leaned forward to thank me.

"Are you better?"

"Not yet, but I will be in a moment."

He came over a little later to tell me he felt much better. At noon, he brought me a cloth soaked in gasoline to clean my fingers. I thanked him with feeling. We said "Bon appetit" and "Good night, see you tomorrow" at the end of the day.

He had a handsome and severe face that intimidated me. He looked less young than the others.

The next morning, I found a croissant wrapped in tissue paper in my box. I called Mustapha.

"Is it yours?"

He shook his head and, as I didn't seem to understand, he said:

"Arezki put it there for you."

Arezki was working further along. In his usual way, he was well ahead of us. When we found ourselves together, I asked him, as I had Mustapha:

"Is it yours?"

"No, it's yours."

Mustapha, who came by, said: "It's for the aspirin yesterday."

"For the aspirin? Come on then, keep it."

"For friendship," Arezki said, looking at me.

I divided the croissant in three and handed each of them a piece.

"Not for me," Arezki said. "I don't eat in the morning."

"I do," said Mustapha.

His voracious look made us laugh. Gilles put his head in the rear window at that precise moment. He looked at me, astonished. Shaken, I picked up my board and quickly got up. But he was already gone. Arezki had seen my embarrassment. He went back to work.

Mustapha called me a few minutes later.

"Hey, Mademoiselle Lise, do you have another aspirin? He's got a headache too."

"He" turned out to be the Magyar. They had no common language, but made signs that they alone understood.

The next day, I found another croissant in my box. Mustapha, who was watching me, urged me on.

"Eat it."

"Is it? . . ."

"Yes," he said.

Getting out of a car, my path crossed Arezki's.

"Monsieur . . ." I began.

He shook his head, smiling, and didn't stop.

I came upon him again a little later; he was arguing with Mustapha. They were speaking Arabic and I had the feeling they were talking about me.

Toward evening, as I stood up from checking some headlights, my eyes met Arezki's who was crouching in the interior. We were both embarrassed, we were avoiding each other, but the rhythm of the line brought us together often.

. . .

One evening, I conjured up his face for me alone and it gave me such pleasure that I did it again often.

We were unable to speak freely with each other. Mustapha served as a pretext. We never said you or I but always he, and we spoke only of him. This ruse took care of our timidity. Mustapha did and said so many silly things that there was always a subject for conversation. And anyway, what could you say in that racket where you had to shout, in that endless getting in and out of cars?

Every morning, I found a tidbit in my box. I accepted it, thinking of the pleasure Arezki must have had buying and putting it there.

I shared it with Mustapha, who waited impatiently for this moment.

Daubat came over one morning and accused Mustapha of tearing his headliners when he hammered the snap-ons. Mustapha protested, shouted, then grabbed Daubat by the collar of his jacket. Arezki jumped out of a car, dragged Mustapha away and made him let go.

They got into the car together. Arezki looked displeased. His words were underlined with menacing gestures.

"He called me a nigger!"

"So what?" Arezki asked. "You can't take that? And what about your father and mother over there, what don't they have to take?"

I interrupted to say that it was shameful when a working man was a racist and called a fellow worker a nigger.

Arezki began to laugh and shook his head.

"If you can't stand that," he said to Mustapha, "how will you stand the rest?"

"We should tell the shop steward," I suggested.

Mustapha made an obscene gesture. But we had lost too much time so we all went back to work.

"It's going to snow," Mustapha said.

He leaned toward the Magyar: "Snow!"

The other man raised his head of thick, very curly blond hair. His pimply red face spelled misery, loneliness, and I thought at the moment, how much these remarks of Mustapha's must mean to him.

I got into the car Arezki was leaving. Looking aside, he said:

"Today is my birthday."

I was surprised for a few seconds, then continued my checking. My muscles, uncooperative at the beginning, were now obedient, but if something unexpected changed the mechanical order, they creaked like old pulleys. The good worker controls each motion and never makes a useless one. And since this rhythm had not been established with conversation in mind, you had to speed up one motion or skip another in order to exchange a few words. You could do it, but at the risk of upsetting order and disturbing your comrades. Therefore, when a man emerges from a car and throws out "Today is my birthday," you forget the dashboard in order to catch up with him in the next car and say, in the din of hammering: "Happy Birthday." And as I was saying this and he was thanking me with a smile, an uproar broke out, so loud that it deafened the motors. Everybody stopped working. The Moroccan, Mustapha and the Magyar jumped into the aisle. Arezki turned to me:

"It's the women."

Gilles was coming in with four girls, and howls rose from the assembly line. Mustapha was gesticulating, shouting, and Arezki pointed to him, laughing.

When the group had passed by, everyone went back to work; but Mustapha, overexcited, came and went, climbed up and down and ended by being carried away by the car up front.

He came back a moment later, and jumped on the Magyar.

"Beautiful woman," he said.

His falling behind didn't seem to bother him. Arezki came up; Mustapha seized his arm.

"There is a woman, right there. She checks locks."

And he whistled in admiration.

"Fine," Arezki said with indifference.

His response pleased me. Mustapha's enthusiasm had annoyed me a little.

During the noon break, the new girls took possession of their lockers in the coatroom. Then they left for lunch; there remained only the regulars who ate there.

"They're putting women on the line."

"It's no worse than anything else."

"They're young."

"Wait 'till you see them in a few weeks."

"Up there, with the Algerians."

"They're putting them everywhere, except in the paint shop."

Lucien had been put in the paint shop four days ago. I hadn't seen him since. I ate quickly and left in the hope of running into him. But nobody was there. The cold fog had emptied the streets. Was he in some café?

At ten to, I walked slowly toward the shop. Fortunately all attention was focused on the new arrivals. I saw Lucien. He was joking with one of the girls who was going up holding on to the railing.

I called to him; he turned around quickly.

"I've been wanting to see you; is there any news? I hear they've put you upstairs."

"I'm O.K.," he said with indifference. And he continued on his way.

"Lucien!"

"Now what?"

"When can I see you?"

He seemed annoyed.

"Come Thursday night," he sighed. "Henri is supposed to bring me some things."

(132)

I got to my station. The Magyar was tightening his belt. Arezki was already there. The four women went by, arm in arm. The youngest was very pretty. She made me think of Marie-Louise. Mustapha, gloriously combed, followed them.

Several times that afternoon, Arezki got mad because Mustapha was making a nuisance of himself with his coming and going.

"For my birthday, you'll come have a drink with me this evening?"

I didn't answer. And he stood in front of me while the Magyar apologized for being in the way. We then saw that we were motionless on the line and were being pulled forward.

Inside me, three mouths opened to speak. One said, "at last . . .," another said "but how? and where? and what if people . . . ?" From the third came a "no," but not as a refusal. The hesitant no when the event you've been imagining for years finally takes place. Seized with apprehension, this mouth said "wait a minute."

"Well?" Arezki asked. He was speaking to Mustapha, who was limping.

"She is beautiful, beautiful. But to talk to, not so easy."

"Forget it," Arezki said dryly. "French girls don't like Arabs."

I took these words as a challenge and, wishing to accept it, I asked him a little later:

"Which birthday is it?"

"Thirty-one."

"Where do you want to meet me?"

His face lit up. He asked me which way I went home after work, where I lived. But he interrupted himself to resume work, for Gilles was coming. He was walking fast and his smock flew behind him. Night was coming on, the windows were dark. The little Moroccan put down his hammer and said "ouf" and rubbed his wrist. Arezki came toward me and signaled me to come near.

"You take the bus at the corner? We'll meet there. I'll get in behind you and we'll get off somewhere along the way."

It seems I went on working until the siren stopped the machines. A workman going by called out to me:

"Hey, you in there, it's over."

In the coatroom, there was a crush. The women were getting dressed and talking in loud voices. But it was a fleeting joy, this release. Down below, in the métro, going home, they would return to another kind of alienation.

I looked for Arezki. He hadn't come yet. I took my place in the queue. Peace was waiting ahead. But now, the storm so long desired rained down on me. Suddenly, Arezki was there. His clothes surprised me. He was wearing a dark suit, a white shirt, but no overcoat, nothing warm. He stationed himself behind me, without speaking, and made a conspiratorial sign. A big Algerian from the assembly line named Lakhdar passed near us. He put his hand out to Arezki.

"Where are you going?"

"I have an errand to do."

We finally got aboard and found ourselves squeezed together on the bus platform. Arezki didn't look at me.

(134)

At the Porte de Vincennes, we were able to move forward.

"Shall we get off at the Porte des Lilacs? Is that all right? Do you like to walk?"

"That's fine," I said.

My awkwardness grew and my companion's silence didn't help. I read from beginning to end the regulations of "The Company" tacked above my head.

Arezki made a sign. We got off. I didn't know the neighborhood. I told this to Arezki; it provided a subject of conversation. After crossing the square, we entered a café, "A la Chope des Lilas." The sign was a brutal green. A large group of men hugged the bar. A few looked us over. The tables were occupied.

"Come," Arezki said, and we threaded our way to the left hand corner where there were a few empty chairs. Arezki sat down opposite me. Our neighbors stared at us. I caught a glimpse of myself in the mirrored column; I was purple and disheveled. I turned down my coat collar and, as I was doing that, I realized what was wrong. I was with an Algerian. It took the look in other people's eyes, the expression of the boy who took our orders, to bring it home. I felt a sudden panic; Arezki looked at me and I blushed, afraid that he had guessed my embarrassment.

"What would you like?"

"Whatever you're having," I said stupidly.

"Hot tea?"

He seemed no more at ease than I. Before taking a sip, I repeated twice: "Happy Birthday!"

He gave me a funny smile and started to ask me

questions. I told him about our life with Grandmother, about Lucien.

"I thought you were younger than him."

"Because I'm small? No, I'm twenty-eight."

He looked at me with astonishment.

"You really love your brother . . ."

"Yes," I said.

And I asked him if he had brothers, or a mother. He had three brothers, a sister and his mother was still alive. He described her as a yellow leaf ready to fall, bruised like over-ripe fruit, her eyesight almost gone. I thought of Grandmother.

To ease the tension, we spoke of Mustapha.

"Would you like to walk a little?" he asked.

We went out. The Boulevard Serrurier. The reassuring night. No one sees us. Cold and in a hurry, people rush past.

I did almost all the talking. Arezki listened, assented, walked, looking straight ahead. Several times, he asked if I was tired. I tried to find something to attract his attention. He agreed with everything I said. I told him about the meeting at the Grange aux Belles.

"If you go to meetings," he said, "you'll get into trouble."

I changed the subject, talked about Henri, Lucien, Indochina, I mixed dreams with the truth. I couldn't stop talking. We walked all the way to the Porte de Pantin. He looked at his watch.

"Are you afraid of walking home alone? It's eight o'clock."

"Of course not."

"I must leave you here. But I'll stay with you until the bus comes."

"How do you go from here?"

"By métro."

"You're not bothered at night by police patrols?"

"Sometimes . . ." he said.

We waited in the shelter. Arezki must have been shivering. He stood stiffly, his hands in his pockets, and looked over my head. When the bus approached, he took out one hand and held it toward me.

"Thank you," he said. "You are kind. I'll see you tomorrow."

The next day, Arezki behaved as usual. I felt a little disappointed that he wasn't more friendly. Had I disappointed him? But I was certain that no one had seen us together.

. . .

In the coatroom, I observed the new girls. The first day, they had worn sandals and drab smocks. But the proximity of men had made them spruce up. One of them had brought a pink smock, another had put glittering barrettes in her hair, still another was wearing flowered mules.

They arrived in the morning, faces madeup and hair arranged, and somehow managed during the day to retire and put on fresh lipstick. There was something there that went beyond coquetry: a display, an instinctive defense against a kind of work that ended by reducing you to the level of a tramp—the nail polish more often than not hid the grime; the dirty hair was beribboned with velvet; they patted the gray sweat with powder. I can still see my neighbor in the coatroom, a woman of thirty-five, not pretty, wrinkled, forced by the regulations to wear a discolored denim uniform, and who, while driving a Fenwick, kept on her pumps.

I felt very isolated in this aviary. Nevertheless, I too became contaminated and withdrew enough money from my first savings to buy a smock. I bought a blue one, piped in white, that came down to my calf.

I only remembered my brother's invitation Thursday morning. Well, that's a good sign. It's like a thorn that comes out gently, without too much damage.

But I'd been stuck again. Arezki seemed to avoid me. The days seemed longer and more difficult.

. . .

I arrived at Lucien's at eight o'clock. Henri was already there and shook my hand hard. Anna asked if I wanted some coffee. Lucien grumbled good evening. On the table were some books Henri had brought. He discussed the situation passionately with my brother. They often disagreed. Henri was trying to show Lucien his contradictions and Lucien, mulish, headstrong, retreated into silence. Anna, sitting on the edge of the bed, was stroking her ankle and looking from one to the other. I was falling asleep and missed my small selfish pleasures, the torpor that comes before sleep.

"You maintain," Henri was saying heatedly, "that the working man doesn't give a damn about the Algerian war. I tell you that it's because they lack the information. If they knew what . . ."

(138)

"Then why do you make fun of the posters, of the slogans on the walls and those who put them there?"

"Because you can do better. Bear witness with your pen. It's been six months," Henri hammered on, "that you've been in there. The working class is twenty thousand leagues under the sea. In another world. Try and learn what's going on there. Through the Party? It demobilizes the masses with its health bulletins: everything is going well, the workers are vigilant, it is getting new members, etc. Can't you report on what you see, what you hear? Describe the relationship between the Algerians and the French at the proletarian level. You intended to do it, you owe it to yourself. But pasting up a poster at night . . ."

"Leave my posters alone," Lucien grumbled.

They were silent for a few minutes. Anna put her slippers back on and got up to pour us more coffee.

What Henri was saying seemed right to me. His somewhat heavy body, his calm deep voice, added to the force of his arguments. But what bothered me was that a part of him found pleasure in these events, dramas and conflicts. He remained part spectator, Peeping Tom even, excited by the spectacle. His psychological insight, his quick intelligence took delight in Lucien.

My brother drank greedily and Anna served him twice. When he had finished and lit a cigarette, he leaned toward me.

"Elise, tell Henri what you think."

"I, but . . ."

"Yes, you, you're not an idiot. You must have something to say."

I said it awkwardly. Lucien interrupted me.

"You see, Henri, neither my sister nor I are good lawyers. A moment ago you reproached me. All right, it is six months since I took this job—from necessity, not choice—and I became excited at the prospect of what I could do. I could bear witness, as you said. Well, today, my friend, I've given up. I can't do it. It's a vicious circle. All day long, I'm like a camera registering pictures. By evening, I've collapsed. The pictures stay inside me. You see, to survive you have to work. So, I put it off. And everyday I get a little more numb. Do you know where they've sent me? To the paint shop. I don't even want to tell you why. So that I'll become disgusted, so that I'll quit. It seems that I sap the workers' morale; I upset them. Even the shop steward is against me. He says I go too far. But I'm not quitting. When I get home at night, I drink quarts of water, I eat and I go to bed. Intellectual effort? Not possible. In six months, I've fallen apart. I'll tell you something else, Henri. If I hadn't been working with blacks, cheek to jowl, I'd have already forgotten them. I would have three francs more, or a half-hour less work, or five minute's rest an hour. But there they are, and for all that I feel exploited and diminished, next to them, I am a privileged person. They are a fuel with no value, an inexhaustible reserve. There can't be more than three or four of us in the factory who see that they are men. No doubt you are right: paste up a poster, scribble on a wall, distribute tracts—a lazy solution. But who makes these posters, who inspires the tracts?"

"You're not a real revolutionary," Henri said.

"You're just a rebel; I've already told you. You're wasting your time. There aren't so many of us and we need people like you. Despite all this, you must do something, take some kind of action against this situation."

"It's taken a bad turn," Lucien murmured. "People are scared. Getting an even break, justice . . . the people have gone over to the side that's winning."

Henri took me home. He had left his car behind the Basilica.

"And what about you, Elise," he asked. "Are you getting used to it?"

I told him no; I was leaving soon, I didn't know exactly when, probably at Christmas.

"Take advantage of Lucien's affection for you, make him quit the factory. He's gotten to the breaking point."

"His affection?" I said skeptically.

"He ought to rest awhile, then look for another job."

"He can't afford to."

"Come on," Henri protested, "just a few days, that's not impossible. He can last two or three weeks without work. What about his medical insurance?"

I didn't answer. There was no point. Between him and me was an ocean's difference. By "lack of money" he didn't mean what we did. He meant giving up the movies, or at worst, gas for his car. But for us it was vital, because there was no one behind or before us. If Lucien stayed three weeks, two months without work, it would be the end. We were no longer at Grandmother's. "You can always find ten thousand francs," Henri said. But only in the bottom of a pay envelope.

"Poor Lucien. He has spent years doing nothing."

"Does he send money to his daughter?" Henri asked suddenly.

Embarrassed, I answered that I didn't know.

"But," I said, "Anna could go to work. That would help."

Henri nodded.

"I'll drop you here?"

"Yes, that's fine."

"He doesn't want her to work. At least for now. Do you know that she came to my house one evening—it was May, I believe. Lucien had been living in Paris six or eight weeks. She had remembered my address. I don't know where she got the money to get this far. But suddenly, there she was, in a state of exaltation that impressed me. She wanted me to tell Lucien that she was dead. She left a letter for him and was gone. We looked for her. Lucien was wild. From anxiety, and also out of a morbid joy over Anna's action. She was killing herself for him. She was playing with her life. Thanks to a friend, we found her in a hospital; people rarely die from an overdose of aspirin. All the same, she had to stay for quite a while. She took on an extra dimension in his eyes. They are very, very far removed from us, don't you think?"

"Yes," I said, looking at the door of the lobby that the night had turned blue.

These far-off places were strange to me. I came to miss Marie-Louise's restful mediocrity. I was afraid of Anna.

.   .   .

"Mademoiselle Letellier, you haven't noticed that all the rear lights are put on wrong?"

Gilles pushed me gently to one side, and when the car arrived in front of us, he looked at the Magyar.

"Do you see?"

He leaned toward him.

"No," he said, just like that.

And, bending down, he showed him.

"Understand?"

The Magyar indicated that he didn't understand that word. Gilles gave him back his screwdriver.

"Get going," he shouted to me. "You'll fall behind."

I got back in the car. Gilles followed and crouched in back of me.

"It's not enough time, is it? You haven't time to check the exterior?"

"Yes sir, it's not enough."

"That's O. K.," he said. "Forget the rear lights. Don't check them any more."

The timekeeper appeared in the frame of the door.

"What's the matter, Mr. Gilles?"

"Your ceiling. Not stretched enough. For two days the checkers have been telling you that."

"Ah?"

He passed his hand over the fabric and wrinkles appeared.

"True. But," he exploded, "look at what you've given me to do the work! Niggers, nothing but niggers. They don't know their job, and talk about lazy . . ."

"Tell me," Gilles interrupted, "are you sure the work has been properly explained to them?"

"What do you think! It's me who explains it."

"All the same, I'm going over to see them."

The timekeeper got out of the car.

"He is a racist, isn't he?" I asked Gilles.

He didn't answer my question.

"I think you'd be better off in the offices," he said. "I'll look into it, in January, after the holidays."

I said nothing, but thought to myself: "After the holidays, I won't be here any more."

Arezki came toward me. I tried to avoid him, but he held out a piece of cotton soaked in gasoline and I thanked him.

"Can I see you this evening? At the bus stop, like the last time. We'll take a walk." He leaned forward to say in my ear: "I want to talk to you."

The timekeeper was looking at us. He was in the car opposite, accompanied by Gilles who was measuring the headliners. I read nothing in his eyes, he was looking at me innocently, but I blushed as if I were guilty. The motors slowed down, the siren delivered us.

"Good," Gilles said, stepping down. "Time's up. Let's go. Are you eating in the canteen, Mademoiselle Letellier?"

"No, in the coatroom."

"You eat a cold lunch?"

That evening, Arezki didn't hurry off before the siren. When he saw me put away my board, he came up from behind and said very fast:

"See you soon. I'll be waiting."

We got off at the Porte des Lilas, like the last time. The trip seemed long.

And we disappeared into the shadows of the Rue des Glaïeuls.

"Shall we walk a while to begin with?" Arezki had asked.

I considered that a bad omen.

It was a short street, badly lit. We walked slowly, Arezki in his jacket and I holding my handbag against my thigh. He was in command and I waited for him to speak. He started with banalities: the cold, the winter, it's good to get out of the factory. I answered without enthusiasm.

"The other evening," he said, "I mentioned a birthday. But I was born in July."

"Oh, yes?"

"Yes. I wanted to tell you, because after listening to you, I was sorry I said that."

"Then why did you?"

Arezki shrugged.

"I don't know. So that you'd say yes."

We had reached the corner of the street. He hesitated over what direction to take. Finally, we returned toward the Boulevard Serrurier.

"It doesn't matter. You were depressed. You wanted someone around. But you don't need to apologize."

"Yes, that's so. I'm keeping you. Perhaps you have something to do somewhere else. Walking in the night, in the cold . . ."

I protested that, on the contrary, I liked it. I thought that he was going to leave me at the corner, I saw the vast street and the shadows all around, people going home two by two, the men carrying a loaf of bread, bottles, people who knew where they were going, home, together, and who could prolong the pleasure of conversation as much as they liked.

"I was afraid I talked too much and bored you. You've been unfriendly since the other evening."

"I?" he said.

He looked at me. He smiled. That rarely happened.

"But how can we talk during work? Besides, I don't want to get you into trouble. If they saw us talking, going out together . . ."

We were in that section of the Boulevard where there were fewer cars, in that corridor of light made by the yellow neon lamps.

He guessed I was more at ease and we discussed our work, our comrades, the assembly line.

"Why do you speak French so well?"

"Luck," he said.

The Porte de Pantin and the bus shelter suddenly rose before us. Now we had to separate. The bus came immediately. As I got on, when we said good night, he turned down the collar of my coat. I drew a hole on the frosted window and I saw him looking to the right and the left before crossing.

.   .   .

Oh sleeping lakes, flowered paths, woods carpeted with fern, fields of wheat where the loved one waits, more golden than the grain, streams we follow hand-in-hand. Old dreams stored away, buried but not dead. This is my lot: the Porte des Lilas, the hill down to the Pré Saint-Gervais; in the horizon, the fading smoke of the sleeping factories, the suburban steppe parched by the cold and the stale air, the half-deserted boulevard where the cars scrape the sidewalks, and next to me, this man with whom for the third time, I wander, as if paradise awaited us at the end.

At the end, the "good night, see you tomorrow," already more affectionate. We each went our way. Our timid conversations remained difficult. Self-assured the minute before, a single word could make Arezki shrink.

To watch the metamorphosis of the trees, to let the eye wander over imaginary paths illuminated by the stars, to drink the fresh rain at dawn, at night the fog, to stand at the window open to a piece of sky, plants in pots, outlines of branches, it makes you—in spite of yourself—different from those who haven't taken the time. Different, not better. But there you are, for the rest of your life, charged with emotions and cumbersome feelings, and as if seen through a kaleidoscope, each event appears stretched, deformed, colored, worked over.

Mutilated by a stunted life, by a fraternal passion and narrow horizons, my acute sensuality, which had found expression only in these nightly contemplations and the mystical joy of renunciation, exploded in the warmth of this secret friendship.

. . .

A fourth time, Arezki whispered, "See you in the evening." But he added a little later:

"Not at the bus stop. I'll explain. Take the métro in the direction of Villette. Get off at Stalingrad and wait for me at the top of the stairs. O.K.?"

That was a long conversation. Mustapha interrupted once; the Magyar passed between us, and from his desk, Bernier saw us together.

Stalingrad, no longer the outskirts but the real city. Arezki found me where he had asked me to wait, in the crowd that marched up and down the stone stairs.

"Come this way."

There were many Arabs. We crossed the street and took the Rue de l'Aqueduc, poorly lit. He led me into a small neighborhood café watched over by an old woman behind the counter.

"Good evening, Mémère," he said, rubbing his hands. "How are you?"

"Good evening, young man, good evening, mademoiselle."

Arezki chose the farthest of the four tables covered with an oilcloth.

"We would have been too cold outdoors."

"Yes."

But I missed the night and the freedom to walk without being seen. Here, we could only move our eyes.

The old woman brought two coffees.

Arezki knew the place. He had come here to eat when he worked in the neighborhood. "With an electrician. I've had many jobs. But that doesn't count, does it? What counts is what you are, not what you do."

I agreed. I didn't dare say that what you did was part of what you were. We talked about Paris. Arezki explained its geometry. I asked him if he liked Paris.

"I have liked it. Now I like nothing."

His eyes flashed in his triangular face. I had never seen him so close.

"Do you like Algiers?" I asked, smiling.

"There is no place I like in the whole world."

When I spoke of the war, his eyes dimmed; he looked away, avoiding mine. The old woman mumbled to herself as she shifted the bottles. It was cosy, we felt safe. Arezki touched my fingers twice. I fell into a silence that lengthened as he smiled at me.

Now, the old woman was showing signs of impatience. Two coffees in one hour was not much business. Arezki looked at his watch.

"I have to go back."

We left, and found ourselves in an intense cold that paralyzed our lips. In the warmth of the métro, Arezki explained that he woud have to leave me there. He would go back on foot, there was a friend he had to see. I said it was all right. He led me to the platform, showed me where to change trains, and the métro appeared. Then he drew me to him and kissed me on the cheek, very fast. I didn't pull away; he kissed me again and let me go. I got into the car, then suddenly, seized with a desire not to leave him, I pushed aside my neighbors and stepped down to the platform. The métro pulled away. I had seen him leave by the stairs to the left. He wasn't there. Where should I go? Several passages opened up before me. One said "Exit." He had said, "I'm going back on foot." The white tiles of the walls were a nightmare corridor in an asylum, a corridor that made you want to run, screaming.

I reached the turnstile. People were coming and going. No Arezki. I thought I saw him to the right. It wasn't him. I went toward the street. Between the pillars of the elevated métro, there were two police cars and a group of men surrounded by cops with tommy guns. I was seeing this spectacle for the first time. Other policemen were herding passers-by. I stood motionless at the foot of the steps, thinking. Was Arezki there, a few meters away, his arms above his head? It was impossible to see anything in the dark behind the screen of police. I was scared. I couldn't move. The black oilskins, the arms stretched horizontally, the black cars, the shiny black gaiters, the black night, the black cartridge belts, the men with black hair, wavy, straight. Arezki is there, I thought to myself. And I prayed he would see me. I was paralyzed with fear. But the people going by didn't seem concerned. Two of the policemen watching the stairs looked at me. I walked up a few steps and turned once again before going through the turnstile. From that level, I saw only the wheels of the cars and a few giant shadows on the pillars where the tommy guns looked as big as cannons.

I wanted to run to Lucien and tell him everything, but I went back to my room and got into bed without eating. I thought of Arezki, his arms in the air. The details of his face I had discovered that night made him more precious to me.

. . .

I went to sleep all the same and woke up late but dressed in such a hurry that I found myself in front of the factory well ahead of time. In the still empty coatroom, the creaking hinges of my locker clawed at my nerves. I ran quickly to my station and sat inside a car to watch the people arriving. Arezki appeared surrounded by the Tunisians. He chatted with them for a few minutes. The Magyar climbed to the line, shivering. He saw me, said "Good morning," a phrase Mustapha had taught him. The little Moroccan said "hello." Daubat and the timekeeper stopped near Bernier's desk as he was wiping away the dust. These few minutes before the line started had the balm of a reprieve. I imagined each time the impossible miracle: Gilles suddenly appearing with a pointer and a giant chart and explaining with his beautiful stern voice the metamorphoses in which we participated with our hands and muscles.

The siren brought the late ones running. The motors started up, the cars moved forward, and, revolving within specified limits, according to well calculated and measured motions (barely discernible turnings of the wheels), we worked toward the sublime end: Production.

Several times, Arezki tried unsuccessfully to talk to me. The long morning dragged on without our exchanging a word. Mustapha and Arezki got into a number of arguments. The latter seemed annoyed and the former tried in vain to make him laugh.

"All right, go," Arezki shouted, "go see the girl up front and leave us to do our work."

Mustapha went off in a huff.

At noon, according to ritual, Arezki brought me the gasoline-soaked cloth. I put down my board and we leaned against the window.

Mustapha joined us. He called to Arezki and the two of them moved off toward the top of the line.

As soon as the siren went off, I jumped into the aisle but, for a change, I stopped near Daubat. Arezki was a few meters ahead of him.

"Well, my little pupil, shall we go for lunch?"

"Yes, but . . ."

I quickly improvised.

"But I wanted to talk to you about my brother."

"To me?" he said, astonished.

Arezki had disappeared in the rush. I gave up trying to join him.

Daubat took off his smock and hooked it to a nail on which hung an immense pair of scissors.

"Watch out, Mohammed, if I catch you touching these . . ."

He was wearing a hand-knit red sweater, and underneath, a brown flannel shirt that outlined an already prominent belly.

"What about your brother?"

"He can't stand the paint. He's in poor health. Can't you ask that he come back down here and work with us?"

"Me? It's Gilles you should ask. How should I . . . He has only to see the doctor or the shop steward."

"So," shouted the timekeeper as he passed by, "what are you two doing?"

Daubat laughed.

"She's talking to me about her brother. The paint shop is making him sick, he wants to change."

(152)

The timekeeper stopped smiling.

"It's his own fault. When he was down here, he had only to keep still. Now they'll leave him up there until he quits."

He stopped to light a cigarette, and Daubat, less brutal, took up the theme:

"I tried to explain it to him. He's young, he doesn't understand life. I told him, forget the niggers, don't get involved in their troubles, do your work, don't argue with the bosses, no politics here. He wouldn't listen, he got angry at everybody, even the shop steward. They had a blow-up here, before you came. He's an agitator, an agitator. The men have had it up to here, and so have the bosses. To them, he's not a useful element; he argues too much."

"Yes, I understand. Forgive me," I said, "I'm keeping you."

"It's nothing at all. You must make him see the light, that's all. Well, have a good lunch."

I opened the door to the coatroom. The women were all there and my usual place was occupied. I approached a girl who was resting her legs on the bench.

"Could you move over a little, please."

She put her feet down, and paying no further attention to me, continued her conversation with her friends. One of them was describing her altercation with the head boss.

"Where I worked before," she added, "it was even worse."

Her profile was attractive, but the corner of her eye

was marred by too many wrinkles. Her hair curled around her ears and revealed where her make-up stopped.

"But at least there were no Arabs," she added.

I blushed, but no one was looking at me.

The girl who reminded me of Marie-Louise had just come in. The resemblance wasn't in her shape or her features, but in her placid and bold expression, her carriage, the way she wore her smock cinched by a wide black patent-leather belt, her small breasts, the glittering earrings. She asked for a cigarette and told one of the girls that the dark-haired boy in the paint shop had brought her coffee.

"They're all dark-haired up in the paint shop," one of them said with a loud laugh.

They all laughed. Up there, almost all the men were black Africans. The girl shrugged.

"Do you think I'd go out with a Negro?"

"You don't seem to mind Algerians."

"Oh, him," she said, "I'll end up smacking him in the face. He stands right in front of me, he stares at me. This morning, he wouldn't stop smiling at me."

"They're women-crazy."

"But the dark one in the paint shop, I like him."

"It's ten to," one of them said.

"O.K.," my neighbor sighed, "I have to do my face."

And she opened her compact. The pains she took belied the irony of her expression.

My neighbor called to the girl—her name was Didi—

because she had left the door to the coatroom wide open.

"I'm keeping an eye on my friend," she said.

In the doorway, with her flowered smock and her golden make-up, with her sparkling earrings dancing on her ears, she brought color back to life. And this glitter, which anywhere else would have seemed loud, gave us in this morose geometry a taste for life. I imagined the stares, the desire her movements provoked. Her smallest motions suggested something erotic of which she seemed unconscious; she displayed herself, like a mouth-watering candy, to the gaze of the famished and then slipped away from their hunger.

I smoothed my hair with my hands and left. The siren went off. I ran with the late ones.

Once inside the shop, there it was again: odors and noise grabbed you and, no matter how hard you fought, they got you in the end. Especially the noise: the motors, the hammers, the machine-tools as strident as saws and, at regular intervals, the heavy fall of metal.

Arezki looked at me only once but his eyes said nothing; they were empty. The day unravelled gently, there was just a white reflection from the widows; the little Moroccan said, "Only one more."

Arezki was far off. His tool box lay on the floor of the car I was checking. I leaned down, rummaged through it, suddenly thinking he might have hidden a message for me. I found nothing and got out, discouraged. The cars were emptying, the noise was quieting down. A few minutes more and the rumbling of the line would die.

(155)

I recognized Arezki's back among the workers who had already reached the door. He hadn't even said hello. I still hoped I would meet him on the stairs, then at the door, finally at the bus stop. But I arrived home without having seen him, alone and unhappy.

I learned the meaning of all those expressions: to feel faint, to be tongue-tied, to feel your heart stop—things I used to laugh at. Every time Arezki passed in front of me muttering only, "Excuse me," every time he let pass a chance to be alone with me, my whole body hurt.

He arrived in the morning, flanked by Mustapha and the Tunisians who worked the headliners. Every noon, he had Mustapha bring me the gasoline-dipped cloth, which the latter delivered making funny faces that didn't make me laugh. He worked several cars away from me. And in the evening, when I got into line for the bus, I deliberately let my neighbors move ahead of me in the hope he might appear. The fairyland of the Pont National left me unmoved, yet the fine and gentle rain transformed the usually drab road into a mirror. If someone jostled me, tears came to my eyes. The headlines of newspapers made me want to cry, and my ragged reflection in the windows, and all the tiny troubles on which I built my grief. But then, what grief, I asked myself when I thought about it rationally? And anyway, I have to leave. I'll see Grandmother again, Marie, Lucien's room.

It will be mine and I'll fix it up my own way.

. . .

Porte de la Chapelle. I went on foot to the residence.

The smell of festivities spread the length of the streets. The coming of Christmas had transformed the shop windows. The butchers, the bakers lighted their displays with electric garlands and wrote on their mirrors enormous inscriptions in white paint on the subject of Christmas Eve. It was violent, loud, living, hot. It took me by the throat; I was agitated, I was excited. A memory came to me: Mr. Scrooge and the quality in Dickens' stories when he is describing the huge turkeys and giant pastries. Mr. Scrooge . . . those were great days. I was thirteen and Lucien six. We didn't have enough to eat and had never seen a turkey. Grandmother described them to us. I read aloud to her and to my brother. He listened, rapt. I had mixed everything up and I believed that I was involved in his passion for these imaginary tales. Raising my eyes after each paragraph, I had seized upon the absorbed and abandoned expression on his face. Flattered, though it had nothing to do with me, dazzled and overwhelmed, I had made the mistake of playing the little mother. Did Lucien still remember Mr. Scrooge?

I collapsed on the small bed as soon as I closed the door and, in a moment, the weariness that had gone was suddenly back; it pinned me to the bed, made me incapable of any motion. I said, tomorrow I'll clean my shoes or launder my blouse. It was too late and I hurt too much. The absurd muscles were taking their revenge. I also said Arezki out loud, and the tears came back.

. . .

Several times, I thought that Arezki was looking at

me. I concentrated on not raising my eyes. The Magyar often smiled at me. He now said very correctly: "Thank you, excuse me, good morning, goddamn." The last was reserved for Bernier.

Arezki was suddenly behind me. I was leaning against the window, writing hurriedly before throwing the page on the trunk of the car, and at that moment he approached. But in the same instant, Gilles crossed the line to speak to me. Arezki froze.

"Mademoiselle Elise," Gilles said, "how's it going? O.K.? Tell me something, your headliners, they've found three more tears you haven't put down."

I panicked. For several seconds, he fixed me with his pure and penetrating gaze.

Leaning toward me, he added: "In January, I'll see to it that you are transferred to the offices."

And he climbed back on the conveyer belt, held on to the hood of the car passing by, and jumped heavily into the aisle.

I looked to my left. Arezki was contemplating his screwdriver. I could hear the beating of my heart. I meant to move away so that I wouldn't seem to be waiting for him, but my legs wouldn't budge. He came up to me and said very fast in my ear:

"Will you wait for me at the bus stop like before? Only, leave a little later, six-twenty, six-twenty-five. O.K.?"

And then he immediately added in a loud voice:

"The car coming up has a torn headliner above the mirror."

(158)

The car went by and the next one came. The Magyar, who was getting off, looked at me, surprised to see me there, motionless. Arezki had rejoined the Tunisians at the headliners without waiting for my answer.

To make the time pass, I washed my hands several times. The women rushed away with no thought for their faces. Another kind of work awaited them for which there was no need to primp. The youngest, or those who had dates, were making their "repairs." No matter what you did, nine hours of the factory destroyed the most beautiful of faces.

"Oh, to quit work," my neighbor sighed as she buttoned her coat.

I protested.

"Why," she said, "won't it be the beginning of the good life?"

"It'll be the end of your life."

"So what? What's in this life for me right now? Rush, watch the time, work. At least I'll have some time, I'll be able to live."

The clock at the Porte de Choisy said six-thirty. Arezki was already in line, but a little to one side. I went toward him. He made a sign. I understood and took a place behind him without saying a word. Lucien came up. He didn't see me and I acted as if I didn't see him. He lit a cigarette and, as he held the match near his face, I caught a glimpse of his wasted profile, the black stubble, the bones.

We were in the same group getting on the bus. Impossible to step back, he must have seen me. I went forward, taking care not to look around. Arezki ignored me. At the Porte de Vincennes, where many people got off, I drew near him. He asked me where I wanted to get off so that we could walk a little. I said, "The Porte de Montreuil." I had noticed on previous evenings a street swarming with people where I thought we could easily lose ourselves.

He got off and I followed. Had Lucien seen me? The thought worried me. We crossed the street and, contemplating two adjoining cafés, Arezki asked:

"Shall we have a cup of hot tea?"

"If you like."

There were lots of people and a lot of noise. All the tables looked full. Arezki went into the second room. I waited near the counter. Some of the customers stared; I felt their eyes on me and guessed what they were thinking. Arezki reappeared and, watching him come, I felt a shock. My God, but he looked Arab! Some of them on the assembly line confused you with their light skin and brown hair. That evening, Arezki wasn't wearing a shirt but a black or dark brown knit pullover that made him look even darker. Panic seized me. I wanted to be outside, in the crowd on the street.

"No room. It doesn't matter, we'll get a drink at the counter. Let's go."

He pushed me toward the corner.

"Tea?"

"Yes."

"Me too."

A boy served us quickly. I blew on my cup so that

(160)

I could drink faster. In the mirror, behind the percolator, I saw a man wearing the cap of a métro employee looking at me. He turned to his neighbor who was folding a newspaper.

"You know what I'd do?" he said very loud. "I'd drop an atom bomb on Algeria."

He looked at me again with a satisfied air. His neighbor didn't agree. He suggested:

"I'd chuck all the niggers in France into concentration camps."

I was afraid Arezki would react. I stole a glance at him. He was calm, or so it seemed.

"It looks as if they're going to put us in shifts," he said.

His voice was assured. He had heard about this from Gilles and checked off for me its advantages and disadvantages. I relaxed. I asked him lots of questions and while he answered, I listened to what the people around us were saying. And I had the impression that he too, as he answered, was following their conversations.

When I passed by him on the way out, the man who wanted to drop the atom bomb took a step toward me. Arezki happened to be in front of us. He saw nothing. I dodged the man without protesting and joined Arezki outside with the feeling of having escaped danger.

The Rue d'Avron stretched scintillating toward infinity. For a few minutes, we were absorbed by the displays.

"So," he asked me with irony, "how are you?"

"I'm fine."

"You've been looking unhappy these past few days. You haven't been sick?"

You can talk, Arezki. You're here. Tonight, I don't need to imagine your face. It's really you, present. I even want—in this setting where we are walking—to tell you about Mr. Scrooge, the turkeys. It is a privileged moment, unreal, suspended over our lives like the garlands hanging across this street. We must speak only careless words that will make us smile.

"Please forgive me for these last few days; I was busy. I had relatives visiting."

"I thought you were angry. You didn't say good morning or good night."

He protests: he nodded to me every morning. And is it all that important? We should, he says, pick a day. A place to meet.

I agree. The stores are further apart. The Rue d'Avron is less scintillating and, down there, before us, it's dark, barely lit. We cross. Arezki holds on to my arm, then passes his arm behind me and rests his hand on my shoulder.

"I'm busy these days. But Monday perhaps . . . Your brother got on the bus behind you. Did you see him?"

"I saw him."

"Elise," he says, "what if we called each other 'tu'?"

I answer that I will try but that I am afraid I don't know how.

"The only man I have ever called 'tu' is Lucien."

"There she goes," he says, mocking me, "she's going to talk about her brother again . . ."

During our first walk I talked, he remarks, only of Lucien.

"I wondered if you were really his sister. Where could we meet next Monday?"

"But I don't know Paris."

"This neighborhood is no good," he says.

And he makes me turn around. We walk back toward the lights.

"You decide and tell me Monday morning."

"Where? On the assembly line? In front of the others?"

"Why not? The others talk to each other. Gilles talks to me, Daubat . . ."

"You forget I am Algerian."

"Yes, I forget."

Arezki squeezes me, shakes me.

"Repeat that. Is it true? Do you forget?"

His eyes bore deep.

"Yes. But you know it. I can't be racist."

"I know it. Rather, I thought it was on account of Lucien and people like him, that this was something a little exotic, mysterious. A year ago . . ."

We start to walk again and he holds me again by the shoulder.

"I knew this woman. I . . . well, I loved her. Every day, she read a comic strip in the newspaper called *The Moor's Passion*. It went to her head. She blended it with the memory of her father who had fought in the resistance against the Germans."

He stops. We are back in the crowd now and Arezki's

(163)

arm bothers me. I am afraid of the people. On the door of a newspaper stand, the evening edition announces "F.L.N. Cell Uncovered in Paris."

Arezki has read it too; his eyes flutter a little.

"Are the reasons for loving," I say dryly, "ever pure? You often have to make do with . . ."

"I don't," he interrupted, equally dryly.

We walk in silence to the métro entrance.

"We must separate, it's late."

I almost say, "So soon."

"Yes, you must be tired."

"Tired? No."

This thought displeases him.

"Please take note," he says gently—and his voice is affectionate—"that for three days, on account of you, I haven't gone to bed."

And, seeing my surprise, he corrects himself:

"No, I should say, I haven't slept. I wanted to see you, but I couldn't. I don't like to speak to you in front of the others. I thought of giving you a message through your brother, but I preferred to wait. Yes, sleep, not go to bed. It's an expression of ours."

"You speak French very well," I say to hide my emotion.

"Talking French is O.K. . . . when I write, I make lots of mistakes."

A police car goes by, its siren loud. Arezki lets go of me. The car doesn't stop.

"It's cold. Let's go, it's time to go home."

He explains the transfers.

"Where do you live?" I ask.

He doesn't answer right away, then he says:

"In Jaurès."

I am sorry I asked. I know he has lied. We get into the same compartment, we sit down opposite each other. He says simply:

"Get off here, take the Dauphine train," and he squeezes very hard the hand I give him.

. . .

I spent the next Sunday in bed.

I slept late. I had read somewhere that sleep makes you more beautiful.

Monday morning, Mustapha and the Magyar arrived late. Mustapha came in first and, going up to Bernier who was watching him, gave him a military salute. It was on the Magyar that Bernier's anger fell. But the Magyar, who was becoming more and more confident, got away and climbed into a car. He saw me and shouted, "Oh la la," pointing at Bernier. Arezki was working quite far away and hadn't seen me yet. If only the line would stop! Time to sit and think quietly. The line doesn't stop and my thoughts fluctuate to the rhythm of my motions. This makes for syncopated anxiety. I catch sight of Arezki and I am reassured. I'm grateful to be aboard this galley with him.

Mustapha joined us as we found ourselves together for the first time that morning. Arezki sent him away under I don't know what pretext.

"Tonight," he said, "I can't. We'll have to put it off to another night, all right?"

The little Moroccan bumped into me hard. Gilles was behind him. Mustapha returned with a box of nails and spilled them in front of Gilles, then without bothering to pick them up, placed himself next to Arezki.

After that, the timekeeper entered the car.

"That's him," he said to Gilles, pointing out Mustapha, who turned around. "I've been watching him. Look. When he hammers, he pulls on the cloth. That's what makes it tear."

Gilles pushed Mustapha aside and took his hammer. He looked closely at the snap-on, the headliner, and began to hammer on the stripping. Mustapha waited, frowning and muttering in Arabic.

Gilles, with a nod, called the timekeeper:

"He has to pull on the cloth to get it under the snap-on and that tears it. Leave an extra three or four centimeters. You cut it too thin."

Mustapha stood up straight, whistling.

Gilles got out and the timekeeper followed him.

"Well, what do you want me to do?" Mustapha shouted. "Do I go on?"

"You go on and you try not to pull too hard."

And Gilles went off.

I was alone in the car. Arezki had left it a few minutes before. I got out of the car and walked around it. The Magyar was installing the rear lights. A creeping fatigue bored into the muscles of my calves. I leaned on the open lid of the trunk. It shuddered and closed. I heard the Magyar shout. He dropped his tool and, faster than I, reopened the lid. But the edge, at this stage in the line, was still sharp. The Magyar's hand and his forearm were covered with blood.

I looked at his bleeding wrist without speaking, and Mustapha, the Moroccan, and a third man looked at it as stupidly as I.

The Magyar held his wrist. The blood flowed freely. With his fingers, he made the motion of knotting a handkerchief he pulled from his pocket. Finally I moved. I took the handkerchief, stiff with dried mucus, and made a tourniquet.

"Come with me," I said.

He followed me. Bernier wasn't at his station. We looked for him. The others were watching and I was glad that Arezki saw me.

"What's the matter?"

Gilles had come over to us. I explained. He took a pass for the infirmary from Bernier's cabinet. He changed his mind and gave me one too.

"Go with him. He doesn't speak French."

We crossed the rows of machines. Nobody whistled. The Magyar was impressive. On the first floor, as we passed the men's room, he stopped and said "piss." He had learned that word too.

I waited for him by the door. He didn't come out. I grew worried, imagining some kind of trouble, and, since no one was around, I opened the door to see what was going on. It smelled strong, like a stable. It was enough to make you sick. The Magyar was washing his hands. He had pulled out his shirttail, moistened it in the running water of the urinal and was rubbing his palms. I made a sign of "hurry, hurry." He smiled and showed me an almost white palm.

On the wall, disfigured with graffiti, there were militant inscriptions carved with a knife.

"Our five francs."

"Showers."

"Up with the Communist party."

Few were obscene.

"Hurry," I said again to the Magyar who was now washing his face with the same piece of wet shirttail.

On the wall to the right, carved in shaky letters, no doubt written in a hurry, was "Vive La Legeri."

It was, of course, "Vive l'Algerie," and I found it touching that the author couldn't even spell what he wanted to glorify. I remembered Mustapha's sign, "Do No Tuch." I'd like to have spoken to Arezki about this.

I explained to the nurse how the accident had happened and I left the Magyar sitting on a chair, examining the sterilizer. His eyes expressed total satisfaction. He must have been congratulating himself on having washed in honor of this warm and clean room. For all these men shunted from factory to home or barrack or sordid hotel, this infirmary was a picture of the sweetness of life, a luxury they could allow themselves from time to time.

I got back to the shop and gave Bernier the pass signed by the nurse.

"What's the matter with him?" he asked.

"I think they're sending him to the hospital."

"These foreigners," he sighed, "they have a talent for accidents."

"It was my fault. I closed the trunk by mistake."

"We must make a report, in case there's a suit. I put Daubat in your place. Get back to work."

Mustapha, Daubat, and some others came to question me. Arezki came too. Between us, there passed a brief inconsequential look. His eyes were always changing and expressed wonderfully his successive states of mind. He had, in particular, one neutral look of indifference that stopped you in your tracks.

Should I confide in my brother?

Was I crazy? I knew perfectly well that I couldn't tell him anything. The words wouldn't come out. And what was there to say? Summarized, locked in words, it reduced itself to four walks in the Paris night, timid overtures, and giant flourishes embroidered by me.

Bernier had an Algerian replace the Magyar. The timekeeper stopped by several times to inspect Mustapha and his headliners.

I had been aware for a long time of the hostility that existed among the workmen. The French didn't like Algerians, or any foreigners, for that matter. They accused them of taking away their jobs and then not knowing how to do them. The shared efforts, the shared sweat, the shared demands were, as Lucien said, "So much crap," so many slogans. Most of them brought their own frustrations and distrusts to the factory. It was impossible to be for the rat hunts outside and the fraternity of the workers inside the cage. Sometimes it blew up and each man hid behind his race and his nationality in order to attack or defend. The shop steward interposed himself with little conviction. The day he brought me my card and stamp, I confessed my astonishment and disillusion.

"There has been so much barbarity," he answered without feeling.

He himself said "niggers" and "Arabs" and resented the fact that they hadn't joined the strike for the five franc raise.

The assembly line came to a halt and the siren went off. Mustapha brought me the gasoline cloth Arezki had given him. It was a signal. He wanted to speak to me.

I picked up my coat and left for the Porte d'Italie. I felt the need to walk and talk out loud. There were gusts of wind that raised your hair on end and sliced the skin of your face, beautiful girls in warm coats who, height of injustice, were made even more beautiful by the cold and their winter clothes, Algerians walking duckfooted in spring jackets with their collars turned up; there were cops at the entrances to the métro checking identity cards, and the windows—from the Prisunic to the most dilapidated grocer—were caught up in a fever of garlands and lights. A happy throng, well-nourished, wearing fur-lined boots and interlined coats, who spent August by the sea and wore spring clothes at Easter, a throng that paid for its leisure with the sweat of its brow, walked, sat at café tables, and looked the other way when into its territorial waters slipped ill-nourished types who wore Easter clothes in November and who, for all their brow's sweat, earned only enough for bread. These species just happened to gather in special neighborhoods—shanty towns, run-down hotels—and, by nationalities: Algerian, Spanish, Portuguese, and, naturally, French. They also fell into other categories: alcoholics, idlers, tuberculars, degenerates. There is something to be said for the ghetto. But sometimes these types managed to sneak up on you in the métro, in the café, and in addition, they were noisy, lost, or disgustingly drunk. And occasionally, in these caricatures of humanity, in these suffering bodies mutilated by misery, in the cold dark rooms, between the dirty laundry and the drying laundry, one of these dregs carried inside him —by luck or miracle—the gleam, the flame, the spark that made him suffer even more. The spirit breathed there as much as anywhere; intelligence either developed or died, crushed.

These thoughts, the cold, my hair blowing around my neck, Arezki's disappearance, the Magyar's blood and the smell of the factory, the four hours on the line stretching ahead, the still unread letter from Grandmother, all this is life. How gentle it had been, the previous one, a little blurred, far from the sordid truth. It had been simple, animal, rich in dreams. I said "one day . . ." and it was enough.

I am living this day, I am living the real life, involved with other human beings, and I suffer. "You aren't aggressive," Lucien would say.

A physical need to talk to him made me turn around in my tracks. I arrived in front of the canteen restaurant. Men were coming out. Gilles appeared, recognized me. I told him I was waiting for my brother.

"Come to think of it, I didn't see him at noon. Wait a minute. I'll be back."

A foreman went by. He was a big man wearing a hat.

From far away, he had seemed terrifying. I had the time to examine his face and I found him much less frightening.

"No," Gilles said as he returned. "He isn't there. He eats at the table across from me and I'm quite sure he wasn't there today."

He asked me if things were going all right, I answered yes and went back to the factory.

Didi, the pretty girl, was standing in the middle of the coatroom under the light bulb, her face raised toward the meager source of light, putting on some lipstick. She saw me and called out:

"Are you the sister of the big dark haired guy in the paint shop? Is he sick or has he quit?"

.   .   .

Anxiety led me to his room that very evening. The thought of seeing Anna unnerved me but I took myself in hand and knocked on their door. It was she who opened it.

Lucien was on the bed, leaning against the headboard and arguing with Henri who sat at the other end.

"What did I tell you?" my brother said in a hoarse voice. "She's come! So," he shouted at me, "you were scared? You thought I was dead?"

"No, but I can see you're sick."

"That's right. I'm sick. I have a cold, idiot. But I'll be back at work tomorrow."

"Well, since you're all right, I'll go."

"Sit down for five minutes," he said. "O.K., your turn, Henri."

Henri read from some sheets of paper he held in his hands. It was an account, inspired by Lucien, of working conditions and methods he had observed.

"Very good. I'll give it to Glottin, who'll put it in the next issue as a 'letter to the editor'."

"You believe in the power of the pen?"

"I believe in the power of publishing under your own name," Henri said dryly.

"But didn't Glottin used to be a member of the Party?"

"So what?"

"Nothing," Lucien said. "He'll sigh, clear his throat several times . . . Those guys, when they quit the Party, they're nothing. It's the Party that stiffens their spines. Once they leave it, they revert to ectoplasm."

"We'll talk about it another time, all right?"

"All right. Anna, get me a lemon."

Anna got up, cut one in half and brought it to him.

"Is that what you eat to get well?"

When I asked questions like that, my voice was, in spite of myself, unpleasant, sarcastic and scolding.

He turned toward me. His smile was radiant.

"And how's your Arab? O.K.?"

He had said it to be vulgar, to annoy me.

"We had an accident this morning."

And I described the Magyar's wound, very fast, to change the subject.

I was ashamed in front of Henri and even more so in front of Anna.

"You're still in Paris, Elise. You've decided to stay?"

"No, I'm leaving at the end of the month, for Christmas."

Lucien put the lemon down.

"You're leaving at the end of the month?"

"I've had news from home. I've got to go back."

I wanted to give him a bad conscience, I wanted to disturb the cloistered life in which he had shut himself up, this room with a view only of the great mass of humanity, the war, the condition of the proletariat, this room walled off from two people in particular, his daughter and Marie-Louise. I wanted vengeance for what he'd said. He understood.

"Arezki will miss you. You know, you've made a good choice. He's the best guy in the whole shop, maybe even the whole factory. After Gilles. But Gilles . . . Yes, the best. But he has an evil temper. I've worked with him; I know. He's thin-skinned, touchy. Gilles realizes it, too."

"I'd like to talk with your Gilles," Henri put in.

Lucien pretended to be falling asleep.

Henri had risen and was stretching.

"I'm leaving you the papers and the pamphlets. If you find any guys to hand them out . . ."

"Sure, the guys who paste. We're good for something."

Anna went out with Henri. She wanted to buy some medicine for my brother. When they had closed the door, Lucien leaned his head back and said:

"He's always wanting to meet somebody."

He added: "He's a drawing-room buff."

I was afraid to stay with him alone. I didn't know how to start a conversation and to say nothing was impossible.

"Somebody was looking for you at noon."

"Who?" he asked with interest.

"The girl who checks the locks. Dark-haired, pretty."

"Yes, yes, I know. Oh," he said, his eyes closed, "a girl without a past."

He sat up again and looked for his cigarettes. Not finding them, he fell back on the bed.

"I don't need it."

I didn't answer. Henri had gone, I had stayed, he was half asleep and wasn't quite sure of the difference.

"And besides . . ."

He said nothing for a long time. When he spoke again, his voice was indistinct, thick with sleep.

"There are those who carry in their souls the weapon that kills love, the very excess of love. They restrict its life by the greedy and devouring way they love."

"So, you're philosophizing?" I said, laughing.

"I'm talking nonsense."

He opened his eyes.

"What time is it?"

"I'm going. It's eight thirty. Take care of yourself. You're thin, you're pale."

"Don't start that again."

He got up. Anna was back.

"There!" she said. And she put a bagful of medicines on the table.

"How much were they?" my brother asked.

(175)

"Three thousand . . . Henri loaned me the money."

"Henri? . . . Finally he's done the right thing," he added. "The redistribution of wealth has commenced."

I reached the door and turned around. The light from the bulb shone on them like a projection. They didn't move as I turned the knob. Once I was gone, their magic would return.

. . .

His left wrist wrapped in a bandage, the Magyar was back. Once again, he screwed on the rear lights.

"Everything all right?" Mustapha asked him each time they passed each other.

"Good," the other answered.

A broken windowpane was letting in the cold and Bernier told us to put some cardboard over it until it was fixed.

"It's been broken for over a year," someone said.

The Magyar worked in a buttoned vest whose collar was layered with grime. I said to Mustapha:

"Why doesn't he wear work clothes? Why don't you?"

"What? What are they?"

"Work clothes," I repeated. "A heavy cotton jacket and pants like . . . Daubat, for example."

"I don't wear work clothes," he said, shocked.

As he got out of the car I was checking, Arezki appeared.

"What about tonight? O.K.? Can we see each other?"

I said I couldn't. I said it coldly, left that car and got into the next one. He didn't try to talk to me again until noon. Then he brought me the gasoline cloth himself. I said nothing. He rejoined Mustapha.

Daubat came down the aisle with some old packing cases. He put one near me. They were for the window.

"I've done half of it. All they have to do is cut it and put it up. Aren't you going to lunch?"

"I was about to go down."

"Is something wrong today. Is it the cold? The work? Have there been mistakes?"

To make him happy, I asked his advice. We went downstairs together. That suited me for I didn't have to go alone through the wolf-whistlers who ate at their stations, even though it was forbidden, and then stretched out in the cars.

Daubat complained about the clanging rhythm of the shop that made meticulous work impossible.

"And of course there are too many foreigners, they don't know how to do it and there isn't time to teach them. Are you eating in the coatroom? Be careful of cold lunches."

The bench—my bench—was unoccupied. I would take full advantage of the moment. If you ignored the walls, the bench and your body took on enormous proportions. You had to stand for five hours in a factory to feel the true voluptuousness of the horizontal position, of hearing only the murmuring voices of a small group of women. The work, the weariness, the hunger, the noise, tortured the body; the stomach, the legs, the temples, the neck—these four most vulnerable points merged into one crushing pain. I watered at the mouth as I slowly munched on my sandwich, while my eyelids quivered and a warm torpor spread from my feet up to my body—this was the incomparable bliss that I arranged every day.

And, as I ate, I tasted the hot tea that Arezki and I had drunk together at each of our meetings. Its flavor blended with the taste of the bread, impregnated it, and I began to regret the morning refusal. I was all the more sensitive to these pleasures, modest though they were, because they were so rare. Those who have everything and consider a feeling of well-being as their right, or who don't consider it at all because it's too familiar, don't know this feeling like drunkenness that creeps through you when you feel warm after having been cold, you're eating something good, you've had some coffee. All your problems vanish, a feeling of power takes over. Suddenly you're invincible because you have a full stomach and dry feet.

The women had stopped talking. A girl had just come in, a redhead, not very pretty, too thin and no longer young. She opened her locker, rummaged around, and, when she had locked the padlock, slipped the key inside her bra.

"How goes it, Irene?" one of the women asked.

"How about you?"

She talked like women who smoke a lot. Her voice was hoarse in the lower register and she drawled in a sensual sort of way. It was her only charm, for her face, full of sharp angles, was hardly appealing.

Irene went out. There were whisperings among the

women. I picked up this phrase: ". . . she goes out with Algerians."

It was the current expression: go out with, always followed by the plural. And it was the final insult: go out with Algerians, go out with Negroes . . .

For a moment, I imagined taking these women into my confidence. I'd share the bench, then I'd say: Hey, what do you think of this? I had a few minutes of satisfaction when I said no to Arezki but now, if I could, I'd take back that refusal. All of you contributed to that no. I'm scared of you. But that hot tea, the touch of his hand when we part, the walk through the night, I can't give these up.

Tomorrow they would say, "She goes out with Algerians." These words evoked lonely rooms where one woman passed through the arms of many men.

He was working as far away as possible from me. However, he sometimes slowed down enough so that our paths crossed, our fellow workers always around us.

"Two more!"

The little Moroccan was relieved. Then I was sad and felt a great bottomless hole before me.

The last car arrived. Arezki got out of it.

"You must put down: torn headliner. As I installed the rearview mirror, I pulled too hard."

"I've fixed it up. I've postponed my brother and I can see you."

"Oh?"

He was surprised. I had spoken so fast that I wondered if he'd actually heard.

(179)

The Magyar, Mustapha, and the little Moroccan joined us. Arezki made me jump into the car.

"Listen. Take the métro to Stalingrad. All right? Get off, take a seat, and wait for me on the platform. While you wait, read a paper folded in front of your face. If any people from here get off, they won't recognize you."

I followed his directions. He joined me on the platform at Stalingrad where I had buried my face in the front pages of my paper. This made him laugh. He tapped on the paper and said we'd go on to Ternes.

"It's near the Étoile. I think it's a good place."

Arezki had dressed carefully. He was wearing a white shirt, a tie hidden by his scarf, and his brown suit, shiny with wear, was spotless.

At last, I was seeing Paris by night, the Paris of post-cards and calendars.

"You like it?"

Arezki was having fun. He suggested that we walk up to l'Étoile and then come back on the opposite sidewalk. It would be easy to lose ourselves and become a part of the scene. To feel one had a place in this beautiful city, to be integrated . . .

We spent some time discussing the Magyar's accident. We were both cold. Arezki glanced toward the cafés as we walked. He must be worrying about their being expensive, I thought. Three days until payday. He must be almost broke, too.

As we turned back toward Les Ternes, he said: "You're cold," and we went into a café whose sidewalk terrace was heated. But he preferred the interior, picked

(180)

out two places and ordered two teas. The process was always the same. Our neighbors studied us in silence for several seconds and it was easy to guess their thoughts. I tried to say to myself: "So what? It's Paris, the city of outlaws, fugitives from all over the world. This is 1957. Am I going to come apart because of a few stares? We are a scandal in this lovely neighborhood. Are these people responsible?"

". . . But where are the police? Look at that guy sitting right next to you in a nice place where you've made a date with a nice girl you're going to take home in the car you've parked nearby . . . and there's an Arab with a French girl! She's French and working class for sure, you can tell right off. We're fighting a war with those guys . . . Where are the police? No, we don't want to make them suffer; we're human. There are camps, places they can be assigned to. Clean up Paris. Maybe this one has a gun in his pocket. They all have."

Every one of their stares said that. The tea had lost the disquieting aroma of the coatroom. It seemed stale and I noticed Arezki's impatience. He made a sign and we left. After that, I realized how much he mistrusted —often mistakenly—those who stared. He saw the police everywhere and was afraid of troublemakers.

In the dense night of the side streets we had taken, I got back my courage. We walked without hurry, a little withdrawn in the cold. Arezki had lost the disconcerting reserve of our first evenings. He still said luck when I remarked on how well he spoke our language.

In the window, on the ground floor of a corner building, we saw a cat watching the street. Arezki began to laugh.

"It's clever of a cat to sit behind a window. When I was home, we had a cat. I was crazy about him, but he always ran away. I wonder what he lived on, what he ate: there were no leftovers."

"What do you want me to tell you?" he said when I asked him about his childhood. "Poverty, poverty, poverty."

He had a brother, strong and resourceful, who left for Algiers and worked successively as a bath attendant, longshoreman, and chips vendor. At thirteen, Arezki had joined him, and he too became a bath attendant. He slept in the Turkish baths. For a while, he was a porter but, thanks to his brother, he never went hungry. At the baths, he had met a compatriot, a young bourgeois who had just sold all his belongings and given the money to the Party, which at that time was still clandestine. This man had glimpsed the flame that burned in Arezki's eyes and fostered it. From then on, driven by a desire to understand and to know, Arezki took to solitary, anarchic study. His brother had encouraged him at first, then one day, after an argument, he sent him back to their village. After that, it was France and the need to survive.

"I haven't been back in six years."

I said nothing; I was thinking of Anna's letter.

Arezki looked at me and laughed, as if he were making fun of me.

"If we're going to start talking about our miseries . . ."

"Ours," I said, "are nothing like yours."

"Yes, I think so too."

After a brief silence, he went on.

"If we keep it secret, we can see each other almost every night."

I didn't answer; I was overwhelmed with joy. We had walked far and now found ourselves in a small square in front of an enormous statue. I stopped and looked at it.

"It's Balzac," I said with glee. "I recognize him. Look, the dressing gown and the cord. Have you read Balzac? Do you like him?"

"Have you read Amrul' Quais? Do you like him?" he asked with a slight edge.

The small square was isolated in the fog. I lived a moment of perfect bliss. It seemed to me that if we left here this joy would fall away.

"Let's go," Arezki said. "You're getting cold. You shouldn't stay here."

I didn't move. I looked at him with a smile. He pulled me to him and kissed me too fast for me to feel anything more than the sudden warmth on my cold face.

Someone broke through the fog and passed in front of us with loud and rapid steps.

"How I love Paris . . ."

"I would have preferred you to say: how I love Arezki . . ."

His voice was mocking. He still held my arms above the elbows and together we began to laugh. I threw quick glances at the statue; I was shivering and put off the moment of leaving.

(183)

"Let's go. Come on."

"Which way?"

"I'm a little lost. That way is Les Ternes. Come, we'll find the métro."

I sighed, "So soon." He pulled me to him and kissed me again with more ardor than before. Hypocrisy made me stiffen up. He let me go, took my hand, and sadly I said good-by to the little square.

The contact of our hands reassured me. He talked in a flat and detached way about the climate of the various cities he'd lived in and I guessed that my reserve had disappointed him.

"When are you free?" he asked me.

His question annoyed me.

"Who is the one who's not free?"

I said this dryly. He took his time, looked at me sideways and answered in a hard tone:

"I thought you were an intelligent woman."

He resumed walking, hands in his pockets, while I floundered and didn't know what to say.

"What cold, what cold!"

I hoped he'd take hold of my hand again.

He smiled ironically.

"What cold, yes. We should have stayed in a café. But a café with an Arab . . . that's troublesome. People look at you. The little dark streets, they're more discreet."

"You're wasting your time." And now I liked the tone of my voice. "It's not me you're talking about. I don't feel that way and you know it."

My anger pleased me. We were standing in front of

the window of a shoe store and the neon lights from the display gave our faces an incandescent glow. Arezki stretched out his arms and I found myself against him.

During the few seconds that this warm and soft contact lasted, my mind wandered and I thought with shock how some night he might kiss me like this in public.

"Don't tell anyone about our evenings together. Tomorrow, wait for me like tonight, at Stalingrad, with a newspaper."

We were about to cross over to the métro entrance when Arezki pulled me back.

"Wait."

He withdrew into the shadow of a porch and watched three men walking back and forth in front of the stairs.

"Let's part here," Arezki said. "I'll see you tomorrow. Get home quickly."

"Why? What about you?"

He seemed impatient and assured me it was nothing, but that he had to leave me. I didn't insist. His expression mystified me. I left him and crossed over. As I passed the three men, I slowed down and looked at them. Nothing about them struck me as unusual. They seemed to be waiting. But when I had gone halfway down the stairs, I stopped and walked back up to see what Arezki was doing. His thread-like silhouette was disappearing down the avenue to the left. One of the men at the métro entrance studied me briefly and then, showing no further interest, resumed his walk around the balustrade.

It was almost eleven when I got back to my room. I

dined on fruit and spent a long time before the mirror above my washstand. I was looking for a change that wasn't visible.

When Arezki joined me at Stalingrad, he stated that we wouldn't go to Les Ternes anymore. It wasn't a good neighborhood.

"We're going to . . . the Trocadéro."

We went to the Trocadéro. We even returned two days later. We walked in the gardens where the freezing fog raised protective walls around us.

We went to the Opéra and circled the building several times.

We crossed the bridges.

We lost ourselves on the streets around Saint-Paul.

We walked up the boulevards toward Saint-Augustin.

Starting at Vaugirard, we ended up at the Porte d'Auteuil.

The Rue de Rivoli we did in both directions.

And the Boulevard Voltaire, and the Boulevard du Temple, and the little streets behind the Palais-Royale. And la Trinité and the Rue Lafayette.

We never returned to the same neighborhood. The smallest incident, a gathering of people, the shadow of a police car, someone who seemed to be following us, and our walk was abruptly ended. We had to part, to go home separately. These interrupted evenings, our conversations cut short, and the anxiety—never knowing, leaving him behind, waiting until the next day to find out if anything serious had happened—these bound me to him in that well-known way where the more fleeting the thing, the dearer it is.

He saw police everywhere. I thought he exaggerated. I protested a bit when he'd say:

"Look. See that guy in front of the window. He's a cop. You don't believe me? I tell you it's so."

"So what? What does it matter?"

We continued our walk.

There were lots of police raids. Arezki dreaded them.

"But you don't break any laws."

"You think that satisfies them?"

And the next night, we changed neighborhoods. I asked no questions. Time passed, we met almost every day. I tried to address him as "tu," for he became angry one night at my continual "vous." I loved to hear him talk. His tongue made a soft little roll when he pronounced his "r's." We passed from serious to gay, we made fun of our friends on the assembly line. I told him about Lucien's youth, I often talked of Grandmother. She had become familiar to him; he knew her faults, her expressions, her manias. Mustapha, Grandmother, Lucien—these people who made up our company helped us to discover each other. Out of shyness, we made use of them to talk about ourselves.

One evening, we were walking in the gardens of the Trocadéro. We found a hole in the shadows and Arezki kissed me violently. With my new ideas, I thought, this is it, now he's going to take me to his room. But nothing happened. Our understanding was miraculous: anyone else would have been more impatient, more audacious. If he wasn't, it was because to the difficult circumstances that already hampered us had been added the calculated pleasure of our moving forward together.

(187)

We observed each other for a long time with growing tenderness. In front of others, we feigned indifference, that game where the smallest gesture, a blink of the eye, an inflection of the voice, takes on intense meaning.

Each time we separated, Arezki swore me to secrecy, which annoyed me a little. Actually, it suited me perfectly.

Rain, sleet, we walked. Paris was an enormous ambush through which we moved with ludicrous precautions. Our love heightened the background of our wanderings. Nothing was ugly. The rain polished the pavement and the lone light of an alley made a prism of the shimmering stones. The squares had a provincial charm and the broken-down sheds took on the look of old abandoned windmills. Our happiness transformed Paris.

On the evenings he couldn't see me, I recuperated. I threw myself on the bed where I sometimes fell asleep fully clothed.

A stubborn reserve I couldn't seem to shed sometimes irritated him. And, because I was afraid he might confuse it with some sort of racist repulsion, I forced myself to act in ways I thought audacious when they were really quite natural.

Self-taught, the two of us, we found each other's company enriching. He had a passion for geography and wondered himself where it came from.

When I talked too much about Lucien, he stopped listening. This disappointed me. Once, when I mentioned the Magyar, he told me gently: "Forget the Magyar and don't smile at him too much."

Once or twice, I asked him indiscreet questions which he avoided with no show of anger. And so I resigned myself to knowing only what he wanted to tell me. We seldom spoke of the war because it was all around us, in the eyes of passers-by, on the newsstands, at the métro entrances, and because we were never sure of finding each other the next day. We talked about the assembly line. Arezki admitted that the strident fury of the noise aroused in him a sexual excitement, as did the din of the boulevards. Silence and calm revived his anguish.

He made excuses for Mustapha and explained from his own experience his friend's behavior toward the girls in the factory.

"When I began to work in Paris," he said, "I was bowled over, my head spun. The girls here have bodies that drive you wild. They are more desirable than our women back home for reasons . . . that have nothing to do with beauty. I went crazy feeling them so near me. I held my head down so that I wouldn't see them move or lean over. The women back home we see so little, here they are barely at arms' length. You can imagine how it is for Mustapha who comes from deep in the mountains . . ."

"And have you loved many of these beautiful women?"

Sometimes he said in a mocking tone:

"Which one of us is the under-developed?"

The days went by. The Christmas holidays came. I paid no attention. Christmas had become an evil day, a day without Arezki; he was never free on Sundays or

(189)

holidays. The week was split up into four happy days and three gray ones.

I pushed back the date of my return and concocted dazzling lies for Grandmother.

Lucien and Mustapha upset the perilous equilibrium. Arezki had said the day before: "Let's go to Saint-Michel tomorrow. You really ought to see it and besides, all the places here are spoiled. I guarantee you, they're full of police. Didn't you see the guy a while ago who got up when we came and stood next to him? So, don't forget. Wait for me at Châtelet. *Châ-te-let.* As usual, on the platform."

The next day, I arrived at seven thirty-four instead of half past, and the guard said, "You're too late, they've taken away the cards. Come back at eight when the office opens."

At first, I was amused imagining Arezki's surprise, his consternation. I'd appear at eight and watch his reaction. This mischievous thought occupied me as I left to take a walk around the factory. I would look up at our shop windows from the Boulevard Masséna. I wondered if Bernier was cursing because he had to take my place. My absence turned me into an important person; everyone would be asking: what's happened to her?

But this pleasure didn't last. As I looked up at the whitened windows of the second floor, a brutal anxiety, a strange impatience made me wish I were already up there. I resumed my slow march around the factory. "It's the dread of having to cross the whole shop alone; it's the fresh air, it's my empty stomach." It was fear, the fear that pummels your stomach with heavy blows and makes you choke on your saliva. At the sight of those high black walls of the fence that separated me from Arezki, I felt sinister visions taking shape inside my head and I could no longer smile at my thoughtless game.

I entered the shop and managed to thread my way to the line. Used to seeing me, the men paid little attention. As I advanced, I took in the whole picture: first I singled out Mustapha who was talking to the little Moroccan and waving his arms.

Arezki saw me. He was getting out of a car holding his tools. He put them down on the floor in the car, began to move toward me, but decided instead just to nod his head.

Bernier had put Daubat in my place. The latter said "Ah" when he saw me, but without warmth.

"I just missed the gate," I shouted.

"You have to go to bed early to get up in the morning," he said without a smile.

Then he stepped off the line and went over to Bernier's desk.

"You overslept?" Mustapha asked.

I smiled and hurried to get into my place. I felt as if everyone was looking at me. Going against his principles, Arezki was waiting for me in the car.

"What's the matter?"

He asked the question without looking at me as he continued to work.

"Nothing. I was late."

"This evening, leave promptly. Remember? Châtelet. I won't have much time and I must talk to you. Don't listen to anybody before I speak to you."

On the surface, it was a morning like any other. Arezki worked as far as possible from me. The mechanical motions functioned well. But Mustapha was looking at me in a new way and so was the little Moroccan and so, farther off and insistent, was Bernier. Something had changed.

At the noon break, I happened to find myself behind Arezki on the way downstairs. Daubat, who was also rushing down, saw me at just the moment when I was shoved against Arezki's back by the hurrying crowd.

I stopped in the women's coatroom and, mechanically looking up, I saw Lucien. He was coming down slowly, pale and rigid like a drunk. The hair on his temples was white and sticky with paint. The expression on his face had been brutalized by his hardening features and fixed stare. This face I had loved so much, had watched so much, disintegrating before my eyes, shocked me. I waited so that I could speak to him.

"So," he said, "you're here. What happened to you?"

He too! I asked him how he knew.

"I came down this morning to look at a car. Apparently, I had messed it up. Bernier stopped me to ask if I knew why you were out. I didn't know. I said no. We went together to look at the car. Arezki was working inside it. I asked him if you were all right last night when he left you."

I looked at him, incredulous.

"You asked him that? In front of Bernier?"

"Yes, in front of Bernier. Why not?"

"What did he say?"

"He spluttered."

"What about Bernier?"

"Bernier? He didn't say anything. Nor the others. Maybe they didn't hear."

"What others?"

"Oh," he said, "you drive me crazy. That little Mustapha, Daubat, I think, someone else too."

I was aghast. Lucien was surprised. Why should you hide? he asked me. Was I ashamed? Afraid?

"You act as if it were a catastrophe. After all, I've seen you several times in the bus at night. True or untrue?"

"You have done something terribly stupid, especially to Arezki."

"Come on, you're not worried about Arezki, you're thinking of yourself. I know you too well. What can you do, it's an accident. When you fall for an Arab . . ."

He was talking too loud, smirking. Had he acted without thinking, spontaneously? Had he treacherously wanted to drive me to the wall and force me, as he had, to ignore what other people would say? When he saw me getting off the bus behind Arezki, when he saw us cautiously turn into the quiet streets, protected by a Paris drowned in fog and the obscurity of seven o'clock, did he think that I lacked daring, dignity, and that I needed a little prodding? And hadn't he taken pleasure in embarrassing the girl whose watchful and disapprov-

(193)

ing eyes he had been forced to bear all these years? What sweet revenge . . . I've got her, he was probably saying to himself. He guessed my panic and looked at me, calm and contemptuous. He, who had burned all his bridges and succeeded in being rejected wherever he went.

Useless to explain. No matter what I said, the harm was done. Luckily, I'd be seeing Arezki that night and we could discuss it together.

I watched intensely the women eating in the coatroom. They paid no more attention to me than usual. That made me feel a little better. But going back to the shop and walking by Daubat, looking Gilles in the face . . . obviously he would know. Everyone would know. "She goes out with . . ." With Mustapha, the Magyar, it wouldn't matter. It was the others I was afraid of.

When the timekeeper came to speak to me in the afternoon, I felt sick. He asked me how the headliners were going. I said they were fine, just fine. Satisfied, he made an innocent joke that reassured me. He didn't know. I listened to his professional explanations with flattering interest. Before anything else, I wanted to gain his sympathy. For reasons I didn't quite understand, I felt guilty and had only one desire: to gain time.

.   .   .

I sank to a bench in the Châtelet station and waited, my mind a blank. Arezki was late. Each time a train pulled in and discharged its passengers, my irritation grew. When he finally arrived, I couldn't unbend. My coldness was infectious. We went out and found ourselves on a bridge. The scene was unfriendly; the water shimmered here and there in the light. Arezki was silent

(194)

and I didn't dare say, "Let's stop for a moment." The empty horizon beyond the river gave an impression of freedom, of space without end.

"Do you know that building?"

He spoke, at last.

"It's the Prefecture of Police. We'll walk around the quay."

I said, with conscious detachment: "Lucien did a stupid thing this morning."

Arezki looked at me; he seemed astonished. "Who told you?"

"He did."

"Why did he do it?"

"It's Lucien all over. He spoke without thinking."

"Yes."

But he was preoccupied and I persisted.

"Is it serious?"

"Serious!" he said. "A little thing like that. Only for you. For me a little, but mostly for you."

"I couldn't care less."

I had shouted it. At that moment, yes. A limp meekness enveloped me and that was enough. Anna said it well when she wrote to my brother: "With you, I feel myself." And I, this evening, I feel myself and I feel the life of this city, beyond Arezki but through him, polished by the shadows opening before us.

Now the rain multiplies the mirages.

"Put your scarf on; you'll get wet."

I like that. He holds my bag, I tie the ends of the scarf under my chin and we move on.

"What do you want to do? It would have been better

to keep it secret. Now they'll make trouble, especially
for you. Bah, it's nothing. You won't change on account
of it?"

I let out a laugh, meant to reassure him.

"If I wasn't so selfish, I'd tell you to quit and look for
work somewhere else. But I like to have you around,
especially in the morning; when I arrive, I look for you,
I see you. Oh, well . . . Let's wait. We'll see."

"Do you like this neighborhood?" he speaks again. "I
was suspicious of it. I like it too, but it's dangerous."

"But there are lots of your brothers."

"She'll never understand," he sighs. "That's exactly
it. It's raiding country for the police. And, besides, it's
not mine. I live in Crimée."

He had told me Jaurès.

"Tonight, the hell with it. Come, let's have a drink."

We walk through streets of the Middle Ages. For a
minute, my pleasure is spoiled by the images evoked:
the alley of the Trois-Chandeliers, our door, the Club,
Grandmother looking for empty crates in the night.
Arezki holds me against him and we walk in step.

Grandmother, the door and the alley disappear.

"We must go inside. It's raining too hard."

On the left side of the little street, there is an Arab
café. The door is ajar. It's jammed, noisy, and there's
music. A man comes out, looks around, goes back in and
closes the door.

"Can we go in there?"

"Are you crazy? It's impossible. I don't live here.
They'd take me for a stool-pigeon, an informer."

My scarf has slipped. We've retreated under an archway. Arezki, let your hair drip, don't wipe your cheeks. You've kissed me. Your jacket where I've leaned my head is cold. The smell of wet leather is intoxicating. The rain keeps coming down. The café door is open again. The music reaches us. One phrase, like a leitmotif, repeats itself. Arezki translates, "Ana ounti: you and I. It's Egyptian." The music is softer; the door has closed. Arezki sighs. I ask him, "Are you cold?"

"No," he says. "It's the thought of separating."

"So soon?"

"Yes, I have to be back early."

The rain lets up; we start walking again. This too swift moment falls like a picture dropped into a box.

The Boulevard Saint-Michel was for me a whole world of symbols. Henri, Lucien, always described it with fascination.

I examined the people on the street. That night, the boulevard didn't seem to live up to its reputation. There were mostly pretty girls window shopping. They didn't seem at all poor. Many areas were crowded with people wearing dingy, dirty clothes as though they were fancy dress. By happy accident, they seemed to mold the girls in the right places and flatter those who needed it.

Arezki pulled me by the sleeve.

"Look at that shirt!"

He pointed to a shirt in the window, white, sheer, silky, expensive.

"I must have that shirt."

"But Arezki, it costs almost a week's pay."

"So what . . . I'll buy it next payday."

"There are handsome ones in other shops and much less expensive."

"They're not the same. Look at it closely. A shirt like that, can you see it on the back of an Algerian?"

He was adamant and I said:

"In any event, it's hardly the shirt of a revolutionary."

"Certainly not."

He looked at it longingly a few more seconds and said, "Come."

"If I could only explain it to you so that you'd understand," he added.

We crossed between the cars and I was silent. Once on the sidewalk, he came to a stop and looked at his watch.

"We won't have time for a drink."

"O. K.," I said, resigned. "We'll do it tomorrow."

"The day after tomorrow. Aïê, aïe," he murmured very fast, "leave me, walk in front."

I hesitated for a moment. He stopped, repeated "move" between his teeth. We had reached a corner where several police cars were parked. We couldn't turn back. I obeyed. Arezki took a step to the left to put space between us and, at that moment, he was stopped.

I crossed mechanically. When I turned around, he was no longer in sight. I didn't want to go without knowing. The cops, spread out in a net on the sloping street, nabbed those who went by, Arabs and those who looked like Arabs. The night life went on on the boulevard, and the students, real or otherwise, walked about or argued.

I had to leave. There was no chance of finding Arezki. He had to be inside one of those big cars and I would only have attracted attention if I'd stayed motionless against the window.

Arezki didn't come to work the next day. Bravely I checked the cars. Various eyes observed me and followed my motions. I looked for Lucien at noon; I had decided to tell him everything. He didn't show up and I didn't want to go to the canteen to look for him.

At two o'clock, when work resumed, Arezki was there. The look on his face said: "Yes, it's me. Patience." I was so happy I contented myself with this message.

Arezki and Mustapha were arguing. Arezki spoke in a low voice and, even without understanding the language, I could tell he was violently angry. Bernier appeared in the frame of the rear window.

"Rezki," he called.

Arezki turned around.

"Why weren't you at work this morning?"

"I was sick," Arezki said.

"Again?"

Bernier got into the car, crouched down and, examining the ceiling, said:

"If you hadn't turned up this afternoon, I was going to ask mademoiselle there to go find out where you were."

Arezki put down his tool.

"Why mademoiselle?" he asked Bernier.

He looked at him angrily; Bernier drew back and got out. Arezki got out too.

Mustapha left the car and stood next to Arezki. For a few seconds, the three of them looked at each other, then two workmen went between them to climb into the car that was passing by and Bernier returned to his desk.

Arezki beckoned to me. We got into an empty car.

"How are you?" I asked very fast.

"O.K. But they held me until this morning."

"Just for an inspection?"

"Sure. When they pick us up, they keep us all night. Try explaining that to a boss. O.K. Listen. Tonight I can't see you. Tomorrow is a holiday, then comes Sunday . . . so, Monday night. Can I call you? If so, write down the number, put it in my box and I'll get it later."

The assembly line went on, life went on, the war went on, and, trapped in these iron chains, we attempted to pluck a few peaceful and tender moments of pleasure.

"Merry Christmas!" Gilles came to tell me.

"Thank you, monsieur."

He held out the envelope with my pay check.

I try to find, and can't, a way to describe what it was like when Gilles was there, in front of you. He made you want to work. He restored the dignity that the brutality of the assembly line and the contempt of the bosses had taken away. He reassured you. Demanding and stern, he had a remarkable sense of justice. He listened to Saîd with the same interest he showed the head of production. He had no affection for any of the workmen but respected each one equally. Finally, by luck, nature had blessed him with this face, its features fine and energetic, its expression direct, open and generous.

At five o'clock, joy ran through the line. "One hour,

(200)

comrades, and it's over! Three days! Tonight is Christmas Eve. We'll start with that, then tomorrow we start all over again. Sunday, we recuperate. And Monday . . . But from now until Monday, it's three days . . . and the end of the paycheck."

"Are you celebrating the holidays?" Mustapha asked me.

"I? No. What about you?"

"I, mademoiselle, I can't. There's the war."

"I can't either. I don't want to."

"We'll see each other later!" he shouted, getting down.

He turned around and bent forward:

". . . if we're not dead . . ."

In the coatroom, the women's joy was noisy. I felt no bitterness. I didn't even envy them. They paid enough for what pleasure awaited them. These few minutes of gaiety, the easy laughter, the dirty smock thrown in a wad brought back the happy excitement of school vacations.

Christmas in Paris, almost mild, rainy; profane streamers, firecrackers disturbing the magic of dawn. I wake with a start. It's the celebrants returning home, a little the worse for wear. Voluptuously, I linger in bed. A sudden pang and Arezki's face kills my joy. I discover the flatness of unshared pleasures. But hope remains, incurable hope, and joy is reborn. I recreate Arezki by myself, with the details that my memory puts together, the pictures fixed in my mind. I can't speak of his beauty; the word would be improper.

Spare, seemingly without muscles, thick veins on his

thin arms, slender fingers, he moves with his calm gait, lowers his neck slightly into his shoulders in that shivering way the Arabs have, walking with a stoop when they're not holding themselves exaggeratedly upright, arms used for balance. His hair, which he treats with great care, shines, curly around the temples, rising in tight waves and lengthening his profile. I try to imagine how his face will change, become more Saracen in the future: hollowed cheeks, little flesh and, above a mouth still red, the hint of a white mustache. I was going to say that his face and expression made me think of some kind of animal. I choose my comparisons: the eyes of a wolf, the eagle's profile. But no, Arezki's face is a human face, always changing; even anger has no effect on its harmonious construction: the long eyelids under the bias of the eyebrows, the slightly hollow temples, the fine chin. The eyes are black, black, black. Velvet, charcoal, jet, anything you like. His fits of bad temper are tenacious. Arezki forgives with difficulty. "I swear it" and "Word of honor" fall ten times in his conversation. He likes the word "brother" and says "our people." Besides, he chooses his words with care, as if he were conferring power on them. He speaks of illness with loathing. He doesn't say "I'm sick" but "I'm tired." The word can bring on the thing. He doesn't dress for protection but for adornment. He likes what magnifies him, brilliant colors that cause the pupils to dilate. Solitary, isolated when he's not with his brothers, he has come to feel superior to those who scorn him. He holes up in his isolation, and his resignation—fleeting—does not come from humility. Imaginative to the point of delirium, his pensiveness and his silence hide the wild waves, the vivid ripples beneath his eyelids.

On the second day of the holidays, my solitude weighs heavy on me. I question myself, I hesitate and then decide. I'll pay Lucien a visit.

I take the bus that lets me off in front of the Basilica. I've bought some cakes I know he likes. It's strange, I don't resent him anymore; I need to feel his nearness. Because of Arezki. I wander around the Basilica until two o'clock with my cumbersome, cone-shaped package. I knock on his door and wait. The door opens, Anna throws herself into my arms with a moan, then pulls back, disappointed. She hadn't expected me.

"Forgive me, I thought it was Lucien."

She turns her face away, but I have an observant eye and take in her swollen eyelids and her nose, red from too much wiping. To escape my searching look, she pretends to dress and turns her back. But her voice betrays the tears she's shed. I ask if Lucien is coming. I anticipate with satisfaction the moment when she has to face me. The same satisfaction I felt earlier when I watched Marie-Louise disintegrating. Shall I prolong her agony? Tell her that I'm staying? She has turned slightly as she steps into her skirt. The sharp angle of her elbow when she tightens the belt, the hollow places on her body awake in me my incurable vice: the need to help, to give succor, to be useful and necessary.

"Things aren't going too well, are they?"

At first she doesn't answer and I feel foolish; then she gives in.

"No, not too well."

She smiles to hide the pain of her admission and her pupils disappear behind the welling tears. She is dressed now and straightens the bed. She calculates, she questions. Will I take her observations back to Lucien? I help her and talk about my brother, his work, the factory, the cauldron he steams in for hours, the startling change in his features, the need to see that he gets rest, food. At first she listens with attention, then I feel her interest wane. She stares at a place on the bed and tries to find in erotic memories the assurance that Lucien will return. Her entire body expresses the desire she feels for him at that moment. If only he'd come back, they'd coil around each other and lose themselves, one in the other. Only there does she feel her being. My arguments sound ludicrous to her. She thinks I've understood nothing. They've had a fight. He left in the night. She waits, she weeps. She is in a hurry to be alone to weep some more. I leave the cakes on the table and get out.

. . .

The machines and motors had slept for three days, but they started up with the first turn of the crank. Our bodies took longer. The first car went by unfinished; the second was missing the snap-ons. By the third, the rhythm was restored.

Arezki surprised me in the car the men had abandoned.

"How are you?" he said. "Tonight?"

I looked up at him.

"Yes, tonight. Everything's fine."

The brief exchange of our eyes, the three simple

words, had lasted but a few seconds. Changed into statues, floating on the belt like a raft on the sea, we were about to be stranded too far from our usual place to remain unnoticed. But Arezki seemed to be in high spirits. He let Mustapha buzz around him, he laughed when the Magyar displayed his neck shorn of its suspect curls, he exchanged a few words with Gilles when he came to inspect the headliners. Twice, he placed his hand on mine and excused himself with a smile of complicity.

I felt better. The behavior of the men around us seemed unchanged. They were always out of breath trying to keep up the pace. The bonus danced before their eyes like a carrot before a donkey. Bernier passed by and passed by again, stopped, left, returned. But that was normal. I noticed only that Mustapha talked to me less easily. The final test was the coatroom. I attracted no particular attention.

Under his breath, Arezki had specified, "Crimée, second stop after Stalingrad."

He was already there when I stepped off the last car.

"Is this where you live?"

He saw my smile, laughed too, and said:

"No, I live at the Goutte d'Or. This time it's the truth. Don't you wonder where we're going?"

I told him I cared very little.

We walked down a quiet street, almost deserted, badly lit. An enormous, very long, very high wall enclosing some kind of factory, rose up along the left-hand sidewalk.

"Mustapha talked too much, like your brother."

I asked him questions. What had Mustapha said? And to whom?

"Mustapha lives on the same street I do. He talked around the neighborhood. At the factory, too; I know because Saïd, the one who does the headliners, repeated it to me. So what! I'm almost glad. I took my precautions; now it's over, no use regretting. We won't hide any longer. Only, you must understand that I have some . . . activities; I'm not always free. I've thought hard about it. What we need is someplace where we'll finally be alone. What do you think?"

I acted as if I didn't understand.

"No, not a café. I meant to say, we need a room."

He continued quickly:

"Your place is out of the question. And I don't live alone. But we have to find something. We're going now to an uncle of mine who lives at this corner. I'm going to try to get him to help us. We'll see what happens."

"Do you want me to go too?"

"Of course, my dear Elise. You're about to enter the brotherhood."

The house looked abandoned. Not a sound came through the walls.

"Of course," Arezki said. "It's the commissariat for the factory across the street. There are only three tenants. He lives on the top floor."

He knocked on the seventh floor's only door. Nobody answered; he knocked again, called out, gave his name. The door opened. A fat and shaggy little man appeared. He greeted Arezki with wails of joy and made us come in. He questioned him about me and Arezki stopped him.

"She doesn't understand. Talk French. I want you to meet Elise."

He gave me a cold good evening and turned to his nephew.

"Please sit down."

He indicated the bed. It took up most of the room. It had iron posts painted white and a mattress so thin I could feel the springs. The tiny room opened onto the roof through a transom whose iron grill hung over the old man's head.

On the floor, between casseroles and baskets, there was a big coffeepot on an electric plate. It was connected by a long cord to the ceiling fixture whose naked bulb was the garret's only light.

Their conversation went on and on. For all his trying, the uncle reverted to his native language. So did Arezki, from time to time. Then he would catch himself and turn to me.

"Please excuse us. It's a habit."

I looked around me; I imagined the garret cleaned and transformed.

They passed each member of the family in review.

I listened patiently.

"My mother is her cousin," Arezki would explain.

And they'd launch into more family gossip of which I understood nothing.

"You must eat with me," the uncle said suddenly.

And paying no attention to Arezki's refusal, he

crouched down and pulled a pot of beans out from under the bed.

"See, it's all ready. I'll reheat it. I want you to eat with me."

Something red was swimming on top.

"It's the seasoning," he explained. He turned toward Arezki and said a few incomprehensible words. Arezki laughed.

"He says the meat is underneath. No, no, we must go."

"You can't leave without eating," the old man insisted.

"And the wine," Arezki said softly, "where do you hide it?"

The uncle froze, mouth open, arms raised. His white, tobacco-stained mustache drew a sharp curve on his worn face; it made him look old and sad. Arezki kept his bantering smile.

"Ah, my son," the uncle said.

He brought his arm down. He now held the pot by its two handles.

"You'll be the death of me. They came, two of them, the other Sunday. I told them, O.K., strike me, kill me, I can't do without it. It's thirty years I've been working in France. Twenty years in the foundry. Ten years I've been a watchman. I have to drink. I'll pay the fine, every week if you insist. But at my age you can't get rid of your habits so easily. I'll pay."

He repeated three times: I'll pay.

"And so?" Arezki asked.

"And so, they fined me. And they told me: you'll be

(208)

fined until you stop drinking. That way, you won't be able to buy wine any more."

He shook his head sadly over his beans.

"You could do something. Go find them and explain. An old man like me. I'm not dangerous."

"Where do you hide it?"

He put down the pot, stood up and went toward the electric plate.

"In the coffeepot. Want some?"

"No. And what if they asked you for a cup of coffee?"

"I'd say: I'll make you some fresh. And I'd go out to wash the pot under the faucet on the sixth floor. They'll listen to you. Tell them I'll pay the fine. Each payday. Just so they leave me alone. I do nothing wrong. I'm all alone, it isn't me that hinders the revolution."

"The revolution," Arezki said gravely, "is a bulldozer."

He made a sweeping gesture.

"It'll go right through."

The uncle had poured himself a glass of wine and was drinking with a sigh. When he put it down empty, Arezki asked him:

"Make us some coffee, real coffee."

With care, he poured the wine into a casserole, covered it with a plate and went out.

"You're not too disappointed with this evening?"

I reassured him. He stroked my cheek.

I drank the coffee with no pleasure, but said it was good.

"It's vile," Arezki broke in. "Take care, uncle, the

wine leaves a taste. Now I'd like to ask a favor of you."

"Anything you say."

When Arezki had finished, the old man whistled. They exchanged a few words, but as they had gone back to their own language, I couldn't follow. Arezki was insistent. The uncle answered with a disapproving grumble.

"What time do you start?"

"At ten."

"We'll go now. Think about it; I'll be back."

"Come eat."

"We'll see."

They embraced four times. The uncle opened the door, held out his hand to me and we went down. Preoccupied, Arezki was silent a long time. At first he answered my questions distractedly, then he exploded. The uncle wouldn't give up his room, lend it, or make a trade.

"If I had promised what he asked, he would have accepted."

"And why refuse him? He's an old man."

"You think I'm too hard. There are rules. A man who drinks becomes dangerous. He talks. If he has nothing to say, he says anything that comes into his mind. He makes himself noticed. Besides, it's the rule and that's it. In front of you is a red light. Crossing is against the law. Among ourselves, we establish red lights. We have everything to learn and we work in the dark like moles . . . But forget it. Come, let's eat. It's too bad, we'll have to find another solution. His beans aroused my appetite, but I was afraid you wouldn't like them. There's a small café that serves food. The owner is from my town. You aren't afraid to be with dirty Arabs?"

Annoyed, I stopped. He pretended to be surprised.

"Come along, touchy one. I'm hungry and you're cold."

At the corner of the street, we were about to cross when he held me back.

"We have to find a room. Soon. Ask your brother, look around where you live. We can't wander around in the night any longer."

I didn't ask my brother for anything. I contented myself with an ardent hope that Arezki would manage to find something.

It was three days before we went out again. He slipped to my side when he saw I was alone and said very fast, "Not tonight, I'm busy. Have you thought about what I said?"

Bernier was observing me. I wrote little notes to Arezki, which I tried without success to slip him. Bernier was everywhere. Prowling the length of the line or suddenly poking his laughing face through the rear window, he seemed bent on tripping me up. He saved all his fault-finding for me, and I couldn't allow myself the smallest mistake. He himself was the favored butt of his superiors, from the boss of the shop to Gilles, from the head of manufacturing to the head of the warehouse. All of them showered him with nasty remarks, reproaches and demands. Only Gilles sometimes condescended to suggest rather than criticize. But Bernier's mean and narrow little soul saw only malice in the foreman. And therefore, he took it out on us and hit out in all directions. Still, we carried on, indifferent, gelatinous or resentful. He had us by the bonus, for he had the power to withhold it. What was the good of becoming an adult, sometimes a man nearing old age, if you were forced back to the childish world of the capricious reward?

I had neither the vocabulary nor the assurance necessary to resist him. Through me, he worked off the stored up resentment he felt against Arezki. It wasn't only him he aimed at, but at all the goddamned niggers who weren't afraid of him and made him run from one end of the line to the other. It was they who were responsible for the reprimands that fell on him. And this man Arezki, so taciturn, whose eyes froze him in his tracks, who was obeyed by Mustapha, by Saïd and the whole lot, he would have dearly loved to humiliate him, and get at him through me.

I lied when Arezki asked if I had talked to Lucien about the room.

"He doesn't know. He'll think about it and tell me later."

I hadn't seen Lucien for several days. He wasn't running from me; I was avoiding him.

We were once again in the street, parading our desires and hopes.

"A room where you could wait for me in safety. Would you like that? If you wouldn't, say so now; don't let me go on dreaming."

"But can you do it? Aren't there obstacles?"

"I already told you. I would have preferred to keep it all secret. Now we have to work it out as best we can."

"Because isn't it,. these . . . obligations which . . ."

I stammered, leaving the sentence unfinished. He smiled without looking at me and without answering.

A bakery, a half-opened doorway, two windows covered with an iron grating, a long crumbling façade, a leaking zinc gutter causing the wall to swell with mold, a bistro with opaque windows in front of which the stones of the sidewalk had disintegrated, all these filed past me on my right during the long silence. They gave it weight, breadth and became its witnesses. For all time, these stones, these signs, these gratings, this chewed-up asphalt would be dyed with a bitter feeling I couldn't fathom: their wretched, stifling ugliness, or the impossibility of being truthful with Arezki? The contradictory desires that tossed me about were drawing me toward deceit. He held my hand tight and every so often carried it to his mouth. His head was half-turned toward me. He talked seriously and listened the same way. At that point, I shook off my paralyzing hesitancy. The obstacles took on an exalting aspect and I remembered my assets: my life had found meaning. But through every chink in my nature, fear and hesitation returned and I didn't lack for pretexts to put off the heroic decision. It was the same with him, but he never expressed it.

At the factory, we kept the same reserve. Arezki permitted himself only one quick sentence to tell me what he was doing that night, which I answered with two words. More often we would just look at each other, or if we were working in the same car, graze each other in passing. Twice, Arezki repeated, as he left me at the end of the evening: "We must have a room."

Feverishly, I said: yes, I'll look, I'll shake Lucien, go see his friend Henri.

As soon as he had left me, I saw the mountains I must move, and felt overwhelmed. I thought of Lucien and Marie-Louise, Anna's letter, the hotel bedrooms. Nothing was free. You had to fight for it.

. . .

"Do you want to come with me next Saturday? You aren't afraid of the mud, the misery?"

"Arezki, I want to go with you everywhere."

"We'll eat in the neighborhood, then go together to Nanterre. I want to see some friends. They're expecting me and I can't let them down."

He introduced me: "This is Elise." They were expecting him. They embraced him. Then began interminable conversations interrupted only by the arrival of some friend or neighbor. They embraced each other. "This is Elise." I shook the outstretched hand, the newcomer sat down and the conversation resumed. I wasn't bored; I wasn't impatient. I watched, I reflected. I felt the peace that comes in the presence, at the sound of the one you love.

So many newspapers, so many witnesses and accounts have since described these places where, penned in, crammed together, hundreds of beings fought to survive. Were I to do it, I would have to repeat the same words, pile up the same adjectives, pivot around the same verbs: wretched over-crowding, physical suffering, sickness, poverty, the cold, the rain, the wind shaking the walls, puddles seeping under the doors, fear of the police, the dark, the inhuman crush, and the misery, everywhere the misery. Only one word was unknown: despair. Everyone said "someday" . . . and no one doubted it. The present, that was the fight for survival. A few stayed and did well. But the larger number, fleeing the suffering multiplied by the war, trying to feed by handouts their starving tribes, came down from the Hauts Plateaux, from the Kabyle villages. Then came the struggle of the immigrant to find employment, not knowing how to read the forms, confused by the din of the city, solicited to the right, to the left, in front, on the walls, everywhere, by pictures, the erotic suggestion of posters, the movies, the lights, stopped, inspected, frisked, inevitably suspect, unable to explain.

The most precious piece of paper, the pass, the safe-conduct, was the pay slip. Without that, the black door of the paddy-wagon remained closed. Without that began the long agony of interrogation, the beatings, the return to the original village which was itself a selection center where they selected with such care that the suspicious ones never got out.

"When I see Mustapha playing with fire," said Arezki, "I get angry. If they kick him out, he may not find other work, and they'll have him shipped out right away."

"But Daubat treats him like a nigger. I've heard him. How do you expect him to control himself?"

"If that bothers him, it's because he hasn't understood anything. You have to be tough, insensitive. If I'm called a nigger or a dirty Arab, it makes me smile. Ask your brother to explain. He'll do it better than me; I lack ability with words."

"You don't lack anything," I said, trying to joke.

And because I really thought it, I added:

"You're an example to the others."

"That," he said, "could make me angry. I think you're making fun of me and I don't like it. I'm like everybody else. I like to punch a few noses, too; I'd like to go out and get drunk when I'm fed up or forget the whole thing; I've sneaked a drink. I've also wanted to cheat the paymaster, and I don't go to the meetings without feeling scared. I'd like to spend my Sundays in bed instead of getting up at six to run around the neighborhood; I don't want to send in reports, be ordered about. There are 'brothers' I can't stand. But it's like loving a woman: you make an effort to please, you shave more carefully, you try to smell nice, you wait up late to see her, you talk to her gently, you carry her packages, you bring her presents. But this requires an even greater love; sometimes the goal fades away, or you think that no one is worth the pain you suffer. We're not saints. We have our own faults and, in addition, those brought out by the kind of life we lead. We argue, we hold grudges, we help each other like fish swimming in the same bowl who can't get away from each other, sleeping in rows, washing in front of each other. Some are cheerful, some are vain, or sly, or naive, or tough, or mean, or timid. They're men. And the miracle is that we've managed to prevent the explosion of a hundred or a thousand people condemned to tolerate each other!"

When he had finished, a man got up, stoked the stove, and lit the gas lamp for the night that falls at five o'clock in winter, plunging into obscurity this city built on mud.

"Please stay for supper," someone said in French.

We had to say yes.

Arezki looked at me. He was about to refuse, saw the small sign I made him, and looked approvingly at me.

A man passed the plates. I was singled out for the newest.

Arezki stopped eating to say: "She's on our side."

One of the men looked at him skeptically.

"She's on your side."

"No, she was on our side before I came along."

Embarrassed, I kept my eyes on my plate.

"Do you know many Frenchmen who are on our side?"

Arezki protested that after all there were a few.

"Workers?"

"Not many," Arezki admitted.

"And you know why they're against the war? Because it's expensive. Not because of us or our kids or our wives. Because they get less steak."

"They don't know the facts."

It was getting late. The gentle light of the gas lamp fell on our faces. When its flame flickered, it painted our cheeks with shifting reflections. On a shelf holding a few pictures, an alarm clock with a panting tick-tock seemed to be telling us, hurry up.

I had to promise I'd come back. When the muddy

paths were behind us, we could hug each other, embrace, and I discovered a delight I had never known before. Arezki sensed it. It doubled his pleasure. We couldn't let each other go.

"We must have a room."

But this time it was I who said it.

. . .

Ten to. I had gone up too early; most of the workmen were still not there. Daubat gave me a half-smile in answer to my greeting. The timekeeper, who was measuring the space between two cars, squarely turned his back on me. So, he must know. I had expected it, but I felt a disagreeable twitch. I stood against the window and took from my pocket the crossword puzzle I'd torn out of the paper the night before. My brother had often made fun of my interest in puzzles. From the beginning, when had he not made fun of everything I did?

The siren. I attached my sheet. "Waves under the sun visor." Needless to put it down; I'd remember it. I mustn't get behind. But the picture stayed in my mind, with its colors, its graceful undulation, evoking fresh air and wide spaces. One of those dreams that saps your strength.

Mustapha made a small sign and I saw Arezki behind him. I stayed in the car.

"Don't move," he shouted in my ear. "Don't look. Bernier is behind me."

Bernier passed by without stopping, saw me writing, looked at Mustapha who, with Arezki's help, was stretching a wrinkled headliner above the door.

"That café we were in yesterday, do you think you can find it alone? I'll be there at eight. We'll go to my place. No one will be there. Have you got it?"

He was watching for me through the window and came out as soon as he recognized me. The café was at the corner of the Rue de Crimée.

"We're going to my place, Rue de la Goutte d'Or."

Goutte d'Or. The name rose in flames. But it was night and there was nothing to distinguish this street from any other.

"We're mad. I'm mad," he exclaimed several times.

I followed him down a hall. He turned around twice to point out an ill-fitting or cracked tile. At the foot of the stairs, he took my hand. I let myself be led. I wanted this stairway to be endless, the silent climb eternal. I dreaded the arrival, the moment when, the door shut, we would rediscover each other under the light. Wasn't it the best part of love, this quiet ascension? He pulled me impatiently, bringing my fingers to his mouth and biting them.

He opened a door and I went in. It was a few seconds before he turned on the light, and I stayed motionless in the dark. Then he turned the switch. The room had two beds, one quite large, the other a folding bed pushed into a corner. How many slept here? On the big bed there was a piece of cloth with large mauve flowers in widely spaced bouquets that filled the room with the smell of new cretonne. The material had the folds and stiffness of something new. Just bought, probably. Bought for me. On the table in the right hand corner

(219)

were several bottles topped with glasses. I looked toward the window, my hands hanging limp.

Arezki came toward me and took them in his. Above his eyelids, his eyebrows almost met in a thick bar. These joyless eyes held at their center the reflection of the light bulb; it was no longer a look of desire. All of a sudden, my presence seemed to crush him. He pointed to the windows which had neither shades nor curtains.

"Wait," he said. "I'll turn the lights off."

Those in the houses across the way were enough to light the room. In the shadow, I felt more at ease. I could pick out the skin, shinier and more brown, around Arezki's mouth. I wished I could speak, but I was spinning around and carried off in a violent eddy.

Arezki smiled. I relaxed a little. He helped me take off my coat, folded it slowly and placed it on the only chair. There was only the bed left to sit on, the bed with its enormous flowers. He pulled me to him.

The flowers dissolved, the walls crumbled, the light paled. He talked fast, using words from his own rough language. I felt caught in the net of his love. I wanted him to go on biting my fingers. I thought of Lucien and Anna, of what was happening to me, and it was like a whirlpool at whose center my life shrank and withered away; the years, the months, the days, those to come and those left behind, suddenly were petrified, and this moment was at the circle's center, round, luminous, shimmering, dazzling, spurting. I let myself slip between his arms, my face crushed against the rough cloth of his jacket. An ear-splitting noise invaded the street below.

"Firemen," I thought to myself. Arezki hadn't moved. There seemed to be several trucks; the noise grew louder and then spun out in a sinister wail and stopped under our window. Arezki let go of me. I understood. The police. I began to tremble. I wasn't scared but I trembled all the same. I couldn't stop trembling: the sirens, the brakes, the banging of the doors and the cold—I felt it now—the cold of the room. Across the street, the lights went out. I didn't know what to do, so suddenly released from his arms. First he put a cigarette in his mouth, then he handed me my coat.

"Take it," he said, not looking at me. "Put it on and go home as soon as the way is clear."

I threw it across the room. In the hotel, there was silence. As we had climbed the stairs, a record player played "L'Aïd, l'Aïd." All the time that Arezki was holding me to him, the music enveloped me. Now it had stopped. We could hear nothing but whistles and the voices of the policemen repeating orders. They climbed the stairs at a gallop. Their heavy feet banged against the treads. There, they'd reached a landing; there they'd stopped; there, they'd started again. Why wouldn't Arezki look at me? He was smoking. He had lit a cigarette and placed the blackened match on the edge of the table. He smoked, looking unperturbed, as if he didn't understand or had heard nothing. They knocked on doors with their fists. With their feet too, it seemed from the noise.

"Police!"

"Police!"

I couldn't speak, I couldn't relax. In the dark, motionless, I listened, and by the sounds, followed, like a blind man, the progress of the search. They were whistling now inside the hotel. Some one shouted an order and the footsteps quickened. They had reached our floor and ran to the exits. The voices took on a strange sound, amplified by the silence of the hotel. The police carried big lanterns whose rays penetrated into the room through the cracks of the worn doorframe. One of them, who had probably been behind, came running up.

"Let's get going with the rat hunt," he joked.

There were a few laughs.

The most terrifying thing was the silence. No cries, no moans, not a single shout, no struggle; just some policemen in an empty house. Then, suddenly, there was a rumbling, then another, a dull sound of falling down the stairs. Then silence again. In the street, some one cried out:

"Get going, get going, get going!"

I got up with an effort and walked to the window. Men were climbing into police vans. A few had on handcuffs. Others, in the line, rubbed their elbows and adjusted their pants. The night was clear, cold, pure. The street light near the car illuminated the scene and the men standing in line. From the window I saw only their elongated heads and the black wool of their hair. ("O race of sheeps' heads, and like them, led to the slaughter . . ." A poem Henri had read to us, when we were awaiting the real life.) One of them, the last one in line, a small man whose hair glistened as he crossed the circle of light, slowed down and rummaged through his pocket. His nose was probably bleeding. He put his head back and mopped it with his sleeve. One of the policemen saw him, jumped on him, seized the little man's shoulders, and, beating his back, threw him toward the wagon. The man missed the step and fell face down on the pavement. I turned away. I couldn't move. Every motion seemed indecent, but I couldn't stand the dark or the silence any longer, nor the acrid smoke coming out of Arezki's mouth that rose, twisted and disappeared. Why didn't Arezki speak? He hadn't moved. This time they were knocking at the door next to ours. The peculiarities of the hotel's construction had relegated our room to an embryonic hall to the right of the toilets. They had visited all the other rooms before arriving at our door. But what were they doing in them? And the others, why didn't they fight back? Why didn't they cry out? I was about to move. I'd go sit down next to Arezki, I'd take his arm, I'd cling to it. A scream rose, brief, smothered. Galloping sounds toward our door. The one who had fought back, had he seen that the exits were guarded? He seemed to be trampling on something, breathing hard and fast, but the others were catching up to him. I heard the collision, the exclamations, the blows, the body dragged along, thrown down the stairs, the bumping against the steps. Somewhere, music exploded, "L'Aïd, l'Aïd." A clapping of hands, a delirious woman's voice, the sound of something breaking, the record player, no doubt.

Now it was our turn. It happened very fast. Arezki

(223)

turned on the light, unlocked the door. They entered. There were three of them. When they saw me, they whistled.

"Put your arms up. Algerian, Moroccan or Tunisian?"

"Algerian."

They felt his pockets, his sleeves.

"Your papers. Your pay voucher. The latest."

"It's in there," Arezki said, pointing to his wallet.

"Take off your clothes."

Arezki hesitated. They looked at me.

"Sooner, later, what does it matter? Hurry up."

I didn't look away. I concentrated on not moving, my eyes focused above Arezki's head, like a blind man who stares without seeing. Arezki had dropped his arms and was beginning to take off his jacket. I didn't want our eyes to meet. My eyes mustn't move from the wall above his head.

"Your papers, Mademoiselle? Madame?"

If only I could stop trembling. To give them my papers, I had to get my coat, lean down, straighten up, so many painful motions.

"You have no right," Arezki said. "I'm within the law, I have no weapons."

"Don't give me any trouble, brother. Take off your clothes. Does an unskilled workman's pay buy you shirts like that?"

It was the white shirt from the Boulevard Saint-Michel; I recognized it. Two more policemen passed by the open door. They guarded a man with handcuffs who was being prodded in the knees by a third.

"What's going on in here?"

The man who had just spoken leaned against the door.

"There's a lady here," said the policeman who was standing in front of Arezki.

The other one gave me a stony look.

"You call that a lady!"

They went out into the hall. Arezki was still flanked by two policemen.

"Take off the shirt!"

Arezki obeyed.

"All right. Get on with it. Your pants. So I can go through them!"

"You've already gone through them."

"Get your arms up!"

At the same time, the one on the left moved the barrel of his gun closer to Arezki. The other one undid the buckle of his belt and the pants slipped down. Arezki now had on only his white shorts. They laughed at the sight.

"Take them off. Some of them hide things inside their shorts."

As he spoke, he shoved the mouth of his gun against Arezki's belly. The other one pulled the elastic with his fingers and the shorts came down.

"When you arrived in France, how were you dressed? You wore a turban, right? With lice underneath? You're doing all right here; you eat, you buy handsome shirts, you please the women. Come, take your pants, and have a good night."

They all went out together. I looked out over the

street where the lights were turning on again. The Parisian Casbah was coming back to life. I tried hard to follow the movement of the clouds in the sky. The worst was yet to come: facing Arezki. I finally turned around. He was drinking a glass of water.

"You're going home," he said in a flat voice.

"Yes, I'm going home."

Sitting on the edge of the bed, he finished his drink.

"I would like to have a glass," I said.

"Take some. It's fresh water."

I went toward him. What was there to say? I wished I knew his language. I got down on my knees. I felt dizzy. He held his hands palms down on the mauve flowers of the bed. Two more flowers. The closed petals were a shiny bronze, the open petals, a dull rose. I took hold of them. The gestures of love were unfamiliar to me. I held them awkwardly not knowing what to do with them. I leaned toward them and kissed them once, in the palm that was warm and fleshy like breasts. Arezki didn't pull back. I kissed them again, drunk on the smell of damp flesh and cigarette, I bit them, kissed them, bit them again, licked them with my tongue. Arezki said a word I didn't understand. I put my head between his two palms.

"Go home," he repeated. "You must go home."

.   .   .

"Lucien, what's the matter? They told me at the residence hall you had tried to find me twice."

"And you weren't there. They didn't know when you'd be back. Henri wanted to see you. For his 'reportage,' you know. He's making a great survey and he was hoping to ask you some questions. You, and . . . Arezki."

"Yes, I got in pretty late. Well, I'm glad to see you. Grandmother has written. She thanks me for the Christmas presents. Marie-Louise paid her a visit. She's living with her sister, but things aren't going well between them. It'll soon be a year since you left. You can guess the rest."

He nodded.

"I can imagine. For the moment, I have more urgent problems. I owe lots and lots of dough."

"Get it from Henri!"

He shrugged and looked at me.

"Henri is no philanthropist. He's a future great sociologist. He's watching me drown and carefully noting down all the details of my agony. And besides, you know perfectly well that Henri is for total anarchy, not for the rescue of the individual. And I am too . . . Henri, Henri," he repeated several times as he moved off.

For a brief moment, I was tempted to run after him. But I was afraid of the irony in his eyes and in his words. He crushed all effort; even his physical appearance, the decomposition of his adolescent's face, the hardening of his expression, the hunger in his eyes, the nervousness of his too mobile mouth discouraged any attempt at friendship. As I climbed the stairs, I wondered if, when he was taken with desire, his face changed, if he found with Anna "the short fifteen minutes of love" she had written about, a different state from the anxious panting which, for him, symbolized love.

(227)

But I was still so profoundly stamped by the emotions of the night before that I was preoccupied only with myself. And besides, love meant one thing to one person and the opposite to the next, so how could you really find out? Anna and Lucien's love I saw as one long wail, a violent commotion in which they were exterminated and reborn, a mad game that isolated them, condemning them to solitude, a drifting ship that never came to shore. I had never fixed with definitive words what pulled me toward Arezki. He had never said "I love you" and I had never said "I love him." Arezki exists. There is Arezki. As there had been Lucien.

Events had played the role of hostile gods and one incident had unravelled the laborious fabric we had spent so many days weaving.

For three days, Arezki avoided me. But I wasn't unhappy. I felt that time must be allowed to pass, to be deliberately lost. Then we could pretend to have too much to say to remember an incident in our past.

I worked under the inquisitive eye of Mustapha who watched me on the side. He no longer talked to me, and since he'd also had a fight with the Magyar, he occasionally let out deep, sad sighs. Daubat often came over to inspect the headliners with the timekeeper. Twice, they talked to me in a gently kidding way that was comforting. I answered them with spirit. It was nice not to be completely excluded.

. . .

Crimée. He said Crimée, at seven o'clock.

We walk along the streets that seem safest, on the

(228)

edge of the dread rectangle of which the Goutte d'Or is the heart. We talk discreetly as we walk, and it's Arezki who risks an allusion.

"Were you afraid?"

"For you, yes."

But that isn't true. I'm lying. I was scared, and when I talk about it, I'm scared again. Lucien, you used to say: "The police . . . the hell with them . . . !" But I say I was scared. I had never understood the meaning of the word "power." Now it's dressed in somber colors, booted, helmeted, belted. They have wide shoulders, strong hands, large weapons. They glisten, from helmet to tommy gun. They are the strong ones.

We enter one café, then another. We walk, we talk, we turn, we cross.

"Let's have dinner together. In a restaurant—it's a dump but the owner's brother is married to my sister."

The presentation: this is Elise. The man has big knobby arms, a long face whose skin is criss-crossed with wrinkles like a waffle. He brings a table up from the rear and serves us generously. We cannot touch each other nor smile, but the mere fact of being together is comforting. A few inquisitive heads turn to look. When the door opens, I turn, for Arezki is facing it. He asks me not to do that here. I talk about Lucien, who worries me. But Lucien's torments really don't interest him. I give him a resumé of Grandmother's letter where, in the last sentence, the poor woman had screamed out her horror of dying in the nursing home.

He listens.

(229)

"What about our going to live down there? We could live together; you'd bring her home. I'd work. I'd love her, she'd love me."

I don't tell him that I doubt it. An Arab . . . my Grandmother's bogeyman.

"But could you leave here? Are you free to go? Perhaps you have important things to do in Paris, responsibilities?"

He leans forward and says very softly:

"At the risk of disillusioning you, I am only a humble militant. It could be arranged. You can be useful anywhere. What do you think?"

I don't think anything. I am torn.

. . .

We run into each other, my brother and I, in the same line waiting for the bus at six forty. Instead of trying to come near me, he makes a small sign. Marie-Louise had written me by way of Grandmother. But at this fresh and virginal hour, I won't tell him.

The various Portes go by. The bus slows down in the traffic that comes out of the Bois de Vincennes. I wipe away the steam on the window I'm leaning against. The sun rises over the stadium at Charenton. In the dissipating fog, young boys in blue sweatshirts are running around the wet track.

The sun rises, their mouths drink in the pure air, and through their pores penetrates the joy of the new morning. They run with taut muscles and long strides while the bus moves toward the Pont National. The sun emerges behind the trains on the siding. The day breaks over the Porte de Choisy, and other boys run toward the locker rooms where they take off their sweatshirts.

. . .

Didi told how she had been in the city the Sunday before.

"To Wagram, to dance."

A few had heard of Wagram. The majority had never left their own neighborhood. They didn't know their city; they were totally ignorant of Paris. The big girl who helped in the warehouse said:

"It's fifteen years since I've been past the Place d'Italie."

I knew only too well how you can spend your life watching it go by. But here in Paris, with its legends of the quartiers and the barricades, I asked myself why and how. The work, the wear and tear, the lack of time, but also a disgusting passivity, quasi-ancestral, added to the clannishness that dried life at its source. The neighborhood movie, the bistro at the corner represented the supreme contact with man. To better yourself meant to have things, to possess. To free yourself signified to acquire. Furniture, a car, after twenty years a summer bungalow. Only then do you begin to exist; you feel you've been admitted.

As she went past, Didi gave me a smile. We entered the shop together and she wished me courage when I reached my place. The men looked at her greedily. She didn't bat an eye when she crossed the rows of men assembled in front of the machines. She liked male attention, even though she pretended to be unaware of the calls and whistles.

"You're asleep," Arezki came over to say. He had caught me with my eyes closed and hands limp.

I was weary. He helped me, pointing out the defects before I saw them. Four separate times Bernier came over, obviously intrigued by this arrangement. But there was nothing he could say; it wasn't against the rules.

"Tonight, go to bed early. Have you thought about it some more? Will you write to your Grandmother?"

I shouted, "Yes, I'll take care of it."

. . .

It was not a good thing, at the start of this year 1958, to be an Algerian in Paris. He was living on borrowed time.

Arrest, unemployment, repression, Arezki felt no indignation.

"It's normal," he said. "There's a war on."

And he laughed at my rebellion. He accepted being a pariah. He sometimes told me about the suffering he had seen or heard about. I reproached him one day for not caring enough.

"A people with five hundred thousand dead. And it's not over yet. You want me to weep over every single one?"

One Saturday, we returned to Nanterre. There was a newcomer sitting in front of the stove, a middle-aged man wearing an old-fashioned checkered suit with large pointed lapels, black with narrow white pin-stripes floating around a stooped shrivelled body. Arezki fell on him. They embraced several times, letting out cries of joy and embraced again as soon as they had finished their litany. Finally, Arezki remembered me and spoke his ritual "This is Elise."

The man had arrived that morning and they both came, he explained, from the same village.

"Si Hacène," he said to the man, "Elise is on our side. When all this is over, I'm going to take her to see our country."

Si Hacène was unmoved. He looked at me with indifference, then continued his conversation with Arezki. It lasted a long time. I never watched a conversation begin between Arezki and his own kind without a feeling of terror. It was like a long thread unwinding for hours whose end never came in sight. This time, Arezki didn't ask Si Hacène to speak French. At one moment, he rose and went outside for a few minutes. Returning to his place, he said almost with joy in his voice:

"You mustn't confuse things. The French don't hate us. Even over there, some of them like us."

Si Hacène's eyes, small, rimmed with black, hardly moving, passed over me. He cleared his throat twice, trying to find the words:

"You believe that?"

He spoke in French.

"They love Algeria, not the Algerians."

"The French love the Algerians the way the knight loves his . . ."

"His mount," Arezki finished for him. "It's one of our proverbs."

Si Hacène had gotten up and taken from the table a

package tied together with string. He held it out to Arezki, who undid it with care. From inside a white cloth, he pulled out several little cakes.

"My mother. She must have deprived herself to send me all this."

He doled out the cakes and we ate while one of the men made coffee.

"She has suffered much, and it was our fault. Her father, my father, my brother . . . and me too."

"They are moving us out," Si Hacène said. "The whole village is being transferred to a center."

"To clean up the region! And this thing, what is it?"

Arezki was holding a small metal box, also tied with a string. Si Hacène smiled. Arezki opened it. It contained earth.

"It's from your mother. She said: he should have a bit of our earth: mint grew in it."

Arezki leaned over, smelled, then pouring the earth into his hands, carried it to his lips and kissed it. But immediately, he rose and picked up the stove stoker.

"I don't want to keep it; this foolishness will make me cry."

When he had removed the lid that covered the stove, he threw the earth into the dying flame; it sputtered and threw off sparks.

We left in the night; coming toward us a man was zig-zagging from one sidewalk to the other. As we came abreast, he looked at Arezki for a few seconds, and said:

"Balak . . . the station."

Arezki stopped, took my arm, and we made a half circle.

"He said to watch out. There is probably a raid at the station. Come, we'll try to find a taxi near the bus stop. I must be back early."

In the taxi, he asked me about Grandmother. I answered that I had written to prepare her. We must move cautiously and not rush her.

"I told you how we lived. She had become used to my freedom."

"Do what you like, but do it. Here, we'll never be able to live together, short of a miracle. You want to, don't you?"

Did I want to! Each time I had to leave him, I resolved to write, then I made it subject to an unrealistic condition: that I would save money. Or I imagined myself telling Lucien everything. But his own affairs were all that absorbed him.

.   .   .

"My dear Elise [Marie-Louise had written], *please send me my husband's address. I've left my sister and have gone back to my parents. The little one has grown, she is pretty, she looks like her father. I'm working as usual. But this is no life. I want to see Lucien. Your grandmother is bored, she is counting on you, and I am, too, for the address."*

I saw Lucien several times without mentioning this to him. He was very excited and explained volubly that "things were starting to happen." Some lawyers had protested to the International Red Cross, the police had seized the plates of a book that denounced the torture, and immediately, several committees had been formed.

When I reported this to Arezki, he said, "Yes, I know." One day I proposed timidly that he put me to work if I could be useful to his people.

He smiled and shook his head.

"Not now. I'd think, and they'd think, that it was simply on my account. And that isn't enough. Even Lucien couldn't do it. That Henri, yes, I have confidence in him. But your brother . . . to me, he's another Mustapha."

I found this opinion of Lucien hasty and unjust. The day after this conversation, my brother created a sensation. From the morning papers, we had learned about the bombing of Sakiet.

At the noon break, Lucien had blown up when he heard the news, and taking advantage of the free period, prepared a kind of manifesto which he read to the workmen gathered around the door. It described the bombs, the murder of children, the rape of a nation, the escalation of the war, the sufferings of a people.

Clinging to a post at the factory entrance, he harangued everyone who came near, asked for all the workmen's signatures, shamed them with their indifference, accused them of complicity, shook them, besought them, implored them, challenged their honor, their class solidarity, their feelings, spoke of their Algerian comrades who had been arrested and tortured, the misery and the fear of the children who were witnesses to the war.

A small group listened. A few left once they'd under-

(236)

stood it wasn't a question of their own interests. Others stayed. Among those listening attentively was a man who called out hoarsely at the end:

"Tell me," he shouted. "Who are you to talk like this? Are you by any chance the man who deserted his wife and child? That's what they're saying at the social welfare office. You're a fine one to talk about morality?"

"Get down," said the shop steward who had been listening at the back. "It's not for you to do this. What right have you? Who do you represent?"

I thought Lucien was going to strike them both.

"You're all a bunch of cowards," he spat out as he got down off the post. "What does my private life have to do with it?"

"A lot, my friend!"

Luckily, the siren dispersed the crowd. Lucien, who was the last to leave, lit a cigarette and went toward the stairs. I caught up with him. I was worried, I wanted to hug him, I wished Anna was there to comfort him.

He turned when I pulled on his sleeve.

"We're in a police state."

"Someone had to say it. You did well."

"You do well when you succeed. When you don't, you do wrong."

. . .

In the questionnaire he filled out the day he was hired, Lucien had not omitted Marie. He had obviously procured her birth certificate and other papers since Anna collected the monthly bonuses due Marie-Louise.

(237)

But an inspector had uncovered the fraud.

When summoned, Lucien swore he was sending the money to his wife.

He came to see me.

"Tell them that you have been sending it and that you misplaced the receipts, or that you slipped them into an envelope."

"You think Marie-Louise will go along with this?"

"Yes, if I write her the right way. Besides, can you see Marie-Louise taking the initiative, filing a complaint?"

Actually, I couldn't. Officials, complaints, lawyers, divorce proceedings, these never have as much force as verbal threats.

"How do you expect to get out of this?"

He didn't answer. I went to his house one night. It was full of books. I noticed a brand-new record player on a chair with several records carefully stacked. The room was barely lit so its sad corners had disappeared. The odor of new books blended with the smell of coffee, and the record, turned very low, evoked the sound of a brook running over polished pebbles. Anna, black and white in the shadows, her cheek held in the hollow of her hand, followed with her eyes the play of the fountains, and the music splashed her with its sparkling drops.

.   .   .

Arezki and I continued to see each other regularly. We went for walks, we had dinner together. It was I who accompanied him back to his hotel. I'd begged him to grant me this satisfaction ever since he'd been arrested after taking me to the métro.

"What time do you finish work?"

"At six."

"And what have you been doing since six? It's almost eleven."

"I went for a walk . . ."

"Come take a walk with us."

They had kept him all that night and the next morning.

I was easier in my mind when I left him in front of his door. He held out his hand, said hello to the man who stood guard at the entrance to the corridor. I left reassured. And as I walked, I composed the letter I would send to Grandmother.

Saïd, who worked the headliners, was fired. He lived in the thirteenth arrondissement. Picked up, run in and held by the police, he was often absent or arrived late.

"What will become of him?"

"The others will feed him. But if he can't find work, I don't know, he'll steal."

Arezki said this with such simplicity that it seemed perfectly natural.

. . .

Impatiently, spring nudged February, and we spent several evenings in the square of La Chapelle. We savored greedily the modest pleasures allowed us. As night came on, the sky exploded; clouds chased each other, overlapped, melted and dissolved behind a wall only to rise again further off in transparent spirals.

"Look at the moon."

Arezki pulled me by the arm. I said, "Oh . . ." with amazement. Then he shook me.

"No, it's the searchlight. Look closer, it's base is hidden by the trees. The mirage of civilization . . ."

And we burst out laughing as we leaned against the back of the bench. Every five minutes the elevated métro fractured the tender evening. The sirens of police cars crossed and recrossed, and our breathing followed their rhythm. We bet each other on when the next flower-bud would open. The palms of our hands rubbed against each other, trying to find the soft hollow. Skin against skin, our fingers vibrated.

But all of a sudden, the grey days returned; cold mornings, horizons limited and opaque, that was March until the 18th, the first clear day after the fog.

It surprised us like an unexpected smile on a sad face. The clouds slowly scattered and the sun finally appeared. We watched each break in the clouds with hope. On that 18th of March . . . At noon, we opened all the windows. At one o'clock, we came back and the cars were warm. The air was mild. It made you want to breathe it in with open mouth. The men rolled up their sleeves. In each doorway, a brown face shone in the light. It happened very quietly. First somebody at the top of the line, banging the steel with his tool, then someone else banging it with his hands, his palms on the hot metal, the sun on the chrome, a thousand suns inside each car, eyelids blinking when the light hit. Motions became slower. You went on with the screwdriver and you drummed a little, then less with the screwdriver and more drumming. Then Bernier rose, the harmless hound, too feeble to bark for long and only too pleased, after he had made his effort, to return to his desk, his papers, his ink and his gothic script.

Very soon, there was a mélée. The men who had fallen behind ran to the start of the line to finish their work, got in the way of others, gave one turn of the screwdriver, one bang of the hammer, and then, back again, late again, rushed for the car already far ahead. Others rested through a whole car, hoping to regain the rhythm. When the car arrived abreast of us, there were too many things missing to go on with the work. Calls, shouts, sham looks of discouragement, everyone searching for a pretext to stop work. Mustapha laughed between clenched teeth, his large nose wrinkled with pleasure. He was delighted with the disorder on the line, the curses of the professionals, their useless zeal. Like a big dog ecstatic in the grass, he lingered in the sun, snap-ons draped around his shoulders, sniffing, hands restless. Somebody shouted: "Cut the current!" A chassis had blocked the elevator door. The car, off balance, had slipped and its hood was headed toward the left. It would take a good half-hour to work it loose. Daubat came toward me wiping his hands.

"I'm going over to look. Want to come?"

I said no, and sat down on the edge of the conveyor belt. No one could see me; I combed my hair. Farther up, the Tunisians were smoking. Arezki was with them.

The chant began at the farthest point of the line. A

long muted call. Opposite us, the hammers answered. They banged, crisply, the same chord. A few hands began to clap. Mustapha ran into the aisle. He had heard it.

"Oh," he said.

He breathed in the air, held it in his lungs. "Oh, oh!" Climbing onto a car roof, he began to clap as he nodded his head.

"Mus-ta-pha!"

Twice someone shouted his name. He clapped still harder. The Tunisians came nearer and so did Arezki. All hands clapped, keeping time to the words Mustapha flung to the sun from the top of his car. A circle of men in Shop No. 76 clapped as they sang, their eyes almost white as they rolled their heads. It was no longer a game; it was, in the purest sense of the word, a liberation, a revenge against the constricted motions of the line, its cramped rhythm. The French workmen made it a point of honor not to come near. There were a few, astonished at the delirium, watching and laughing. I saw Lucien. He'd come down too. He wasn't smoking; he listened, he heard. He drank in this music born, like a river, of a thin, sad note, dragged out, trembling, hesitant, staccato, quavering: the plucked string of the gambri, always the same note, prolonged, painful, a pin stuck in the flesh that grows into a hole as the note swells and the string snaps. No doubt, if he'd dared, he would have moved to the quickening rhythm of the hands. They banged the metal at the front and rear of the cars, an enormous metallic drum where long bronze fingers glided covering

Mustapha's voice, then stopped when the boy, like a muezzin, intoned the drawling "elbi el-bi" of all Arab laments. He sang, he banged, he gasped, his eyes drowned, drunk with the sound of his own voice. He was once again the shepherd sitting under the olive tree, watching over his skinny sheep, he climbed down the yellow rock in his bare feet, a little shepherd in rags who, with a single note, opened, lacerated the flesh of those around him, this race of the exalted, breathless dispossessed, heads waving on the wand of their bodies, balanced in the music's wind. When you thought you'd grasped the rhythm of the clapping—twice with the left hand, once with the right, once with the left, twice, once —when you were about to join in, the rhythm broke, the river curved; the song flowed now in a cascade of cries and beats, now thin like its original note and, without plan, stopping suddenly, taking up again the calm, long torrent of unexpected eddies; if you weren't in on the secret, the magic of this music, you entered it at cross purposes, always against the current.

Seated, my throat choked, almost trembling, I pinched my legs to keep from crying. Mustapha wailed a plaint, his short little arms raised up, and the sound tore us to shreds.

Daubat circled the group. Tonight he'd say to his wife: "Today, I had to put up with a concert by the niggers." The other one, the timekeeper with the glasses, probably thought: "My son is over there, while they're here, singing and having fun." Those over there who should have accepted them, had, instead, rejected them, these men who proclaimed at their congresses "Workers of the world, unite!" They're savages, and their music is savage. "Norafs," they called them. A worse label than the yellow star on the hearts of Jews. The men with knives in their pockets, good-for-nothings, thieves, liars, savages, cruel, filthy—norafs. This evening, the newspaper would report, "Some North Africans assaulted a grocer's wife." And, further down, under an edifying picture, "Some French Moslems salute the resident minister." In both cases, dogs. Either good, faithful dogs, affectionate and loved, or mad dogs. That's all; nothing more. Nothing could ever make Daubat, or the timekeeper, or most of the others, admit that the "norafs" were their equals. Theirs was a lost generation. You'd have to take the next one, Marie's, and, as Lucien had hoped, begin again with her.

I felt some small screws land on my arm. I turned in Arezki's direction. He was at some distance, in the circle, in the song. I felt more screws. This time, I caught him. He was throwing them adroitly so that no one had noticed. He turned his head around and his eyes met mine. Of course, we'd demolish what stood in our path! One day, there'd be no need for a room to hide in. I picked up a screw, aimed carefully and hit his back. Everyone saw me.

A short siren. The line was about to start. The circle broke up. Mustapha got down. Daubat moved up and caught him.

"See what you did?"

A big streak blackened the yellow paint. Mustapha, still in ecstacy, grabbed the collar of his uniform.

"If you tell the foreman, I'll wait for you at the exit, I'll slice open your belly and I'll eat your flesh."

Daubat grew pale. He believed him. Arezki caught Mustapha, and pushed him against the car, talking to him violently. The boy moved away and muttering under his breath, picked up his strips.

Slowly, work resumed. We had a few minutes to let ourselves be rolled along, sitting on the edge of the car for that never-changing voyage to the end of the line.

. . .

Gradually, the circle contracted. Expressions became hostile. The timekeeper no longer smiled at me. Daubat held out his hand without warmth. In the coatroom, I had made no attempt to become friends with my fellow workers. Sensitive to the extreme, I suspected their silences, their inquisitive glances.

There remained only a few scattered islands where I felt comfortable. I counted all those who didn't know: Gilles, the shop steward, the girl with the locker next to mine who lunched outside and drove a Fenwick, a few more who worked in the parts shop. With them, I felt at ease, I felt bursts of affection, I talked to them gratefully. And when I was on what I thought to be a safe island and caught an insistent glance, a mixture of irony, disbelief, curiosity and contempt, I lost confidence, I became confused.

Didi was cruel. When she talked to me, she called me

Aïcha and as soon as I entered the coatroom, she clapped her hands like one possessed and sang "Allah! Allah!" I should have laughed.

Arezki said, one evening when we were talking about it:

"What do you want? To the French, we are sexual brutes, and to us, the French are champions of . . . refinement. Some of them couple for these reasons. I ought to point out that there is often disappointment on both sides. The legends . . ."

He called me Hawa when we were together. He also said it when he was talking quietly or kissing me.

I didn't ask what the name meant. I preferred not knowing and invented various translations.

One afternoon, at five o'clock, Gilles signaled me to follow him. When we'd reached the door of the shop, he told me not to get excited. Lucien had had a hemorrhage; he'd been taken to Bicêtre, where I could go to see him that evening.

He offered to go with me. I had a date with Arezki. I asked to go back to the line and finish my work first. Surprised, Gilles let me go. I went over to Arezki. I told him the news even though Bernier was in the back of the car with the timekeeper. Arezki understood. He said loudly:

"I hope you'll have good news for us tomorrow."

.   .   .

We drank in silence. I knew Gilles would be curious. It was one of those rare and perilous moments that makes or breaks a friendship. I didn't like the smell of beer. However, I had to drink it bravely. Gilles had a bald spot that showed when he leaned over to light a cigarette. His jacket suited him less well than his big white smock which camouflaged the thickness of his body.

"Do you feel better?"

He was asking for the third time.

"Yes, monsieur," I said.

I looked at him gratefully. He touched my hand, which was resting on the edge of the table.

"You were pale at Bicêtre."

"But I'm used to hospitals. I'm all right."

He was drinking fast. He seemed very thirsty.

"I like your brother very much."

"You're one of the few . . ."

"Why one of the few?"

And he began to laugh.

"A lung condition, you get over that. When I came back from Germany, I had a punctured lung. And look at me today!"

"Yes, I know, monsieur."

"Don't say monsieur all the time!"

It was my turn to laugh and I felt better. I had to drink. I tried a big gulp. I couldn't empty the glass.

"There's a comic side to our lives. They could sing about us, 'The Two Orphans.' At the end of each couplet, we're back at the hospital. I have the impression sometimes that the earth revolves in one direction but Lucien and I in the other, like the balancing act in a circus."

(247)

Gilles had emptied his glass. He looked through the window. I guessed he hadn't liked what I'd just said.

"In one sense, it's not so bad," he said. "He'll be taken in hand, treated, cured. It will take a few months. From now until then . . ."

The waiter came by. Gilles called him. I thought that we had to finish up and leave. I drank the rest of my glass with one swallow.

"Another half-pint," Gilles said. "What about you, Elise?"

So that the evening might go on, I accepted. I needed to talk the way I had that first evening with Arezki. A need to tell everything, the past, the present, the bad and the less bad. (And now that you know, make sense out of it and then tell me about yourself!)

I described Anna, Henri, Marie-Louise; I talked about what I knew: the posters in the night, the meetings, the paint shop, the cauldron; and about what I guessed: the exhausting conversations with Anna, the late hours, the lack of money. I came to the scene in front of the factory.

"I heard about it," he said. "The day after, at the canteen when I said hello, he barely answered. We were in sympathy at the beginning. He interested me. We also had our quarrels. He, you, all the others, hate your work. I don't agree. What you do you must do well. You do it slap-dash, you gripe. I understand the reasons. You sell your arms, work, and for so little. But you should respect your work which is partly the others'. Looked at from another angle, isn't the assembly line beautiful?"

I protested: "And the speed-up?"

"Yes, yes. I'm with you there. I put up a fight. But you destroy my weapons because you do poor work."

"We do poor work because we haven't enough time."

I shut up. The beers were in front of us. A juke box played: "Julie, Julie la rousse."

"How did you both end up here? Nobody ever looked after you, gave advice, helped? You've set off in the wrong direction."

I knew I was blushing. I felt the sweat under my arms. I tried to stay calm and let Gilles do the talking. He told me about Lucien at the beginning, his naïveté, his excesses. I knew all that. He told me about his mistakes and explained the reasons. He didn't deny the workers' racism; he blamed it on our mechanized society which ground men down, on the system and its workings.

"If the nigger didn't exist, we would have to invent him. Understand: face to face with an Arab, they are able to assert themselves. Add to that their ignorance, their lack of culture, the fear of anything that doesn't look like them, the war, above all. All that has to be skillfully removed by long and patient work, and not through brutal action, confrontation or anarchy."

He hadn't convinced me. I identified with my brother; his excesses were mine. Made bold by the beer, I asked him if he had agreed when the Party censured direct aid to the militant Algerians.

"I agree with decisions that have been weighed, analyzed and discussed. You must always be prudent.

Some make a revolution just for themselves, or for barely admissible interests. Are you in a position to judge who this revolution really represents?"

"All those who have the guts to fight for it."

He gazed at me so hard that I had to turn away.

"Elise," he said.

"Yes."

I saw that there was affection in his eyes.

"You must come over to our side, believe me. Alone, you'll get nowhere. For ten years you'll be rebels, then one fine day, you'll become resigned. Who knows? You'll move over to the other camp . . . Do you know," he went on, "that I blamed you once for your attitude toward that little guy of the snap-ons?"

"Mustapha? Yes, I remember. I hadn't put down his mistakes."

"I call that . . . maternalism."

"But that's my attitude toward life."

"You must change it. Why don't you see if you can discuss it sometime with Arezki, the one who installs the rearview mirrors."

So, he didn't know.

"I already have several times."

"He got along well with your brother at the beginning. But it didn't last."

The mixture of sounds, the beer, the freedom of our conversation, pushed me toward confession. Then, at the last minute, I held back. If I'd said, "Listen . . ." I foresaw that his view might change. Inevitably, he'd think: there it is, her too, it's the bed. Who would try to understand? Who'd want to? He, I, all of us, judge everything so fast. That's the way it is. We take the first explanation because it makes things simple; it satisfies our need to conform.

"Listen . . ."

"Yes."

"Listen, you've made yourself late bringing me to Bicêtre. I wouldn't like to . . ."

"You're right. I must be going. My wife wouldn't worry, but . . . you ought to get to know her. She's a militant, you know . . . and," he said, buttoning his jacket with difficulty, "if you need me to help your brother . . ."

. . .

Lung cavity, fever, red with fever, red blood, X-rays, sputum, bacillus, hospital, charts, medical insurance, examinations, visits, injections, tortuous labyrinths and the culmination: the sanatorium.

Lucien didn't stay long at Bicêtre. He went back to his place and I went to see him twice. If he didn't welcome my first visit, he seemed happy enough with the second, even though Henri was there, outrageously optimistic the way you think you ought to be in the presence of a sick person. He had to go away, there was nothing else to do. "Three months," Henri shot at him. "That's nothing." "They tell you three months and keep you six." "And so? Read, rest . . ." Anna said nothing. She hoped Lucien wouldn't go away. I looked at her with loathing, thinking, "Wretched, wretched girl, she's the one who contaminated him. She's the carrier, with her unhealthy, sallow scrawniness. Her mother died of it."

"Aincourt isn't so far. We'll see you every month."

"Ah, not that," he protested. "Save me from that!"

His eyes couldn't rest; they kept making the rounds of the room, object by object, then they started all over again. Physical collapse, the need to escape, to fasten onto something: he gave in quickly and said, "I'll go." He closed his eyes, stirred to find the cigarettes he was forbidden, and slapped himself on the thigh.

"It's your turn to play. I'm going to watch."

He entered Aincourt the 15th of April. His resigned departure created the miracle Arezki had hoped for. Lucien left me his room. Anna agreed to the exchange. She took my room at the residence and I occupied, oh, sweet revenge, the place from which she had chased me.

"Fifteen thousand for a girl who isn't working. It's impossible. Take the room and give it back to me when I get out."

She took the records, the record player, the books. Thus our life was like the jungle; its pleasures and joys born of the sorrow of others. While they were arranging between them the practical details, my eyes caressed the table, the bed, the window from which we'd watch the hills turn from blue to purple.

. . .

Gilles stopped by to ask for news of Lucien. I tried to be restrained, dry, brief, but he guessed my emotion. He sent me toward the car coming up; when I got out, he was still there, but Mustapha was talking to him and waving his arms, so I stayed to one side. A little later, as he was crossing the aisle, he looked in my direction.

The 20th of April was a Sunday. I had hurried Anna's departure; she was unable to close her suitcase, she said, because of a pair of high-heeled shoes that would poke into the fragile top.

"Why don't you carry them in your hands."

"Of course. You're right."

I regretted my lack of sympathy, which was a response to her fake humility. I saw once again her face swollen with tears, just as I'd seen it the 1st of January. Tonight, I said to myself, it will be the same. I saw her in the small room in the residence, soggy with sobs smothered in the eiderdown.

As he was leaving, Lucien had taken me aside.

"If you can, help her at the beginning. Henri is going to try to find her something to do. Don't leave her alone. That's all I ask. I'll make it up to you when I get out. They say they teach you a craft down there during your convalescence."

But I couldn't decide to sacrifice my first Sunday. For two days, I lived in preparation for Arezki's coming, the total freedom that four walls give . . .

He had said: "I'll call for you. It's great being able to call you. I'll tell you whether I can come. It's wild in the neighborhood. Fifteen arrests. All of them valuable men!"

In the afternoon, I lay in bed the way I'd seen Anna lie in bed, and I let my hair down so that I'd resemble her even more. I read a little, went to the window, went back to find once more the comfort of my dreams.

Arezki had called at noon. "No, I'm not coming. I explained it to you. It's impossible for me to go out today. I must stay here. Tomorrow, tomorrow evening for sure."

I had to wait until Wednesday. Arezki came into the shop in the morning, walked straight to the assembly line, squeezed my hand hard and stayed near me until the siren started the motors.

"Don't worry."

He read my bad humor in my face.

At last, Wednesday, he whispered: "Crimée, at seven."

I quickly picked up my board and pencil. Mustapha was working in silence. I asked him what was wrong.

"Oh, nothing."

Daubat, passing down the aisle, asked after Lucien.

"I don't know anything yet. I'm going to telephone tomorrow. He has a bad case."

"It's the paint shop! Too bad, a young man like him."

Daubat had heavy, reddish, grainy pouches under his eyes and his cheeky voice was more gentle.

"It's not going so well with me either," he said. "In the morning, I can hardly get up. I can't wait until I retire."

And everybody repeated that. Everybody dreamt of it. To retire!

.   .   .

"Hawa, you're mad at me. But you have no right to be. I've asked you, begged you to go away with me to your home. We could have lived with your grandmother. Yesterday I could have done it, I was free

(254)

. . . or almost. In the underground, you're somebody, then you're nobody, then you're somebody again. Think of it, fifteen brothers arrested, the whole neighborhood disorganized; but no matter. The war won't go on forever. You're my Hawa, this evening I'm free. It's going to be a little more difficult than before, you know, but we'll work it out. That's all right with you, isn't it?"

What did Hawa mean?

"So we're going to see each other less often?"

"A little less often, yes. But longer each time, since we have the room."

As soon as we arrived at Saint-Denis and made the tour of the shops to buy food for our dinner, he lost his spirit. In front of the hotel door, I said:

"Softly now. They don't know me very well yet."

But the manager, who was coming down the stairs, crossed our path and turned around at the same moment I did. With the door closed, Arezki put down the bread and fruit. Looking at the bed, he heaved a sigh and sat on it to light a cigarette.

Then he pulled me to him.

"Hawa, please, go down and buy some wine. I need a drink tonight. Will you?"

We lingered over dinner. Arezki had rediscovered his gaiety. He saw himself coming two or three times a week.

"You must also leave the factory. But wait a little longer."

I talked a lot. Arezki stretched out on the bed with the glass he had not emptied.

"Leave the dishes . . . come to me."

(255)

And I knew the pleasure of giving pleasure. We'd left the window open and the night air awakened us.

"Turn on the light," Arezki said.

He began to smoke thoughtfully. Because of the room, I wasn't sure whether we were us or Lucien and Anna—whose gestures I had assumed. We talked until dawn when sleep overcame us again.

"I wanted to refuse . . ."

Arezki was talking in a thick voice.

" . . . but had I resisted, they would have struck me in front of you or they would have taken you too. I saw it all in a couple of seconds."

"What are you talking about?"

He was already asleep.

The alarm clock shook me. I dressed on tiptoe without turning on the light. Arezki was still asleep. I went over to look at him. To protect his eyes from the feeble light of early morning, he had wound himself in the sheet from which escaped a few black strands of hair. The room was growing light, objects were taking shape, their outline still gracefully vague. Arezki stirred. I ran to the bed. We looked at each other in silence.

The manager saw us leave together as he emptied the garbage outside.

Arezki bought a paper and without reading it, shoved it under his arm. I took it away and pointed to the news of the war. He shrugged. Before the bus stopped at the Porte de Choisy, he squeezed my fingers very tight and I did the same to his.

The siren was trailing off as he took his place on the line. I had already been there several minutes exchanging banalities with Mustapha. I was suddenly seized with rapture and all the feelings of desire I hadn't felt during the night flowed through me. I thought of grabbing his arm if our work happened to throw us together alone, and to kiss the crook at that delicate place where the swollen veins cross, in the hope that this unusual, oddly-timed gesture might tell him the depths of my attachment.

Ever since Lucien's departure, and in spite of Arezki's presence, I'd been feeling isolated. My brother had never been of the slightest help, but to know he was there, nearby, gave me assurance. Bernier tried in vain to find us at fault, following Arezki with his eyes when he came near me. If at that moment I had committed a professional error, he would have penalized me without mercy. I made mistakes that morning. Gilles didn't hide his irritation. I took his scolding in silence, while Bernier stood by relishing it. At recess time, Gilles sought me out. He took me to a chassis and pointed out the dashboard. I had let it pass by without putting down the defect which was very apparent.

"You see what's wrong?"

"Yes, it's not the same color."

"There you are! And I could show you others. What's the matter? Are you sick? Are you worried about Lucien? You know, Elise, to get involved to the point of despair will get you nowhere."

Seeing that I didn't want to answer, he let me go. I was leaving the shop when the shop steward stopped me.

"You shouldn't let him get away with it. A boss,

even Gilles, has no right to keep you after the bell."

"He was concerned about my brother."

"In front of a car you were checking?"

I left him and went down to the telephone. First I called Anna at the residence, but she wasn't there. Then I asked for Aincourt. I couldn't get a word about my brother's condition.

I dragged myself the whole afternoon from one car to the next, and that evening, I went back to the room and the bed where I fell asleep without undressing.

The next day, the manager gave me a letter Anna had left.

"I take advantage of the occasion to remind you," he grumbled, "that it's forbidden for people to sleep here who aren't registered. Especially . . . foreigners."

. . .

"Elise, I went to Aincourt yesterday, but it was the therapy period and I couldn't go near him. They reassured me. We have been authorized to visit him on May 4th. I've told Henri. He'll drive us there."

. . .

"Will you come, Arezki?"

"No, what would I do there?"

"You'd get to know Henri, Anna—and I know Lucien would like to talk to you."

"No, not Henri, not Anna. I don't want to know anybody."

. . .

He came Sunday, as he had promised. He had telephoned me the evening before, but the presence of the manager made it difficult to talk.

"Elise, are you mad at me? Please bear with me if you love me. Do you love me?"

"Yes, of course."

"I'll come tomorrow. I'll be free in the morning, and I'll stay until Monday. Is it all right with you?"

"Yes, sure."

We smoked the same cigarette. Arezki cheated, inhaling two puffs, then he passed it to me and I cheated too for all I did was puff enough to keep it lit. We had not yet turned on the light even though night had invaded the room. While the cigarette was glowing, we watched each other furtively. I didn't know the time; I guessed it was late. I didn't dare interrupt this nocturnal siesta which Arezki seemed to enjoy. He sighed and I asked him:

"Arezki, what's the matter? You seem unhappy. Didn't we want a room? Now we have it. We're here together. What makes you sad? What's missing?"

"Yes, that's it. Something's missing. It's hard . . . I haven't the imagination. I can't visualize the future any more. Dreams won't come any longer . . ."

"And the present doesn't interest you?"

"I feel as if it were already past. Can you understand that?"

I touched his hair. The contact made me quiver. For years, I had wanted to touch Lucien's hair. When he was small, I combed it myself and I loved to plunge my fingers in it, proud of its thickness, of its shiny brown; then one day, he pushed my hand aside violently, and I never stroked it again.

"We'll be like the dead of seven thousand years ago."

"What?"

I had sat up and looked at him, black death mask whose contours were outlined by the lights from the street.

"No, don't be afraid. It's a verse from an Arab poet; I've forgotten the beginning. He says you must live for the moment. They write that way in peaceful times or when the danger has passed. We too live for the moment. Turn on the light, Hawa. Have you anything strong to drink in this room?"

I got up and looked in the cupboard under the washstand. All I found was a tiny bottle of rum such as you buy to flavor crêpes. It had been opened and I poured what was left in a big glass. Joking, I tried to lift up his head and make him drink. I didn't like his mood; it made me uneasy.

"Do you like the color blue?"

"Yes, a lot. But there are several blues."

"The seas, a mixture of green and blue. But you've never seen the sea?"

"No, never."

"Someday you'll see it, and next month I'm going to bring you a dressing gown in the blue I like."

"A dressing gown, Arezki. You do so have an imagination! To want things is to imagine them."

"And when you speak loudly, you convince yourself!"

"What you really are is tired. I guessed it from the

(260)

way you fell on the bed when we came in. How do you live? When do you get any rest?"

He asked me to pass him the cigarettes he'd left in his jacket pocket.

"I run all over the lot, to the right, to the left . . . The cops are strong, you know . . ."

He smelled the glass, tasted it and put it down without drinking.

"I don't like rum. Too bad; give me whatever else you've got, it doesn't matter what."

The small lamp Lucien had installed gave just enough light under its red lamp shade to soften the angles of his face. When Arezki smoked, he became talkative. But I was a bad listener. I wanted to defend myself against him, I rejected despair and closed the door to shadows. He talked. He straightened the red shade and uttered his complaints in a quiet, low voice. Like Lucien, he said that the body didn't count, that you must use it and abuse it, and that weariness, late hours were important. He said that the struggle, in effect, was teaching the brothers to wash, not to spit in the métro, to band together, to distrust everybody, to deceive, to oblige, to obey.

"Men," he sighed, "you can't imagine what they're like. Me, me first of all. Here, I drink; elsewhere, I punish the man who drinks. War isn't good for men."

I encouraged him; I reassured him. Besides, wasn't the war reaching its climax? There was a hint of a shift in the general opinion, an attack of conscience.

"Where?" he broke in. "In Elise, in Lucien, in Henri? How many does that make?"

I protested, and he wanted to make me happy, so he said I was right.

"Come to me. But close the window. Don't you find it cold? Tell me some stories."

We often resorted to the trick of telling stories. Stories about Grandmother, the port, the Kabyle landscape, set objects, set people, harmless, comforting. The ruse worked. And then one word, one sigh, one regret brought us back to the crux of the matter.

"I won't be able to see you the whole of next week."

I looked down and asked: "Saturday?"

"No, not Saturday, you know that."

"Do you think the government is going to fall?"

"Which government?"

"The French one, of course. Lucien said before he left that that would change everything."

"When are you going to see Lucien?"

"Next Sunday, with Henri and Anna. Do come with us."

He made a face and said:

"Too bad . . . we could have spent all Sunday together. I would have come early in the morning."

I didn't answer. A long silence held us apart. Then I saw that he had fallen asleep and I covered him.

. . .

In the evening I opened the windows of the room where, alone, I waited for night, and the glow of the twilight gave me what I needed. I turned on the light only as dusk was fading into night. Until Friday, I held fast to my plans, not wanting my brother to feel that Anna was his only resort. Then, on that morning, I slipped near Arezki and asked him:

"Would you come Sunday if I stayed here?" He assured me he would, and I decided to give up the visit to Lucien.

During the noon break, the shop stewards distributed leaflets in front of the factory entrance. They'd been turned away a few days earlier by the management, and were now asking us to attend a meeting that evening. "The promises are never kept. They only make them to take the heat out of our demands."

We were only a handful that evening when the union men outlined the situation. One of the workmen in the shop who was standing behind me whispered in my ear:

"And your buddies the Arabs, where are they?"

Not a single foreign workman was at the meeting.

. . .

I lied shamelessly when Anna called me. The excuse I gave smelled of fraud. And while I was speaking, I realized how much I loved my brother and how much giving up this trip meant to me. Anna was obviously delighted. I could hear it in the tone of her voice. She promised to stop by on her return and give me all the news.

I waited for Arezki all day Sunday. He didn't come. Around six o'clock, someone rattled the door. Anna came in and, without sitting down, gave me an account of her visit to Lucien, which was cut short by the various treatments he had to take. Her eyes sparkled, her voice trembled with happiness as she reported his plans. He wanted to leave. He had declared he couldn't go through another three months without her. "One more month and I beat it." She thought I'd protest in the name of wisdom, reason, health. I contented myself with asking if he was very disappointed that I hadn't come. A stupid question which was answered by the mocking twist of her lip:

"The next visiting day is the second of June."

"I'll go then, you can be sure."

At eight, Arezki telephoned and said:

"I'm on my way."

I was angry. I was certain he had lied.

He didn't try to pretend.

"Yes, I did it on purpose."

"Did it give you pleasure?"

"Yes."

He was relaxed that evening. We planned several outings, for a future that stretched into infinity.

"Also, you must quit work. But wait two months until the holidays."

I thought: "And what about Grandmother?" I didn't say it, and I didn't talk about my brother either. For me as well, dreams had stopped.

.   .   .

A letter to Lucien, which he didn't answer, a few evenings with Arezki, outside or in the room, kept me occupied until Tuesday, the 13th. That morning, Bernier came over to tell me, without losing his cheerful smile, that I had lost my bonus.

"Your work is poor, very poor. We have to check your checking. You forget defects, you can't turn your head, you must look at the car and not at the person in the car."

I asked him what he meant by that.

"What I mean?"

Arezki was right near us, listening.

"Judge my work and nothing else, please."

"You think I'm afraid," he shouted, "because your Arab is listening?"

I had to keep Arezki out of it. I should have prudently beaten a retreat, but losing all control, I threw my board and my pencil on the floor, shouting that I'd go see the shop steward. I was no longer afraid, other people's expressions no longer bothered me. Bernier turned to Arezki.

"Just what are you up to? You've really gone to her head, haven't you? Is it you who's pushing her?"

I didn't hear Arezki's answer. He maintained later that all he said was "leave me alone." But I saw him brush past Bernier, who was barring the way. Bernier grabbed the collar of his shirt, and Arezki, in order to free himself, pushed him against the car that was moving up. Bernier wasn't hurt, but he staggered and sat down on the moving belt.

"You're going to get fired for this."

He got up, aided by Daubat, who had mysteriously appeared, and went off to the glassed-in office of the foreman.

At noon, Arezki was called to the office and informed that he was dismissed. He left the shop without speaking to me, having shaken hands with a few Tunisians and Mustapha, who, after lunch hour, gave me a piece of paper. Arezki would be waiting for me at Crimée.

He was standing with his face to the light which hit him just under the eye sockets, outlining an eyeless mask, unmoving and sinister.

"I am unemployed!"

For all his laughing and making little of the incident, I could see the consequences. To my questions, he answered:

"Yes, starting tomorrow, I'll look for work."

"I'll leave too. Without you, I can't stay there."

As we were leaving, someone said in a loud voice:

"It appears there's been fighting in Algiers. It's just been on the radio."

The news hardly distracted us from our preoccupations. I went home alone around nine, and for the first time in a long while, I cried. I'd have to go out the next day with a bloated face after a night spent in tears. I had promised Arezki I'd hold out until the end of the month.

"When I have a job, you can quit. We mustn't both of us be without money at the same time."

At the Porte de Vincennes, I found a place to sit and opened my paper. But whether from weariness or worry, I couldn't understand the importance of the events that were taking place. Without Arezki, without his face over there between the steel and the iron, I had the feeling of being naked in the cold. The days left behind seemed the very peak of happiness. At the end of the day, Gilles went by in the company of the men in white smocks.

I felt I had to leave and explained it to Arezki when I met him in the Place D'Italie. We walked for a bit; the weather was fine. The situation was serious, he told me, and I could see it in the size of the headlines in the evening papers. He hadn't found work yet. He'd go the next day, here, there, and without question, he'd find something. This was to reassure me.

Suddenly the events went to my head. I spoke of them with an excitement that made Arezki smile. At that particular moment, I was less anxious over his situation, preoccupied as I was by what was in the newspapers, the discussions at the factory, the frequent telephone conversations with Henri and Anna. We lived those days with intensity, persuaded that the hour had finally come when some fantastic upset was about to take place, satisfied to be "in the thick of it." We didn't quite know what "it" was, but inside we felt indispensable, alert, finally useful. I wrote to Lucien every other day. He answered. The news that had penetrated down there was driving him crazy. He spoke of "throwing everything up and coming." He was out of it. At the factory, the mood had changed. I can still see Gilles in the park where the cars were backed up between the Portes d'Ivry and de Choisy. Around him, a little group. He called to me, he told the others, "She is in a good position." He gave the numbers: "In such and such a shop, there are five members of the Party, in number seventy-six there are eight." Gilles said, "What counts is not how things were yesterday; it's how many we are today." Even Daubat gave up his lunch break to come. Many came, women too. Gilles beamed. "In France, there is an ancient republican tradition. It is aroused when there is danger." Only a few intractables refused to sign the petitions, the resolutions, the calls to action, the testaments. Something was flowing the length of the line, something heavy, warm, reassuring that bound us together, what Gilles baptized the brotherhood of the workers. This enthusiasm and these transports heard their swan song on the 28th of May.

Arezki scoffed. "It's useless. It's too late."

I resented his skepticism and disbelief.

On the 27th of May he telephoned. I was finishing dinner. We hadn't been able to see each other that evening; he was busy.

"Everything's O.K. I've been promised something the fifteenth of June. It's not certain yet. But there's hope. I'm going to try to come tonight."

"Tonight?"

"Yes. In a half-hour, an hour."

I thought about the manager and his objections.

"Come after eleven. No one will see you."

"That's too late. It's the time when they pick you up. Too bad, we'll see each other tomorrow."

"There's the demonstration tomorrow. I don't know when it will be over."

"Ah, the demonstration!"

I let the irony pass.

"O.K., I'll do my best to come after eleven. If I'm prevented . . ."

"Telephone me tomorrow. Please come tonight,

(268)

Arezki. But watch out for the manager. What if I went out and waited for you someplace? We could come back together. It would be more sensible."

"No, wait for me in the room."

But I waited in vain. On the 28th, I woke up in a state close to drunkenness. I opened the window, looked out at the street, the smokeless horizon, the orange line above housetops that heralded a hot day. We worked until twelve. I missed Lucien. I imagined him in the greenery of Aincourt, as cloying as a sugar refinery to eyes starved for asphalt and pavement. Then we left in a group for the métro. To make our way in, we had to squeeze between the shoulders of metal-workers, postmen, masons. At each station, new groups tried to find room in the bulging cars. The same people who in the evening quarreled over being tripped or nudged, laughed and called each other comrades. The métro rolled on, like a river where countless streams of men converged, carrying streamers, placards, rolled up banners, flags. A few, the oldest, wore red neckties. I was surrounded by workers I had classed as nasty types, the factory racists, and my over-excitement was such that I wanted to ask their pardon for having misjudged them. I didn't yet understand that they were eternal followers in the wake, no matter which way the wind blew. Very small among all those men, I closed my eyes with joy. I was preparing the account I would give Arezki. Would he still laugh if he could see the ocean that was submerging the Place de la Nation?

Gilles came over to me.

"So, Elise, this is it."

"Yes, this time, I think it is."

"It's like thirty-six," Daubat said behind me.

"The students . . ."

They were folding their banners. Liberal Arts, Medicine, University of Antony . . .

"Look, there's Renault!"

The spearhead of the working class advanced to the sound of applause.

We walked as far as the République, arm in arm, shouting slogans. We could have walked a lot farther. At the République, a young madman climbed the statue and draped it with flowers. The whole of Paris, heart and soul, was there and it would have been impossible to break it up. Helicopters were flying over the crowd. Someone behind me said:

"What if they drop paratroopers?"

"Let them come!"

We were saving the Republic, we had the numbers, invincible and united. The boy who had just spoken vaguely resembled Lucien. He was different in the firm and calm expression on his face, his stronger body. In his eyes, you could see the joy, the enthusiasm, and I thought to myself: "There goes a successful Lucien."

I stayed until the end, to the moment when the sight of the deserted square began to undermine my confidence. On my reluctant way home, I stupidly kept repeating: "res publica, public thing." Arezki didn't phone, but it hardly mattered, I was too tired. When I woke up, the sun was in the room. I looked at the time;

it was too late to go to the Porte de Choisy. Too bad, the morning was done for. I walked back and forth in the sun's rays several times. I felt an intense sense of physical well-being. It seemed as if a new era was opening up and that the night before we had staged a kind of revolution. I went out, bought several newspapers and fresh bread for lunch. I cut out the pictures in *L'Humanitâ* and put them away for Lucien. The steam of the coffee rose up in the sun's rays, which had now reached the table. The fresh bread made crumbs as I broke it, and this minute of idleness prolonged the thrill of yesterday.

Looking through the newspapers, I learned of Lucien's death. I got up, I ran to the mirror where I looked at myself, holding my face between my hands. I went back to the table, looked for the key, went down to the telephone. I called Anna. She wasn't there. Then Henri. "He's out," answered the landlady. I went back up, I opened the door, I pushed the bolt, I looked at the cup and the crumbs of bread. The paper was there, vicious like a snake, and I didn't dare to touch it. I got down on my knees, I said: "Lucien, Lucien, Lucien." Seized with nausea, I rushed for the washbowl, only to spit; I opened the shutters, I gazed at the newspaper and after a long while picked it up. It was on the last page, the "News in Brief," under the heading: "Tragic Accident on The Outskirts of Mantes." I had to wait again. My eyes refused to read the slender lines, the ones that reported:

"On Wednesday morning, at about four o'clock, a

young man on a motor scooter met his death on the outskirts of Mantes. The driver of the milk truck that struck him was questioned by the police. The victim, Lucien Letellier, age 22, was undergoing treatment at the sanatorium of Aincourt. The scooter he was driving had been stolen from one of the institution's employees. According to the evidence of the man driving behind him, the young man was going very fast and without lights. When the man honked his horn, he increased his speed. Unable to stay on the right, he ran into the truck coming in the other direction. Death was immediate. It is not known what the young man was fleeing in the middle of the night, or what was his destination."

I wasn't suffering yet. I was able to leave, to go to the post office where I sent a telegram to Arezki. "Come right away, it's urgent. Elise." Neither Henri nor Anna were at home. I called Aincourt. They told me Lucien was at Mantes.

I went back toward the hotel walking on the sunny side as if it could still give me pleasure. Then the wound opened, and what poured forth emptied me of all substance, leaving only grief. I climbed the stairs hurriedly, and once in the room, buried myself in the sheets to stifle my sobs. The time passed. Arezki didn't come. I only met up with Henri that evening. He knew. Anna knew also. She was with him, she was, he said, mad with a grief that was tragic, obscene.

"It's horrible, Elise. I still can't believe it. Lucien! He was coming to Paris, wasn't he? It was mad. For a useless demonstration. You read the evening papers? Of course you can count on me. We'll go down together tomorrow. Be strong; like you've always been. See you tomorrow, don't move, wait for me."

Had Arezki forgotten me, couldn't he come?

I waited for him to open the door so that I could throw myself against him and weep. In the morning, I found myself still in bed. I had slept and dreamt of Lucien. A beautiful colorful dream in which we were arguing over nothing. When Henri knocked on the door, I was ready. I left a message with the manager, who accepted it grudgingly. Arezki might come while I was away; he had to be told.

"Please," I asked Henri, "can we go by the Goutte d'Or?"

And I explained why.

I entered the hotel alone and climbed up to the room where the police had found us. I knocked. I waited. The man who opened questioned me rudely.

"What? What do you want?"

"Arezki. I want to see him."

"He isn't here."

Then I began to cry, and I told him, as if he could understand:

"Lucien is dead."

Suspiciously, he pushed the door but I persisted.

"I must see him. My name is Elise. I have something to tell him. It's serious."

He was very ugly. He had a squint.

"Where is he? Could you give him a message?"

He didn't understand the word, for he said:

(273)

"What?"

I wouldn't give up. Then he made up his mind.

"They picked him up Tuesday night; in the métro."

"Ah, yes?"

"Yes. That's it."

Of course, that's it. One is taken, another comes to take his place. "The revolution is a bulldozer. It pushes on . . ."

A little old man with a long mustache was climbing the stairs.

"Do you know Arezki?"

"I don't know anybody."

I was too hot in my heavy skirt. It was sticking to my calves. Henri was waiting at the corner, taking in the smells of the Casbah while talking to a suspicious Algerian who was trying to get away.

"He was arrested. Tuesday evening. Do you want to wait for me? I'm going to see Feraht."

It was the restaurant where we had eaten several times. "His brother is married to my sister . . . "

"I'll go with you, Elise."

Feraht knew nothing.

"So many have been picked up . . ."

"Where did they take him? How can I find out?"

"Well," he said, "La Villette, or . . ."

"I can't go with you, Henri. I've got to find out."

"But you won't find out anything. Who's going to talk to you? The police? All you can do is wait; maybe they'll release him."

I suddenly thought of Mustapha. We stopped at the

Porte de Choisy and I waited for the closing siren. I ran when it went off and got to the door just as the guard was opening it. People stared at me because I was sweating and breathing hard. Mustapha went by. I clutched him.

"They picked him up Tuesday with Slimane. Slimane was let out yesterday."

I begged him to take me to this man Slimane.

"I can't. I don't want to be fired. Arezki didn't have his pay slip."

He explained where Slimane lived and excused himself:

"I have to eat."

I was tempted to run after him to tell him about my brother's death. But what good would that do? He had become hardened, just like Arezki. He would open wide his small eyes, I'd have to tell him how and when, on the sidewalk, in the full sun, in full view of life.

Henri, always accommodating, drove me to the Rue de Chartes, to the address given by Mustapha.

"It's not only his pay slip," said Slimane. "Yes, if he'd had it, the police might not have kept him, but . . . I can't tell you anything. I don't know anything."

"Tuesday night, around nine, he called me, he said: I'm on my way . . ."

"I know. I was with him. We were talking in a café, and then we walked as far as the métro. It was there they picked us up."

"What happened then?"

"After that, I don't know. I was all right. I didn't see

where they took him. They sorted us out. We weren't together after that."

"Come," Henri said, "be reasonable, Elise. We must leave for Mantes. You're not going to get anything more. When we get back, I'll help you if you like. You must be patient."

We arrived in Mantes Friday toward evening, and Monday morning, we set off again for Paris. Henri had been a great comfort. I did exactly what he told me. My grief was decent, showable. I felt only a mutilation that our various motions, the comings and goings, from Aincourt to Mantes, Mantes to Paris, helped to anesthetize a little. Henri said I mustn't see my brother, that there was no point to it, that only his young beautiful madman's face should be in our thoughts. I assented docilely. It seemed as if I were preparing a ceremony for Lucien, from which he was absent, but nothing like the void, or death.

Monday morning at nine, we left Mantes. I thought of Lucien, fleeing, crazed by the sound of the horn, thinking himself pursued, clumsy, shaking, nervous. "What madness," Henri had said. "For a useless demonstration . . ." Was it only for that? Hadn't the need to see Anna hastened his decision? To this last hypothesis in which he didn't believe—Henri had answered impatiently:

"But Anna was a part of the whole!"

.   .   .

There, in that flat landscape, the adventure of his life had ended. His life a failure, his death ludicrous. The young heroes of the day died on their speeding motorcycles and he killed himself on a scooter. So, nothing would remain of his end but a caricature, without the slightest romance. He had wanted to be a part of it; he had thought Paris would thunder; Paris had only yawned. There was nothing left of Lucien except what was in us, who had loved him.

"So what?" he would have said in his caustic voice. "What then?"

.   .   .

We were going through a town when I saw on the sidewalk a small boy carrying two loaves of bread in his arms, rushing to cross the street. A song my brother had learned when he was about twelve came back to me. He sang it over and over in his room, on the staircase; he whistled it to my face like a challenge:

*"Hanz de Tchloquenoque has everything he wants
And what he has he doesn't want
And what he wants he doesn't have*

*Hanz de Tchloquenoque says anything he wants
And what he says he doesn't believe
And what he believes he doesn't say*

*Hanz de Tchloquenoque goes where he wants
And where he goes he doesn't stay
And where he stays he doesn't like.*

"Hanz de Tchloquenoque," I used to say, "that's you."

And for a long time, to his vast displeasure, that's what I called him.

. . .

"Here's Paris. I'll drive you straight to your house, O.K.? We'll take the outside boulevards; it'll be quicker."

Henri had understood that I didn't want to talk and had been silent since our departure. "Here's Paris." The words woke me up.

From Mantes, gracious city, to the Pont de Saint-Cloud just after the tunnel that starts and finishes the expressway, the green of the trees and the fields, the sky's indecision, gray here, rose further on, and all those hours I had just spent among the whisperings in the hospital corridors, in the administrative offices, this trip to Aincourt where I was given everything Lucien had left, the three awakenings at the hotel when I opened my eyes to the barking of a dog or the chatter in a near-by courtyard, the terrible picture crushed a dawning sense of joy and left me stupidly inert, ears buzzing and my breath bitter, its texture a mixture of all the images and emotions that had enveloped and separated me from the living. "Here's Paris." The cloth tears. The countryside and the soft wind in the trees, anticipating the summer to come, prolonged still further the funeral ceremony and its capacity to appease. But here begins the city's overflow. A clock marks the time. The streets are rectilinear and without mystery. The horizon now is a fragment of sky between the many buildings. It is decidedly blue. It is going to be hot, and the women are wearing dresses without collars or sleeves. Some Arabs are digging a sidewalk. Once we've passed the viaduct at Auteuil, the traffic grows heavier. This is Paris. Delivery trucks, trailer trucks, buses, it's the start of a day. From the Porte de Versailles, we move slowly and I examine the people on the sidewalk to my right, as if they could answer my questions. It's because here, in the noise of the city, in its colors and mixtures, I've found Arezki again.

Now the buildings of the "Cité Universitaire." The red brick of their walls reminds me of the English colleges, the way they looked in my brother's school books. Between two pavilions, a garden gives to the whole a quality of fullness. Lecture halls, rooms from which it must be possible to see the distant roses amidst the green . . . , because of that, because of the old stones and a few students walking toward the boulevard, I tell myself that Arezki risks nothing. Farther along, coming out of the Moroccan pavilion, a boy yawns, his collar open. He stretches his free arm. And even if Arezki didn't come back, I'd rouse Paris. There are lawyers, newspapers. A man's life, that matters here. A few would rise up to cry out, protest, make demands. The 28th of May was not a dream.

At the Porte de Gentilly, the road goes gently downhill. The concrete of the stadium steps is blinding in the sun. On a sign, I read "Poterne des Peupliers." It reminds me of gallows. Articles 76 and 78: "Attack on the internal and external security . . ." They won't let go all that fast.

We pass a monument made of white stones: "TO FRENCH MOTHERS." The homage, the veneration, they come later, when it's too late. The slope flattens out toward the Place d'Italie. I know it too well; I barely look to the left toward this old whore of a factory where I read the inscription "Automobiles; Wood-working machines." I feel as if the unnerving noise of the assembly line were reaching out for me. I smell the warm metal.

When we begin the descent toward Charenton, the vibrating motions of the car—the boulevard is being repaired—throw me from hope back to anguish. And memories are mixed in as we pass the square of La Limagne. Arezki used to say "de la Limace." He also said: "Le Mont de Pitié," and I loved this last word.

On the Pont National, at the sight of the water, I think about the bodies that float under it. Bodies that are thrown in on nights of big riots, in the paroxysm of hatred; the bodies of the weak who have talked too much and whom death punishes. Out of place in this area, L'Auberge du Régal watches those pass whom no red light stops.

On the Boulevard Poniatowski, buildings rise to circle Paris with their pre-war ugliness. Unfriendly houses with rough façades, dull stones, shapeless doorways, large interior courts no sun could ever reach; there lives the workers' aristocracy aspiring to the bourgeoisie. Crushed and constricted by indifference, by new ideas, what price the life of an Arab here? The love of order oozes from these buildings. He's been sent away, sent back into the war. I could cry, but who would hear me? If he's alive, where is he? If he's dead, where is his body?

(280)

Who will tell me? You've taken his life, yes, but what have you done with his body? At the Porte de Vincennes, the boulevard comes to an end and a vast housing project takes over: new apartment buildings with terraces shaded by blue and orange awnings. They suggest hot afternoons where you drink from frosted glasses while listening to a record. Who will think of Arezki?

Henri slows down still more. We're behind a truck that belches its exhaust. Montreuil is at my right and the Rue d'Avron opposite. The stalls of les Halles challenge a painter's palette. The rows of fruit, the pyramids of vegetables tear the fabric of my hopes. In front of the mounds of garden produce, thousands of ants act as a rampart before the displays.

On the hill between Bagnolet and Les Lilas, the car struggles between two buses. A road gang at the Porte de Ménilmontant is taking time off for a drink. Tomorrow, one of them won't be back and fifty will appear to pick up his shovel. There are so many, there are too many, inexhaustible reserves, forever replenished.

After Les Lilas, on the curve going down toward the Pré-Saint-Gervais, you see before you Aubervilliers, pale in the heat haze. On the barren esplanade, a curious solitary church attracts me. But now Henri is driving very fast and it's only after the Porte de Pantin that we reach the slums of that other Paris that comes to Paris only for the 28th of May. Not dangerous, easy to control, easy to satisfy. We enter the tunnel under the Porte de la Villette. I have a presentiment that I will never see Arezki again.

"Thank you, Henri."

"If there is anything I can do for you, please call me. I'll telephone you one evening about your friend. I don't think Anna wants to see you right now, but she mustn't be left alone. What do you think?"

I didn't think anything. Anna's grief left me cold. Henri didn't insist.

The next few days, I slept a great deal. Sleep came and I absorbed it like a tranquilizer. Between two bouts, I went to the factory to wind up my affairs. Seeing the assembly line again—the shop—would have stirred up emotions so I stayed in the personnel office. Told of my presence, Gilles came down. His compassion, controlled because it was sincere, was touching, but I didn't go so far as to talk to him about Arezki. He understood the events of the past few days with remarkable lucidity and faced the future without a sense of discouragement.

"You're going? It's decided?"

What else was there to do? I gave myself two weeks before leaving; I'd go everywhere, I'd knock on every door. It no longer cost me anything to go into a café full of men, question them, be seen and judged. I accused myself with severity, remembering my hesitations, my second thoughts which had throttled the realization of our plans. But all the time that I was heaping accusations on myself, I knew I couldn't have acted differently. Arezki had loved me knowing all this, not fooled by my promises. He hadn't pressured me, knowing that time and physical attachment would bind me to him with ever increasing strength.

I went to see the uncle one evening. He received me coldly. He wanted no complications, he said he knew nothing, not even that Arezki had been arrested. His right cheek, from his eye to his nose, had purple bruises. The coffee pot had disappeared; I wondered where he hid the wine now.

I went back to Feraht, but he had learned nothing. He made me sit down, brought me an orangeade and we talked about Arezki, the war. His pronouncements had a terrifying dryness, and the words torture, death, suffering went hollow as they left his mouth. He knew that one day he'd be arrested and it would then be his turn to learn to shut up. Arezki's disappearance was natural, it was part of a fatal logic, and I was alone in being affected by it.

"My opinion is that they've sent him back. That would be bad. Not many get there. Perhaps he's in prison here? How can you tell? Maybe they found compromising papers on him, but that would surprise me; he was too careful. Perhaps someone turned him in? There are those who rat. It's not easy when you're alone with them, your hands tied . . . It isn't the café counter any more . . . there are no witnesses."

I wanted to leave him my address, my home address, since I was going there. He refused.

"No pieces of paper, no addresses! It's too dangerous!"

.   .   .

And finally I went to see Mustapha. In front of him,

(283)

I dared to cry. My grief crushed him. He agreed to take my address and if Arezki reappeared one day . . .

"If I'm not dead," he added.

There was one last question to ask him.

"What does Hawa mean?"

"What?"

I repeated, making an effort to pronounce it properly.

"Hawa? That's Eve."

"Thank you."

When I told her I was leaving, Anna asked hurriedly: "What about the room?"

"You can have it back if you want it."

Her voice on the phone became even more of a whisper.

"I don't like the residence. I'm going to work soon, and . . ."

"Come on the twenty-second. My bags will be packed. I'll give you back the key."

"See you soon."

She was the first to hang up.

. . .

I refuse to imagine what awaits me. The sight of Marie-Louise is already unbearable; unfairly, her sorrow fills me with horror. She is a victim and I loathe her. I foresee too that I'll be harsh with Grandmother and that, after the first expressions of sympathy are over, I'll avoid all conversation.

I'll have to go to work, and I'll undoubtedly pick one of those bread-winning jobs where human relationships are non-existent. The real life will have lasted nine months.

. . .

Anna has just left. The room, my life. Will I ever see her again? She excused herself.

"I'm very early, but I had to do it. I'll take the key. All you have to do is shut the door. I won't forget you, Elise. Yes, I'm working. The post office takes on temporary help every summer. I must go; buses are few on Sunday. I'm leaving my suitcase on the chair."

She touches me with her cold hand.

She has just closed the door and in order to see her a last time, I lean out the window and follow her with my eyes. She crosses the street and walks toward the alley opposite the bus shelter. A car backs out slowly. It's Henri's. He opens the door and she gets in.

The black pit of loneliness isn't sucking her in yet. But to what kind of branch has she attached herself? I feel for her. She will suffer. One day, Henri will cut her off. Lucien will remain the bleeding wound of her sex and her heart.

"That's you in thirty years!" he had sneered in front of an old hag. With Henri, she has a few weeks, a few months. He will come to see her in this room. The manager won't mind. On this same bed, each of us will have known "the short fifteen minutes of love." Anna is using Henri as balm on her wound. The lovers to follow will be only that—bandages on a wound, the wound that was her life, badly constructed, congenitally

(285)

crippled. But after each man, the wound gapes more.

What was the power we lacked? Where is the flaw that would not permit us to dominate what is so easy to call fate? To what degree are we guilty? These beautiful flowers growing among the weeds will only have served to make funeral wreaths. What we had to defend, what we were to conquer, we leave behind us. It's Henri and those like him who will fight in our places. What will they do with the victory they win? What will relieve me of the turbulent tide of my thoughts? Sorrow shadows me, hovers over my future, lurks in my memories. It waits to attack me but I'll divert it and I'll defend myself. I'll drive it from me down to the last image. And under the ashes, hope will hold on. I don't know where it will push me. I feel it. Indistinct, unformed, impalpable, but here. I will hide inside myself, but I won't die.